W9-CBC-322

**Praise for *New York Times* bestselling author
Brenda Jackson**

"Jackson is a master at writing."
—*Publishers Weekly* on *Sensual Confessions*

"Brenda Jackson is the queen of newly discovered
love.… If there's one thing Jackson knows how to
do, it's how to pluck those heartstrings and stir up
some seriously saucy drama."
—*BookPage* on *Inseparable*

"Jackson's characters are wonderful, strong,
colorful and hot enough to burn the pages."
—*RT Book Reviews* on *Westmoreland's Way*

**Praise for *USA TODAY* bestselling author
Catherine Mann**

"Catherine Mann certainly knows how to reach
your heart through her characters."
—*Fresh Fiction* on *Honorable Intentions*

"A charmingly passionate tale."
—*RT Book Reviews* on *Rich Man's Fake Fiancée*

BRENDA JACKSON

is a die "heart" romantic who married her childhood sweetheart and still proudly wears the "going steady" ring he gave her when she was fifteen. Because she believes in the power of love, Brenda's stories always have happy endings. In her real-life love story, Brenda and her husband of more than forty years live in Jacksonville, Florida, and have two sons.

A *New York Times* bestselling author of more than seventy-five romance titles, Brenda is a recent retiree who now divides her time between family, writing and traveling with Gerald. You may write Brenda at P.O. Box 28267, Jacksonville, Florida 32226, email her at WriterBJackson@aol.com or visit her website at www.brendajackson.net.

CATHERINE MANN

USA TODAY bestselling author Catherine Mann lives on a sunny Florida beach with her flyboy husband and their four children. With more than forty books in print in over twenty countries, she has also celebrated wins for both a RITA® Award and a Booksellers' Best Award. She writes for the Harlequin Desire line. Catherine enjoys chatting with readers online—thanks to the wonders of the internet, which allows her to network with her laptop by the water! Contact Catherine through her website, www.catherinemann.com, find her on Facebook and Twitter (@CatherineMann1) or reach her by snail mail at P.O. Box 6065, Navarre, FL 32566.

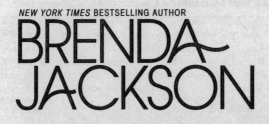

NEW YORK TIMES BESTSELLING AUTHOR

BRENDA JACKSON

In Bed with Her Boss

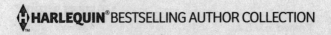

HARLEQUIN® BESTSELLING AUTHOR COLLECTION

If you purchased this book without a cover you should be aware that this book is stolen property. It was reported as "unsold and destroyed" to the publisher, and neither the author nor the publisher has received any payment for this "stripped book."

Recycling programs for this product may not exist in your area.

ISBN-13: 978-0-373-18083-7

IN BED WITH HER BOSS
Copyright © 2014 by Harlequin Books S.A.

The publisher acknowledges the copyright holders of the individual works as follows:

IN BED WITH HER BOSS
Copyright © 2007 by Harlequin Books S. A.

RICH MAN'S FAKE FIANCÉE
Copyright © 2008 by Catherine Mann

All rights reserved. Except for use in any review, the reproduction or utilization of this work in whole or in part in any form by any electronic, mechanical or other means, now known or hereafter invented, including xerography, photocopying and recording, or in any information storage or retrieval system, is forbidden without the written permission of the publisher, Harlequin Enterprises Limited, 225 Duncan Mill Road, Don Mills, Ontario M3B 3K9, Canada.

This is a work of fiction. Names, characters, places and incidents are either the product of the author's imagination or are used fictitiously, and any resemblance to actual persons, living or dead, business establishments, events or locales is entirely coincidental.

This edition published by arrangement with Harlequin Books S.A.

For questions and comments about the quality of this book, please contact us at CustomerService@Harlequin.com.

® and TM are trademarks of Harlequin Enterprises Limited or its corporate affiliates. Trademarks indicated with ® are registered in the United States Patent and Trademark Office, the Canadian Trade Marks Office and in other countries.

Printed in U.S.A.

CONTENTS

Dear Reader,

Finding love in the workplace can put a person in a challenging situation. And when the object of your desire is your boss, you're definitely in for a test of your courage and endurance while trying to engage in a discreet yet steamy love affair.

My two characters discover their attraction is too much to handle, but are ripe for passion of the most intense kind. They also discover along the way that sexual chemistry isn't the driving force behind their attraction. It's something bigger and stronger. It's something they can't continue to deny.

I love weaving stories of passion and romance, and placing two unlikely people in a situation where they have to finally realize that, sooner or later, love is going to get you. I had fun writing this story and I hope you have just as much fun reading it.

Brenda Jackson

IN BED WITH HER BOSS

New York Times Bestselling Author

Brenda Jackson

To Gerald Jackson, Sr.—thanks for being
the special man that you are.

To all my readers who enjoy a good love story
that centers on family.

To my Heavenly Father, who shows me each
and every day how much he loves me.

"Withhold not good from them to whom it is due,
when it is in the power of thine hand to do it."
—*Proverbs 3:27*

Chapter 1

Opal Lockhart glanced around the crowded backyard and smiled at the many family, friends and invited guests she saw. There was nothing like an annual family reunion to bring everyone together. This one seemed even better than the last, because she and her sisters had a lot to celebrate.

First, she had a new job she loved, although things would be better if her boss didn't have such surly behavior most of the time. Her sister Pearl, who at twenty-five was two years younger than Opal, had sent her new demo tapes to several gospel labels all over the country. And then there was her eldest sister, Ruby, twenty-nine, who had gotten a superior rating on her most recent job-performance evaluation. That would definitely keep Ruby first in line for a promotion with her present employer. Everyone knew how important moving up the corporate ladder of success was to Ruby.

But the biggest blessing of all, as far as Opal and her other two sisters were concerned, was that their twenty-one-year-old baby sister, Amber, had finished another year in college, which she was attending part-time, and had set a record by not changing boyfriends more than three times since the last reunion.

She smiled as she glanced over at Amber, but her smile quickly turned to a frown when she saw her youngest sister openly flirting with several of the male guests, most of them from the family's church. Opal glanced over at Ruby, who met her gaze and nodded, indicating she, too, was aware of Amber's outlandish behavior.

Opal was about to go have a word with her sister when her cell phone vibrated in the back pocket of her shorts. She quickly pulled it out, and her frown deepened when she saw the caller was her boss. Why on earth would he be contacting her on a Saturday?

She moved to an area of the patio away from the noise—mainly the heated discussion going on between her sister Pearl and Reverend Wade Kendrick regarding the woman's role in a Christian household. Reverend Kendrick, who was only twenty-eight, was their church's new minister. A former "gangsta," he had found faith when he had overcome a personal tragedy.

Opal was thoroughly impressed with him and thought he was a dynamic speaker. Already the congregation had increased tremendously since he'd arrived. And because he was a rather handsome single man, a lot of the unwed female church members were vying for his attention. At least, everyone but Pearl was. It seemed she and Reverend Kendrick butted heads on just about every topic.

Opal slipped onto an empty bench and flipped open the phone. "Hello."

"Ms. Lockhart, this is D'marcus Armstrong. I hate bothering you at home but something of importance has come up and I need you to meet me at the office in thirty minutes."

Opal glanced at her watch. "Mr. Armstrong, my sisters and I are hosting our family reunion and—"

"I regret the interruption but I do need you at the office, otherwise I wouldn't be calling." His tone indicated there would be no discussion on the matter. "You should be able to return to your family function within the hour."

Opal sighed. Now was not the time to make waves with her boss. This was her last semester at the university in her quest for a business management degree, and her employment at Sports Unlimited was part of her internship. She even planned to stay with the company after graduation and take advantage of the good benefits and the potential for advancement.

Having no choice, she replied, "All right. I'll be there in thirty minutes." Disappointed, she clicked off the phone.

"Don't tell us you're leaving."

Opal turned around and saw her sisters Ruby and Pearl standing behind her. At least Pearl was no longer debating issues with the new minister. Before her cell phone had gone off, being the diplomat in the family, Opal had thought about intervening in the heated discussion to smooth a few feathers that appeared to be getting ruffled.

She met Ruby's gaze and said, "Yes, I'm leaving but just for a little while. Something has come up at the office."

"And why didn't you tell that boss of yours that you don't work on Saturdays?" Ruby said, a little miffed. "I swear, that man is a tyrant."

Opal couldn't help but smile as she stood up. "Really, Ruby, D'marcus isn't that bad. He has a business to run and wants to continue its success. All those extra hours I work are justified. I *am* his administrative assistant, so he depends on me a lot. Besides, I can certainly use the money if I plan on moving to another apartment complex."

"The tenants around your apartment are still partying every night?" Pearl asked.

"Yes, and the landlord acts as if there's nothing he can do. I had hoped the situation would get better, but it hasn't. My building has become known as the party building."

Pearl smiled. "Umm, maybe I ought to move in when you move out. There's nothing like a good party every now and then."

Opal shook her head. Good at heart, Pearl enjoyed giving the impression that she was a wild child, but Opal knew better. Her sister's party-girl ways were just a facade. Opal had a feeling that, in reality, Pearl was someone still trying to find her purpose in life. More than anything, Opal hoped things worked out for Pearl with those demo tapes she had sent out.

"I can handle a good party every now and then," Opal decided to say. "But there are limits to one's tolerance and endurance."

"Things really must be out of hand if you're complaining," Pearl said. "Everyone knows you rarely complain about anything. You just roll with the flow."

Opal couldn't help but smile. It was a known fact that of the four Lockhart sisters, she was the hopeless optimist. No matter what the problem, she believed the result would end up positive.

She then thought of the problem she had detected before answering her phone. "Did you say anything to Amber about her behavior?" she asked Ruby.

Ruby shook her head. "Are you kidding? And have her not speak to me again for weeks? No, I didn't say anything to her, but I did ask Luther to say something. She usually listens to him."

Opal nodded. Luther Biggens, whom they had designated as cook for the day, was a family friend. His father and theirs had been the best of buddies when the two had been alive. A military man, Luther had left the navy SEALs after suffering a disabling leg injury. Now he managed his family's very profitable chain of mega automobile dealerships.

"I hope she listens to him," Pearl said glancing out across the yard. "I don't think Megan Townsend appreciates Amber flirting with her fiancé."

Opal sighed. "Well, let me go. I won't have time to go home and change so I'm going to have to wear what I have on," she said, glancing down at the shorts and T-shirt she was wearing.

"You look fine," Pearl said. "Besides, it will do D'marcus Armstrong good to see you in something other than a business suit. Maybe now he'll take a notice to you. You have great-looking legs, so you might as well flaunt them."

Opal rolled her eyes. "I don't want him to notice me.

I just want him to pay me well for the job that I do and give me a good evaluation at the end of my internship."

"Hey, if I were you I would want him to notice me," Pearl said chuckling. "The man might be a tyrant, but he's definitely a hunk, and a rich one. Tall, dark and handsome are the things dreams are made of. If I were you—"

"But you aren't me," Opal said, laughing. "Just make sure our family and guests continue to have a good time. Let everyone know I had to leave for a while, but I'll be back in an hour."

"If you're not, just make sure Mr. Armstrong knows your sisters plan on coming over there to get you," Ruby said.

Opal returned her grin. "Okay, I'll make sure he's aware of it. I'm sure the last thing he wants is the Lockhart sisters showing up causing problems. I'll be back later." She dashed inside the house to get her purse.

D'marcus Armstrong stood at the window of his office on the fifteenth floor and looked down into the parking lot below. His administrative assistant was arriving and she'd made good time. He had asked the ever-efficient Opal Lockhart to be there in thirty minutes and she had arrived in twenty.

He watched as she got out of her car and began walking toward the entrance of the building. He had told her he needed her services right away so the only sensible solution to meet his demand was to come dressed as she was.

And much to his displeasure, he rather liked it.

He didn't want to admit that he'd often wondered

what she looked like in something other than those business suits she liked wearing. It was plain to see she had a very curvy figure in addition to her attractive features. But she was not one to flaunt them. Instead, she kept trying to keep them well hidden. Her shoulder-length hair was usually worn pulled back in a bun and her face, more times than not, was devoid of any makeup. However, there was something about her that always managed to catch his attention anyway. Even the way she would arch her brow when she questioned him.

He released a deep breath trying to recall at what point he had become attracted to Opal. Lord knows he'd tried not to notice certain things about her, but nothing seemed to work. So he'd tried putting as much distance between them as possible, which wasn't easy given the nature of her job.

He continued studying her, watching as she tossed her hair back from her face, and he suddenly realized this was only the second time he'd seen her hair worn in any style other than a bun on her head. He didn't want to admit that even from fifteen stories up, she looked good.

"Hey, I'm tired of waiting for this meeting to begin."

At first D'marcus refused to turn around to acknowledge the comment that had been made. Dashuan Kennedy was trouble. He'd known it from the first, yet his partners had insisted that they hire him to play for the Detroit Chargers, the professional basketball team of which D'marcus was part owner.

"Armstrong, are you listening to me?"

It was then that D'marcus turned around. Skimming the other two men in the room, his partners in the ownership of the Chargers, his gaze immediately settled on the man reclining in the largest chair as though he owned it. "To be quite honest with you, Kennedy, no, I'm not listening to you. But it will behoove you to listen to what the other owners and I have to say once this meeting is underway. Since you've been sidelined by your knee injury, you have done nothing but cause us problems, and, frankly, I'm within an inch of giving you your walking papers."

Kennedy stared back at him, and a cocky smile touched his lips when he said, "That's bullshit and you know it. You can't afford to let me go. Have you forgotten who was the MVP for most of last season? If you have, Armstrong, I'm sure these two men here remember." He smirked, indicating the team's other owners, Ronald Williams and Stanley Hennessy.

"That might be true," D'marcus replied. "But I'm sure, like me, they feel you can take that MVP and shove it, because we're sick and tired of having to defend your behavior to the media. This time you have gone too far. Drugs and breaking team rules are two things that we won't tolerate even if you're Michael Jordan reincarnated."

The smirk on Dashuan's face disappeared. "When my ankle heals and I start playing this season, you'll know that I *am* the team and, without me, you can kiss the championship goodbye. Like I said, I'm sure these men know my worth, even if you don't."

Anger rose in D'marcus's face. Evidently Kennedy had forgotten that D'marcus owned the controlling interest in the Chargers. He decided he'd heard enough from a player who didn't know the meaning of *teamwork*. He was about to tell him that just as Opal walked into the room. Upon seeing her, an inexplicable calmness settled over him. Not liking the sensation, he shifted his glance to the two men sitting at the table.

"We can start the meeting now," he said, coming away from the window to stand in the middle of the room. "My administrative assistant has arrived."

Trying to focus on the meeting to make sure her notes documented the entire proceedings, Opal stared down at her notepad. She hadn't been surprised when she'd walked in to see bad boy Dashuan Kennedy being taken to task by D'marcus. This wasn't the first time Kennedy had gotten into trouble and she had a feeling it wouldn't be the last.

She glanced up just as the sun shining through the window hit D'marcus at an angle that highlighted his looks. At the age of thirty he was a self-made millionaire who, in addition to being part owner of the Chargers, was CEO of Sports Unlimited, which was a conglomeration of sport franchises.

As she stared at him, she had to admit that Pearl had been right in what she'd said earlier that day. D'marcus was a hunk. At six foot two, he had medium-brown skin, dark eyes, a clean-shaven face and short-cropped brown hair. Heads turned whenever he walked near women. And she was no exception. For no reason, he could make heated sensations flow through her whenever she was in a room with him.

The majority of the time he barely noticed she was alive, going about the job of making his company successful. Unfortunately, she was always quick to notice him—how well the clothes he wore fitted his body, how muscular and toned that particular body was, how the deep, husky sound of his voice could make her think of things other than business.

Even now, dressed in a polo shirt and a pair of jeans, he looked good, and she noticed as he moved around the room how the denim of his jeans stretched across muscular thighs and a firm butt. He also had a pair of lips that were very expressive. During the three months that she'd been working for him, she'd been able to decipher his mood just from watching his lips. And they were lips that were now moving again, she noted as she turned her concentration back on what he was saying.

"I think that should wrap things up as far as what we'll say during the press conference," D'marcus concluded. "And I hope you understand, Kennedy, that if you cause us any more problems, you run the risk of ending your career with this organization. Understood?"

Opal watched as Kennedy narrowed his eyes. It was plain to see D'marcus had pissed him off.

"Yeah, I understand," he responded in a clipped tone as he stood.

"Fine. We expect you at each practice session and preseason game regardless of whether you play," D'marcus added, his expression tight and his tone of voice direct.

"Whatever," Dashuan angrily threw over his shoulder as he left the room.

It was Opal's opinion that D'marcus had handled the situation remarkably well, but then she wasn't surprised. As his administrative assistant, she had seen him in action several times with both domestic and overseas buyers, and it always amazed her how astute he was in his business dealings.

"I appreciate you coming, Ms. Lockhart. I know it was unexpected."

She blinked, then noticed the other two gentlemen had left, leaving them alone in D'marcus's office. She stood. "No problem. You said it would take less than an hour and it did." It then occurred to her that this was the first time her boss had ever shown his appreciation for anything. Usually, although she tried her best, they seemed always to be at odds with each other.

"Do you need me for the press conference later today?" she asked as she inserted her notepad into her desk drawer for when she'd type the notes for Monday morning.

He shook his head. "No, I'll have the task of explaining why one of my key players was charged with possession of an illegal substance. Dashuan, of course, will no doubt be thrilled with the hours of community service he'll have to do."

She nodded as she gathered her purse and placed the straps on her shoulder. "All right, then."

He glanced at her T-shirt. "About your family reunion…"

"Yes?"

"I apologize for having to call you away from it."

Now he was apologizing. This was another first. She shrugged. "No big deal, I told them I'd be back in an hour and I will be. I'll see you on Monday."

She moved to leave and then turned back around. She knew he intended to remain at the office awhile, so she said, "We have plenty of food. Barbecued ribs, baked beans, corn, potato salad, all sorts of desserts. If you'd like, I can drop off a plate for you since I know you'll be here awhile."

D'marcus, who was about to reach for the phone, stopped abruptly and narrowed his eyes at her. "I don't need you to do that, Ms. Lockhart," he said rather harshly. "If I get hungry I can very well order something up or stop what I'm doing and go somewhere for a meal."

Although she should not have been, Opal found she was taken aback by his tone of voice. She really should be used to it by now. "Excuse me for making the suggestion, Mr. Armstrong."

As she turned and walked out of the room she wondered why she even bothered trying to be nice to the man.

Chapter 2

"I'm glad you made it back," Colleen Richards said when Opal stepped out on the patio.

"I told everyone I would," Opal said, mirroring her smile. She and Colleen were more than first cousins of the same age. Opal considered Colleen her very best friend, as well. And Colleen's sister, Paige, was Pearl's best friend and roommate.

Opal glanced around. It seemed the crowd of guests had thinned. "What happened to the church group that was sitting over there?" she asked.

Colleen rolled her eyes. "Thanks to Amber, they left. I think a few of the sisters got disgusted with her brazen behavior. Megan Townsend left first, hauling her fiancé out of here so quick it almost made your head spin. And then when Amber started trying to flirt with a few others, their significant others hauled them away, as well."

Opal sighed, shaking her head. "I thought Ruby asked Luther to talk to her."

"From what I understand, he tried but it didn't do any good. He told Ruby that Amber said her flirting was harmless." She shrugged. "It seems she was determined to get into mischief today."

Opal glanced around the yard. "And where is she?"

Colleen chuckled. "When most of the single men left and she couldn't do any more damage, she and that girl she was with left, too. She said they were going clubbing later."

When Colleen fell silent, Opal released a deep breath. There was no way around it. She, Ruby and Pearl needed to have a serious conversation with their baby sister.

"Oh, and I might as well be the one to tell you that you were the topic of speculation among your sisters after you left," Colleen said, smiling.

Opal lifted a brow. "What sort of speculation?"

Colleen chuckled. "I tried to tell them D'marcus Armstrong wasn't your type, but Pearl and Amber are convinced you should go after the man. He's handsome, rich, looks good in his clothes, so they're convinced he'll look good out of them, and they think you're what he needs."

Opal rolled her eyes when she thought about how she and D'marcus had parted ways just moments ago. "Trust me, I am not what that man needs."

"That's what Ruby said. She doesn't think he's the type of person you should get involved with. He's too moody. But Pearl and Amber said with all that money he has, they think you should be able to forget his moodiness."

Opal shook her head. "Those two *would* think that way."

"The three of them did agree on one thing, though."

Opal truly didn't like the sound of that. "And what would that be?"

"They think you have a crush on the man."

"What?"

"Just telling you what they said. I didn't agree with them, of course."

"Thanks, Colleen, I appreciate that."

"But now they do have me thinking."

Opal turned toward her cousin. "Thinking about what?"

"You are the most easygoing, tolerant and optimistic person I know. You always look on the bright side and usually don't let anything ruffle your feathers. But D'marcus Armstrong has been doing just that."

"There's only so much any one person can take, Colleen. I'm not a saint."

"No, but why is he getting next to you? If he's that bad, just quit."

Opal released a groan of frustration. "Mr. Armstrong is not all that bad, really. I think his bark is worse than his bite, and part of me wants to think he deliberately tries getting on my last nerve."

Colleen arched a brow. "Why do you think he would do that?"

Opal shrugged. "That's the way some bosses are, I guess. They like to be in control. He just has a rough-and-gruff demeanor. I'm getting used to it. But trust me when I say that I don't have a crush on the man. Of course, I think he's good-looking and all that, but he is not someone I want to get to know personally. I like my space and I'm sure he likes his."

Colleen nodded. "What do you know about him... personally?"

"Just what the gossip mill around the office says. He was raised by an aunt and uncle after his parents were killed in a car accident when he was six. He was engaged to marry his high school sweetheart in his last year of college when she was killed in a boating accident two weeks before their wedding."

"Oh, how awful that must have been for him."

Opal nodded. She knew that Colleen, who was pursuing a degree in psychology, was probably trying to figure out if D'marcus's past had somehow had an effect on his present state.

"You're back," she heard Pearl say behind them as she came out of the house carrying another bowl of potato salad. "What was so important that The Hunk had to call you away?"

"Nothing important," she said quickly. Because of the often confidential nature of her job she never divulged any private information. "He just needed me to take a few notes for him." And to change the subject quickly she glanced around and asked, "Where's Ruby?"

"She's inside trying to bring order to the kitchen," Pearl responded over her shoulder.

"I'll be back in a minute," Opal said to Colleen. "I need to talk to Ruby about something."

As she entered the back door into the kitchen, she paused. Ruby, who had fixed most of the food and gotten the meats ready for Luther to grill, was sitting at the kitchen table while Luther massaged her shoulders.

It seemed her sister was taking a much-deserved quiet moment.

Opal smiled. Not for first time, she wondered when her eldest sister would finally open her eyes and realize that, although they claimed to be only friends, she and Luther were meant for each other.

She went back outside. She shook her head when she found Pearl and Reverend Kendrick involved in another debate. As long as this one didn't turn as heated as the last, it should be okay.

She noticed the couple who owned the house next door, Keith and La Keita Hayward, had arrived while she was gone, and she decided to go speak to them. As she walked crossed the yard, she glanced back and studied the Tudor-style single-family brick home. Located in inner-city Detroit, it had always been a home filled with love and warmth.

After their father's death, she and her three sisters had been raised by their widowed mother, and their family had been one of the first African-American families to integrate into the neighborhood. Despite the urban blight that now surrounded the area, they had remained in their majestic family home basically on principal, not to mention their shoestring finances. Now everyone but Ruby had moved out. Opal couldn't help wondering what would become of their home if Ruby ever decided to go live someplace else. Would they sell the house? Rent it out? Or, now that it was paid for, would they leave it as a place they could come back to whenever they felt the need to escape and chill? Whatever decision she and her sisters made would be the right one.

Her thoughts then drifted to D'marcus. She couldn't help but wonder if he was still at the office and if he had gotten something to eat. She knew how easy it was for him to work through lunch. Then she remembered the chill in his tone when he'd dismissed her offer of food. Well, as far as she was concerned, it was his loss.

She sighed deeply, thinking that she should be used to his curt and unfriendly nature by now. But there wasn't a day that went by that she didn't hope his attitude would improve. So far it hadn't.

As she stopped in front of the Haywards, she smiled and quickly decided that D'marcus Armstrong was the last person she wanted to think about. She refused to let his behavior completely ruin her day.

D'marcus tossed aside a file he'd been working on and glanced over at the clock. It was after five already. Where had the day gone? He heard the growling of his stomach and immediately thought of all that food Opal had named when she'd offered to bring him a plate from her family gathering. Maybe he should have accepted her offer. But part of him felt he'd done the right thing by not doing so.

He leaned back in his chair as he picked up the framed photograph of the young woman. The woman who was to have been his wife. The pain of that loss was still with him even after six years. Tonya had been the one thing he had wanted in his life, the person he had loved with all his heart, and he'd lost her in one afternoon, two weeks before they were to marry. What really had torn him in two was finding out that at her death she had been a month pregnant with their child.

He hadn't just lost the woman he'd loved, but also the baby that would have been theirs.

He placed the photograph back on his desk and walked over to the window. It had been a beautiful day, warm for the first week in October, although the forecasters were predicting a cold front sometime next week.

His gaze swept the empty parking lot where Opal's car had been parked earlier. Part of him regretted his rude behavior to her. That same part knew there was no excuse for it. But another part, the part of him that had been protecting himself for the past six years, refused to agree. It believed there was an excuse. Opal Lockhart was a woman who could wiggle her way inside a man's head and heart if he wasn't careful. She was the first woman since Tonya who had ignited even a spark inside him. What was so sad was that he hadn't been trying for that spark.

She had worked late one night, her first week with Sports Unlimited, and he had left the office for the day. He had gotten as far as the third floor when he remembered that he had left behind a file he needed to take home to review. He had returned and walked into her office area to find her standing at the window in deep thought. Because of the long day, she had taken off her shoes and jacket, and the fashionable scarf was no longer around her neck. He had stood studying her. Without knowing he was there, she released her bun and ran her hands through her shoulder-length hair. Without the jacket he'd seen her small waist and the delicate curves of her hips. She had looked beguiling, sexy, a total turn-on.

For the first time in six years, he had felt long-buried sensations. Sexual chemistry to a degree he'd never known before had nearly driven him to take her in his arms. Instead, he had regained control of his senses and left. But from that evening forward, he'd made it a point to make sure he placed distance between himself and his administrative assistant, and he took on a gruff demeanor to make sure things stayed distant. The last thing he needed was for the two of them to get too friendly with each other. The only woman he could ever possibly love had died six years ago.

Moving away from the window, he returned to the chair behind his desk. He would work for another hour or so before he called it a day. On the way home he would stop at one of the fast-food places and grab a sandwich. Usually he didn't stay all day at the office on the weekend, but after the press conference, he had decided to get a head start on next week's work.

He cringed in anger every time he thought about Dashuan Kennedy and his poor attitude. Players like him gave any game a bad name. He definitely wasn't any kid's role model. In fact, as far as D'marcus was concerned, whether they won or lost, the Chargers probably would be better off without Dashaun. There was no doubt Kennedy was a gifted young basketball player—but he was one who had some kind of a chip on his shoulder. D'marcus felt whatever issues Dashuan was having extended beyond his badass ego problem. Frankly, D'marcus was ready to trade him, but the other two owners saw Dashaun as their hope for the coming season.

He felt a strange prickling sensation and looked up,

surprised to see Opal standing in the doorway of his office. Before he could open his mouth to ask what she was doing there, she entered and placed a take-out box in front of him.

"I know what you said, but I couldn't see myself letting you starve. If you don't want to eat it you can trash it," she said, before turning to leave.

"Why?" he asked before she had reached the door. When she turned around, his eyes flicked over her with a cool expression. "Why did you come back? With the food?"

She tilted her chin and he saw a stubborn glint to it when she said, "Because I refuse to become a grouch like you. Life has been too good to me this year for me to do that."

"Then I suggest you count your blessings, Ms. Lockhart."

To his surprise, she smiled. "Trust me, Mr. Armstrong, I do. Maybe it's time for you to start counting yours."

His eyes narrowed at the boldness of her statement and before he could give her a reply, she was gone.

Opal quickly stepped onto the elevator thinking she could probably go ahead and kiss her job goodbye. However, today her boss had gotten on her last nerve. Maybe she was out of line for returning with food, but she had known he wouldn't take the time to eat anything.

Part of her wondered why she even cared, but she did. Once the crowd at the reunion had begun dwindling, that part of her that was too filled with kindness to let even someone like D'marcus Armstrong not share in such a wonderful meal had decided that, no matter what kind of attitude he had, she would not let him dictate hers. By nature she was not a mean-spirited person and she refused to let him turn her into one.

As she made her way through the parking lot toward her car, she glanced over her shoulder and looked up. D'marcus was standing at the window in his office staring down at her. She sighed, deciding she would report to work on Monday as usual. If he asked for her resignation because of what she'd said, there was nothing she could do about it. But he'd needed to hear what she had said. He of all people should be counting his blessings.

As she got into her car she forced any worries about next week aside. Tomorrow she would go to church and say a prayer for him. She would also make sure she got all the spiritual preparations she needed for when she saw D'marcus Armstrong again.

On Sunday morning Opal sat in a pew beside Amber and Ruby in the Lakeview Baptist Church. This was Pearl's Sunday to lead a song, and they were all excited. Reverend Kendrick would be delivering the message after the scripture was read, and Opal felt she needed to hear the word today, more so than ever.

D'marcus Armstrong might have pissed her off something awful yesterday, but that hadn't stopped him from invading her dreams last night. Some of her thoughts had been downright corrupt, and a lot of what she had imagined them doing together was shamefully sinful. And, to make matters worse, she didn't even like the man. Not to mention there was a good chance he would be kicking both her and her job to the curb tomorrow. Her sisters would refuse to believe that she, of all people—someone who never lost her temper—had actually gone off on D'marcus Armstrong.

She cleared her mind of the issues facing her with her boss when Pearl stepped up to the mic to sing. The church was packed—not unusual for the first Sunday of the month. And Opal thought the choir's new robes looked really nice.

Pearl began singing "What a Mighty God We Serve" in a way that only Pearl could do. Within no time, the church was rocking, people were standing on their feet rejoicing, getting caught up in their own testimonies to the fact that God was truly awesome. Pearl and the choir members were singing out of their souls, but it was Pearl's beautiful voice that was stirring things up, causing jubilation to spread throughout the congregation.

After Pearl's song ended and the scripture had been read, Reverend Kendrick stood before a packed and electrified house. "I want to thank Sister Lockhart for that song, because while she was singing I was sitting there thinking about just what a mighty God we do serve."

He paused to glance over the congregation, and for some reason Opal thought he looked at her a little longer than the others. *A guilty conscience will do that to you,* she thought, shifting in her seat.

"How many of you ever pause to not only think about how mighty God is," Reverend Kendrick continued, "but also about all the many blessings He bestows? Most of us just assume we're at where we are in our lives because we are deserving. Well, that is not the case, because none of us are deserving. We have all sinned at some point in our lives. Some of us are still sinning."

Opal hoped no one saw her blush when she felt her cheeks get a little warm.

"But God loves us anyway," Reverend Kendrick continued. "He forgives us, and we have to find it in our hearts to forgive others, even those we may feel don't deserve our forgiveness."

D'marcus Armstrong suddenly flashed across Opal's mind.

"But we have to forgive them, just like our Father constantly forgives us," Reverend Kendrick went on to say.

Opal shifted in her seat, thinking it was too bad D'marcus wasn't at church today. If he embraced the concept of forgiving and forgetting, then she wouldn't have to go to bed tonight worrying about whether she still had a job tomorrow.

Reverend Kendrick interrupted her thoughts by saying, "We should especially forgive those who don't deserve our forgiveness, and continue to pray for God to work to change their hearts. And I'm standing before you as a living witness that miracles can happen. You just have to believe that they can."

Chapter 3

Monday morning, Opal was seated at her desk when D'marcus arrived. He glanced over at her, gave her a curt nod as he crossed the room to his office.

"Mr. Armstrong, the minutes from Saturday's meeting are typed and on your desk. I've also saved them in an electronic file."

At her words, he'd slowly turned toward her, and now she quickly searched his features for any indication that she was about to be fired. He wasn't smiling—not that he ever did—but aside from that, she couldn't gauge his expression. Part of her wanted to believe that he had gotten over what she'd said and that it was water under the bridge. However, she knew some men would consider her words disrespectful.

"Thank you, Ms. Lockhart, and please hold all my calls until noon."

"Yes, sir," she added with a quick smile of relief when it appeared he wasn't going to let her go.

"And, Ms. Lockhart?"

She swallowed, thinking perhaps her relief had been premature. "Yes?"

"Thanks for dinner on Saturday. I enjoyed it very much."

She blinked. He was thanking her for dinner? Gracious. As Reverend Kendrick had said at church yesterday, miracles could happen if you only believed.

D'marcus tossed his briefcase into the chair and let out a ragged sigh. He wasn't sure just what he planned to do about Opal Lockhart. Because of her very efficient nature, she had become a vital asset to him, but as far as he was concerned, just as he'd told Dashuan Kennedy on Saturday, anyone was replaceable.

But while sitting in this very office on Saturday evening enjoying every mouthful of the food she'd brought him, he kept thinking that Opal Lockhart was a woman who could remind a man each and every time he saw her that there was more to life than work.

When she had shown up with the food, she had still been wearing what she'd had on earlier, a pair of shorts and a T-shirt. Although the length of the shorts could be considered decent, they had still shown her lovely legs. For the second time that day, she had stirred his hormones and for a split second as he had stood at the window and watched her leave, he had been tempted to call her on her cell phone and tell her to come back up to his office.

D'marcus grimaced. He was glad he hadn't made such a move. That would have been the worst thing he could have done. His mind knew that, but at the moment, his body wasn't so sure. He counted backward, trying to remember the last time he'd been intimate with a woman, and was surprised to recall it had been well over eight months. It had been just that long since he'd socialized in any way. Lately, he had spent the majority of his time adding more stores to his portfolio, which required a lot of his time and concentration. No wonder he was beginning to notice just how downright horny he was now.

There was one way to fix his problem. Tonight when he got home he would check his address book to see which one of his female acquaintances who knew the score would go out on a date with him that weekend. A date that would eventually end up with them sharing a bed. If getting laid was what he needed, then he would take care of the problem—and soon.

Opal picked up the phone on the first ring. "Sports Unlimited, Mr. Armstrong's office. Opal Lockhart speaking."

"Ms. Lockhart, this is Mr. Stone, manager of the Viscera Apartments."

Opal smiled. "Yes, Mr. Stone?" She hoped he was calling with good news.

"It appears I'll have a vacancy within a few weeks."

Opal's smile widened. "That's certainly good news." Once she had made the decision to move, she had decided to check on the Viscera Apartments. They were a lot nicer than her current place and only minutes from the office, which meant a lower gas bill. Of course, the rent would be higher, but she was a firm believer in getting what you paid for. And right now, she was tired of paying for sleepless nights in the party building.

"So I take it you're still interested?" Mr. Stone was saying.

"Yes, most definitely."

"All right. Then you can come by this afternoon with your deposit. We require two months in advance."

Her eyebrows raised. Two months rent was a lot and not what she'd assumed. "Two months?"

"Yes. That's our policy. If you don't think you can—"

"No, there won't be a problem," she said quickly. She would take the money out of her savings, but she would have to replace it quickly if she still intended to get a new car at the beginning of the year.

"Good. I'll see you this afternoon."

"Okay, Mr. Stone, I'll see you then."

Opal had just returned from lunch when D'marcus buzzed her. "Yes, Mr. Armstrong?"

"Ms. Lockhart, could you step into my office a moment, please?"

"Certainly."

She gathered her notepad. He hadn't been out of his office since he'd shut himself in there this morning, nor had he called out for her assistance.

She opened the door and walked into his office. He had removed his jacket, and the sleeves of his shirt were rolled up to his elbows. A ton of files were spread out on his desk.

He glanced up when she walked in. "We might be adding two other stores this week," he said in a tone of voice that was all business.

"Congratulations."

"Thank you. And while it's good news for me, it might not be for you, Ms. Lockhart."

She swallowed tightly. Maybe she had told Mr. Stone prematurely that she would be taking the apartment. There was no way she could afford it if she didn't have a job. "Why would you say that?" she asked as she sat down in the chair across from his desk.

"Because it will require you to work longer hours for the next two weeks. Of course I will pay you generously for any overtime."

Relief spread through Opal. Little did he know, she considered what he was saying as good news. The extra money would help replace what she was taking out of her savings to cover the security on her apartment. And she couldn't discount the fact that, if she impressed him by doing a good job, it would be a way to move up in the company. She would have her degree in the spring and there were plenty of opportunities for advancement within this company.

"Will you be able to work additional hours, Ms. Lockhart?"

She met his gaze. "That won't be a problem. When will they start?"

"Tomorrow. Three extra hours every evening this week, except for Friday, should be sufficient. And let's do the same for next week, although I want to throw Monday night into the mix."

"That's no problem."

"Good. Now, I need to go over the stats for the Savannah store with you. I should have asked you to bring that file in here with you."

"I'll go and get it."

Opal stood and quickly walked out of the office.

As soon as Opal left, D'marcus leaned back in his office chair. Her scent was still in the room. More than once, he had noticed the fragrance and had yet to put a name to it, but he definitely liked it on her.

No, he mustn't think about how much he liked that particular perfume on her or how good she looked today in her business suit. Professional but still sexy. She never wore anything to call attention to herself but her clothes did it anyway.

He thought about all that he knew about her from her employment records. Both of her parents were deceased and she was the second oldest of four daughters. She lived in an apartment in a fairly decent area of town and she had turned twenty-seven her last birthday. He gathered she was close to her siblings and enjoyed staying in touch with her family. The family affair she had attended on Saturday attested to that. He also knew there were great cooks in her family, considering the food she had brought to him. What he'd told her was true. He had totally enjoyed every mouthful.

He glanced up when she returned to his office. "All right, I'm ready, Mr. Armstrong."

Her words stirred something deep within him, something directly below the gut. That part of his body definitely needed help and he intended to get it this weekend.

"Okay," he said, straightening up in his chair. "Let's get started."

"So you have to spend more time with The Hunk?" Pearl smiled at Opal as she sat down at the kitchen table. Ruby and Pearl had dropped by after work as they usually did most Monday afternoons. Amber would join them every once in a while but lately she'd been taking classes at the university on Monday nights. Opal had been excited to tell them the good news about the apartment. Then she told them about the additional money she'd make working extra hours the next two weeks.

Opal rolled her eyes. "I'll be working overtime but Mr. Armstrong wasn't specific as to whether he would be staying late or not."

"Why would you fall for such a tyrant?" Ruby asked, grinning.

Opal shook her head. "First of all, I haven't fallen for anyone and, to be quite honest, D'marcus Armstrong isn't a tyrant. He just happens to be a very demanding boss. There is a difference."

Ruby lifted an arched brow. "And do you have a crush on him?"

"Of course not. Where did the two of you get such an idea from?"

Before either of her sisters could answer her question, her cell phone rang. Standing, she pulled it from her purse and checked the caller ID. It was Colleen. "Yes, Colleen?"

"Did you get the apartment?" her cousin asked excitedly.

Opal smiled. "Yes, I put down the deposit today," she said, deciding not to mention to anyone how much of a deposit it was. But she did tell Colleen about the overtime since they usually went to prayer meeting together at church on Wednesday nights.

"Maybe you can get Mr. Armstrong to go to prayer meeting with you," Colleen joked.

"Sure, but don't hold your breath," Opal replied, wondering if D'marcus even went to church.

A few minutes later, after ending the call with Colleen, she glanced across the table to find her two sisters staring at her with smug looks on their faces. "What?"

"You do have a crush on him," Pearl said.

"I do not," she persisted.

"Yes, you do. You get this funny little smile on your face each time you mention his name. Just like you did just now, while talking to Colleen."

"You're imagining things," Opal said, taking a sip of her tea.

Ruby smiled at her over the rim of her cup. "Okay, keep your secrets, but you can't fool us. I agree with Pearl. You have a crush on your boss."

One thing Opal had discovered about her sisters while growing up with them was that if they truly believed something trying to convince them they were wrong was nearly impossible, a waste of good time. So she decided not even to try anymore. In time, they would discover their assumption was incorrect.

Later that night, when Opal slipped between the sheets in her bed, she tried drowning out the sound of the loud music playing next door by thinking how nice her new apartment would be. She thought of the time she would spend decorating and how, since the new place was more spacious, she would no longer feel cramped.

She glanced at the clock on her nightstand. It was ten o'clock. She wondered if D'marcus was still at the office or if he'd already gone. He had been on an important international conference call when she had left. She breathed in deeply as she recalled how she'd stuck her head in his office to let him know she was leaving and found him sitting on the corner of his desk talking on the speakerphone.

Once again, she had been struck by just what a good-looking man he was. Even while conducting business, he spoke in a deep, husky voice that actually had made her pulse race. And the way his trousers stretched tight across his firm, muscular thighs had made her heart pound in her chest.

She had silently mouthed the words, *I'm leaving now,* and he had held her gaze and nodded, letting her know he'd understood what she had said. For just a heartbeat, she'd thought their gazes had held for a moment longer than necessary, but now she was sure she had imagined it.

She turned on her side, thinking how wrong her sisters were about her feelings for D'marcus. She would be honest and say she was attracted to him, but that was as far as it went. And, as she had told Ruby and Pearl, she wasn't sure he would be staying late with her over the next two weeks, but if he did, she was determined that things would be kept on a strictly professional basis. She couldn't imagine him having it any other way.

Chapter 4

D'marcus released a deep breath before taking a sip of coffee as he stood at his office window and watched his ever-efficient administrative assistant walk across the parking lot.

There was a businesslike tilt to her head, and her walk was brisk and measured. He glanced at the clock. She was early. Usually he arrived after she did so he never knew exactly what time she arrived at work each day. He wondered if coming in at least an hour early was the norm for her or if she had done it today because of all the work she would be tackling this week. If coming in early was a habit, she definitely hadn't been recording it on her time card.

He frowned. He was a person who believed in paying his employees for the work they did and the hours they worked. He would definitely have a discussion with her about it.

He glanced back out the window and watched as another one of his employees, Ted Marshall, from the accounting department, conveniently began walking beside her. D'marcus stiffened inwardly when he noticed Opal smiling at something the man had said. Were the two dating? For some reason the thought irritated him. He knew that Marshall was divorced and, from what D'marcus had heard from his last administrative assistant, Marshall thought himself quite the ladies' man. Definitely not the type of person Opal needed to become mixed up with. He shook his head, thinking, who was he to determine who his employees should be involved with?

He moved from the window and sat behind his desk, staring at the files spread across it. He had more to do with his time than be concerned with the love life of Opal Lockhart.

Opal drew in a sharp breath when she sat down at her desk and realized Mr. Armstrong had already arrived at work. Usually she had plenty of time to get settled into her work before he got there.

While her computer booted up she went about watering the plants in her office. There were a number of them and she intended to keep them alive and healthy.

She turned when she heard D'marcus open the door to come out of his office. She flicked a glance in his direction and immediately studied his face, wondering just what sort of day she would have. His expression was unreadable.

"Ms. Lockhart."

"Good morning, Mr. Armstrong."

"I have an off-site breakfast meeting this morning with the other two owners of the Chargers. I should be back in a few hours. Then you and I need to get together to discuss the inventory for the two new stores."

"Yes, sir." She tried not to notice how nice he looked from the toes of his expensive shoes to his dark suit and white shirt. The man was immaculately well groomed and sexy as sin.

"We may have to work through lunch, so I suggest you order us something."

Opal raised an arched brow. "You want me to order something for lunch? For both of us?"

"Yes, by all means. I need your assistance the better part of the day, but I don't want to rob you of your lunch. And I might as well eat something myself since I plan on working rather late tonight."

She nodded. He had just answered the question that had been tugging at her mind—whether he would be working late each night, as well. "Is there anything you prefer? Any particular type of sandwich?"

He shook his head. "No, but I prefer they hold the mustard."

"Yes, sir."

"And, Ms. Lockhart?"

"Yes?"

"Do you come in early every day?"

"Just about."

"Then make sure you're adequately compensated for any extra time you spend here by including it on your time card," he said curtly, and then he walked away.

D'marcus glanced up when Opal entered his office carrying bags filled with their lunch. He quickly got up and walked around the desk to relieve her of them. It didn't help matters that he had to stand close enough to her that he got a good whiff of her perfume, the same perfume he'd found to be totally seductive.

She glanced up at him. "Thanks."

He nodded and took a step back. "No problem." He placed the bags on his desk. "What do we have?"

She smiled. "Turkey sandwiches, cream of broccoli soup and iced tea."

"Sounds good. Let me clear an area on my desk so we can pull everything out of the bags."

Opal lifted a brow. He wanted them to sit in the same room together and eat? She'd assumed they'd be taking a break and she would be going back to her desk to eat.

He must have seen the strange look on her face because he asked, "Is something wrong, Ms. Lockhart?"

"No, but I assumed you would want to eat lunch alone."

He shrugged. "Normally I do, but I'm expecting a call from Bob Chaney any moment and I'll need you here to jot down what he says when I place him on speakerphone."

He then eyed her for a moment and asked, "Do you have a problem doing that? If so, I can ask Human Resources to send me one of the women from the typing pool."

"No, I don't have a problem with it."

"You sure?"

No, she wasn't sure, but she wasn't about to tell him that. "Yes, I'm sure."

"Good."

He then proceeded to clear his desk before coming back to sit behind it, leaving Opal to set out the lunch.

"We basically got the same thing," she said, handing him his sandwich, soup and tea. "I'm not crazy about mustard, either."

He glanced over at her when she took the chair in front of his desk and scooted it up closer to share the desktop with him. "What else aren't you crazy about?" he asked.

She started to say "demanding bosses," but thought better of it. She had said enough on Saturday. Even now, she was surprised he hadn't given her her walking papers. "In the way of foods, I've never developed a fondness for squash."

"Umm, I like squash."

She stared at him and watched as he took a big bite out of his sandwich and slowly began chewing it. A strange sensation passed through her stomach when she thought about him opening his mouth that wide over hers, devouring it as greedily as he was the sandwich.

She quickly gave herself a mental shake, wondering where such a thought came from and demanding it never return.

"Is something wrong?"

She blinked when she realized he had asked her a question. "No."

"Then why are you staring at me like that?"

She swallowed, not knowing how long she'd been staring. Never before had she been mesmerized by a man's mouth. So she said the first thing that came into her mind. "You seem hungry."

He chuckled and she blinked again. This was the first time she'd ever heard him chuckle, and the dimples that came into his cheeks almost made her drop the cup of iced tea she was holding. "If I seem hungry, Ms. Lockhart, it's because I am. I came into the office early today, so I didn't get a chance to eat breakfast."

"Oh," she said. Instead of meeting his gaze she bit into her own sandwich and tried concentrating on just eating it.

"I hope your family isn't upset about the extra hours you'll be working."

She washed down the food she had in her mouth with her iced tea before saying, "Trust me, they understand."

"What about Ted Marshall?"

She did glance up at him then. "Ted Marshall in the accounting department?"

"Yes. I saw the two of you walk in together this morning and assumed that you were seeing each other."

She shook her head. "I barely know the man. We just happened to be in the parking lot around the same time and walked in together. No biggie."

D'marcus stared at her for a moment while she lowered her head and continued eating her sandwich. What on earth had possessed him to bring up Ted Marshall's name? He was not the type of employer who got into his employees' personal business. It really wasn't any concern of his if she and Marshall had been dating. It was their business as long as they conducted themselves decently in the office.

A few moments later, his phone rang. It was Bob Chaney and, as far as D'marcus was concerned, he had received the call right on time. He wasn't sure how much longer he could have endured being alone in the same office with his very attractive administrative assistant.

* * *

Opal glanced at her watch. It was close to eight o'clock and she had just completed filing all the electronic messages. It was time to call it a day, but before she left, she needed to check with D'marcus to make sure there wasn't anything else he needed her to do. They had been busy in his office with numerous conference calls until around five that afternoon. She wondered where on earth the man got his energy. In addition to his regular business, he had received a couple of media calls regarding Dashuan Kennedy's incident that past weekend.

Before logging off her computer, she picked up the stack of papers she needed him to sign. The door to his office was slightly ajar so she walked in—and stopped short. He was leaning back in his chair, asleep. This was another first. Today at lunch she had seen him smile; now tonight she was watching him have a peaceful moment. The expression on his face was relaxed, unstrained and calm. She walked farther into the room and once again noticed the framed photograph of the woman he usually had sitting on his desk. Earlier, when he'd spread out the files on his desk, he had placed it in a drawer.

Curiosity made her move toward the desk to pick up the photograph and look at it. Something she had never done before. For some reason, he always placed it in the drawer when he left each day.

The woman was simply beautiful and Opal immediately knew she had to be the fiancée he'd lost, the one who had gotten killed in a boating accident two weeks before their wedding. She then wondered if Colleen was right and if D'marcus's less-than-friendly attitude could be the result of a broken heart.

"What are you doing in here?"

Opal jumped at the sound of the gruff voice, nearly dropping the papers out of her hand as she quickly placed the frame back on his desk. She swallowed against the tightness in her throat and said, "I have papers for you to sign."

He straightened in his chair. "But that doesn't give you the right to bother my personal belongings, Ms. Lockhart."

"I'm sorry, Mr. Armstrong, but I was curious." She then added, "She was beautiful."

Instead of accepting the compliment, he stared at her with ice-cold eyes. "You had no right to touch that photograph." The anger in his voice almost made Opal's pulse go still.

"I said I was sorry, sir, and it won't happen again." Anger tainted her voice, too. She was a person who respected everyone's privacy and she hadn't meant any harm. It wasn't like she was planning on stealing the darn thing.

"These need your signature," she said, handing him the papers. He took them from her and the room got extremely quiet. The only sound was the shuffling of papers. He handed them back to her and she turned and quickly walked out of his office, closing the door behind her.

As soon as Opal left, D'marcus stood and shoved his hands into the pockets of his pants. He walked over to the window and glanced up at the sky. Damn, what was wrong with him? It seemed he didn't miss a beat when it came to chewing out Opal Lockhart about anything. He could understand her being curious about the photograph, especially since he went to great pains to lock it up each night. And she *was* his administrative assistant. There was nothing on his desk that she shouldn't be allowed to touch.

He inhaled deeply. What was there about her that seemed to bring out the worst in him without her even trying? In fact, if he was honest with himself, he had to admit she was the most easygoing person he knew.

He heard her shutting down her computer for the day and knew he had to apologize for his behavior. Grabbing his jacket off the rack, he headed for his office door.

"The man is a tyrant, just like Ruby said," she muttered to herself as she buttoned up her jacket. As predicted, an October cold front had moved in, changing the weather overnight. She'd even heard there was a strong possibility Detroit would be having its first snowstorm by the end of the week.

"Who's Ruby?"

D'marcus's question snapped Opal around. He was standing against the wall with his arms crossed over his chest, staring at her. "Excuse me?"

"I asked you, who's Ruby?"

Opal stiffened slightly. Evidently, he'd heard her muttering to herself. She tilted up her chin and said. "Ruby is my eldest sister."

He nodded. "And she thinks I'm a tyrant?"

Heat flooded her cheeks and she couldn't look at him any longer. Instead, she looked down at her purse to get her car keys out. "Yes, that's her opinion," she said softly.

"And evidently yours, as well."

She lifted her head and met his gaze again. "Not until tonight. Before now I just assumed you were demanding, like most bosses."

D'marcus stared at her in silence for a moment and she stared back, refusing to look away. "Okay," he finally said. "Because of my actions tonight I probably deserve that. I apologize."

For the second time that day Opal felt her pulse go still. He was actually apologizing to her again. Before she could say anything he continued, "In the future I will try not to be a tyrant, as well as not being overly demanding."

His words surprised Opal and she didn't know what to say. "If you're about ready to leave, we can walk out together," he continued. "I'm not sure the parking lot is well lit. Be sure to contact someone in the maintenance department tomorrow about replacing those bulbs with brighter lights."

"All right." After taking the keys from her purse, she came from around her desk and waited while he turned off the lights. She should have assured him that she would be safe walking to her car alone, but her head was still whirling from his apology as well as the promise he'd made.

They caught the elevator in silence and walked out of the building without exchanging any conversation. She was surprised he knew exactly where her car was parked and walked her straight to it. He stood back as she opened the door and eased into the driver's seat.

"And don't forget what I said, Ms. Armstrong. I want you to be compensated any time you arrive at the office early."

"Okay," she said, rolling her window down. She couldn't help but stare at him for a moment. It seemed his gaze was focused on her lips. Heat flowed through her at the thought, and she quickly diverted her gaze from his and started her car.

She glanced back at him to say, "Good night."

"Good night." He stepped back as she put her car in gear and pulled away. She couldn't help looking into her rearview mirror. He was still standing there, staring as she drove off.

Chapter 5

Opal released a sigh of gratitude as she sat at her desk. Ever since Tuesday night D'marcus had kept his word and tried to be a more reasonable boss. He actually used words like *please* and *thank-you* a lot more often than ever before, and a couple of times he had actually smiled while talking to her. But then, he had reason to smile. They had gotten word yesterday that two additional stores would be opening in California.

That meant they'd been extremely busy with various conference calls and contracts that had to be readied and faxed out. She and D'marcus spent most of the time either together or with his lawyers. She enjoyed watching how he handled business. He was a self-made millionaire and his sports franchise was growing by leaps and bounds, making him even richer.

"Ms. Lockhart, could you step into my office, please?"

Opal smiled. The courtesy words were beginning to come more naturally for him. At first they'd sounded clipped and forced. "Yes, sir, I'm on my way," she said, grabbing her notepad.

She walked into his office to find files spread out on his desk, which was becoming a norm. Thank God for her organizational skills or he would never be able to find anything. In fact, a few days ago, he had complimented her on them when he'd looked for a file while she'd been at lunch. Her unique filing system made things a lot easier to find, especially for him.

"Yes, Mr. Armstrong?"

He glanced up and met her gaze, and, as always, she felt a tingling sensation in the pit of her stomach. She wished for once he would come to the office looking any way but desirable. Let his hair grow longer, go unshaven, acquire a scar or two, get a broken nose. But she had a feeling, even with those imperfections, he would still be handsome.

"I have to be in San Francisco next week," he was saying. "With four stores opening in the next couple of months I need to be closer to the action."

She nodded, understanding completely since all four new stores would be opening in California. She also knew he had satellite offices in several states. "So you won't need me working overtime for you next week," she said, stating the obvious and thinking that was the reason he had summoned her to his office.

"Yes, that's right. However, I will need you to go to California with me."

She blinked, certain she hadn't heard him correctly. "You want me to go to California with you?" she asked.

"Yes. San Francisco, California."

She tried to keep the nervous sigh from escaping her

lips. She knew of administrative assistants who traveled with their bosses all the time and loved it and considered it as one of the perks of the job. Even Ruby traveled with her boss occasionally and considered it an opportunity to shine. But Opal had never given any consideration to the thought that Mr. Armstrong would want to take her anyplace with him.

"Will there be a problem, Ms. Lockhart?"

He recaptured her attention and she met his gaze. She'd never tell him the "problem." "No, there won't be a problem, sir."

He nodded. "Good. I plan to fly out first thing Monday morning. You can probably return on Friday. I might stay for a few more days visiting relatives."

"I'll be ready to fly out Monday morning." She told herself it wouldn't be that bad. They'd be on a crowded plane, then in busy meetings.

He turned back to his files, then looked up as she was about to exit. "Oh, Ms. Lockhart, I forgot to tell you. We'll be taking my private jet."

What was wrong?

When he had mentioned her accompanying him on that business trip, although she hadn't protested or declined, Opal had seemed surprised and even nervous. In fact, when she'd left his office, she had appeared downright rattled. He smiled. And here he'd thought that nothing could ruffle Opal Lockhart…except his tyrannical, demanding behavior.

He chuckled when he remembered what she'd said to him. She had been deadly serious in explaining her feelings. He had seen it in her eyes, the depth of her honesty. That had been one of the rare times he'd conversed with her and hadn't been studying her lips. There was just something about the shape of her mouth that always tempted him.

She had a way of putting every male hormone he possessed on full alert whenever she entered his office. God knows he had tried to ignore it, avoid it, find ways to become immune to it, but so far nothing worked. Even without trying, she had a sensuality about her that he found totally irresistible. And what he found so astounding was that she was unaware of the depth of her appeal.

The other day, while sipping his soup at lunch, he had found himself glancing across the desk at her, and part of him had imagined sipping on her instead. He definitely had one hell of a sexual ache and he hoped his date this weekend was what he needed to cure him.

He tossed aside the paper he'd been trying to read. Taking Opal to San Francisco with him wasn't a smart idea given his attraction to her—an attraction he just couldn't kick. But he did need her there. In this stage of his business negotiations, he needed someone he could depend on and he'd discovered since she had come to work for him that he could definitely depend on her. Not only was she well versed in the handling of business affairs, she had a good grasp of marketing and advertising, customer service and public relations, as well. She was a natural when it came to people skills. She got along with everyone at the office, and, more than once, he'd received compliments on her behalf from clients and business associates whom she had treated well.

Somehow, he would get through a week of spending

the majority of his time in her presence. Hadn't he done so this week? Still, there was something about being away from the office that seemed to put a whole new light on things.... But he refused to let it. Opal was his employee and nothing more. And once he had his date this weekend with Priscilla Tucker, his need for sexual release would be taken care of and he would be fine.

The last thing he needed to think about or consider was sleeping with his administrative assistant. That was something that could not and would not happen. He had to make sure of it.

"Give me one good reason why you don't want to go out of town with D'marcus Armstrong, Opal," Colleen was asking her. Opal had called her cousin and invited her to lunch after D'marcus had told her he would be out of the office at a meeting.

Opal pursed her lips, thinking. "Because I really need to stay here. I'll be moving in a couple of weeks and I need to start packing things up."

"And from what you've told me, you'll be back in time to do that. When you took this job, didn't the person in Human Resources tell you there might be traveling involved?"

"Yes, but after meeting D'marcus and seeing what kind of attitude he had, I figured I'd be the last person he would take anyplace."

"And why not? You're efficient and good at what you do. You've become very valuable to him. From what I see, the man is definitely wheeling and dealing and his business is growing like wildfire. He would want someone familiar and dependable to assist him during this time."

Opal nodded, knowing everything Colleen was saying was true. But…

"Be honest with me, Opal. What has you so rattled? Why are you so bothered by the thought of spending a week in California, sharing a hotel with D'marcus Armstrong? And note I said hotel, and not hotel room," she interjected when Opal arched a brow. "I've traveled with my boss before."

Opal rolled her eyes upward. "Yes, but he's married."

Colleen chuckled. "Yes, and, at times, I hear they can be the worst ones, although Mr. Matherson has never gotten out of line with me. But just because D'marcus is single shouldn't make a difference. Unless…"

Opal glanced across the table and asked, "Unless what?"

"Unless you do have a crush on him like your sisters think."

"Wrong. Like I told you before, I find the man attractive, but that's as far as it goes."

Colleen leaned closer over the table and looked her in the eyes. "You sure?"

Opal broke eye contact and took a sip of her hot tea. "I'm positive."

"Okay, so when do you leave?" Colleen asked, leaning back in her chair.

"Monday morning."

Colleen nodded. "That means you'll have to do all your shopping for the trip this weekend."

"Shopping?" Opal said, now getting really rattled. She hated going shopping. She usually shopped seriously at Christmas and purchased enough outfits to last for the coming year, unable to understand why women would constantly go to malls as if it was an addiction. Her three sisters shopped enough for her, thank you.

"Yes, shopping. Surely you don't plan to take your regular clothes."

Opal frowned. "And what's wrong with my regular clothes?"

Colleen grinned. "Your wool suits are fine for this climate, but I think they'll be too warm in sunny California."

"Fine, I have some summer suits."

Colleen nodded slowly. "Yes, and I've seen them."

Opal's frown deepened. "And?"

"And do me a favor and get some new things. Come on, Opal, a couple of new outfits won't hurt. Remember, in this business, it's the entire package that has to impress. Not only does D'marcus Armstrong want an efficient secretary, I'm sure he wants one who dresses the part."

Opal lifted her chin. "I dress professionally."

"Of course you do, but I want you to spruce up your outfits a little more. What can it hurt?"

"My bank account."

Colleen laughed. "Hey, with all that extra money you're making from the overtime, you can afford to put a dent in it."

As soon as Colleen went back to her office, she got Opal's sisters, all three of them, on the phone via conference call. "I need the three of you to help." She then explained the situation.

"Opal's going to San Francisco?" Amber said excitedly. "That's really cool. Wish it was me."

"Me, too," Pearl said. "There are several recording studios and well-known restaurants I'd love dining at."

"I would concentrate on hitting the stores and then take a ride across the Golden Gate Bridge over to Sausalito," Ruby said thoughtfully.

"Well, I'm sure all of us have ideas of what we would like to do in San Francisco, but my major concern is Opal. You guys might be right. Although she denied it, I think she might have a crush on her boss."

"And you sound like that's good news," Ruby said tersely. "The man is a tyrant."

"Maybe," Colleen said. "And, given time, if anyone can change him, Opal can."

Everyone agreed with that.

"Okay, what do you need us to do?" Amber asked.

"I want you to help me coax Opal into going shopping for more clothes. I mentioned it, and she was against the idea."

"And, while we're at it," Pearl was saying, "what about persuading her to do a complete makeover? It's time she stopped wearing that friggin' bun on her head. She has beautiful hair. I'll schedule her an appointment at my hair salon."

"Umm, and a manicure and pedicure wouldn't be so bad, either," Ruby was saying out loud.

"Okay, then, we'll all make this a group effort and, no matter how much she tries to fight us on this, we will remain a united force, right?" Colleen asked.

"Right," the sisters said simultaneously.

"Good. This will be Operation Opal. When D'marcus

Armstrong sees her on Monday morning, he won't believe his eyes."

"When Opal sees herself on Saturday evening, she won't believe her own eyes," Amber said, giggling. "I can't wait."

And neither could the others.

On Friday Opal received a call from Amber at work telling her she needed to talk to her about something important. Since it was the one day D'marcus had decided they wouldn't be working late this week, she immediately arranged to meet with her sister at a café in town. When she arrived, she not only found Amber waiting for her, but her other two sisters and her cousins, Colleen and Paige, as well.

She lifted a brow. "What's going on?" She immediately thought the worst. Was Amber going to break the news that she was pregnant? And, if that wasn't it, she thought, was someone sick?

Ruby evidently saw the look of panic on her face and quickly said, "Nothing is wrong, Opal. We just want to talk to you about something."

"About what?" Opal asked, taking a seat.

"About your trip to California," Pearl said.

"What about it?" Opal asked, crossing her arms over her chest. If her sisters were going to try to talk her out of going, they'd better think again. She'd figured out how much she would be making on the trip, and that car she wanted to purchase at the first of the year would be a dream she'd make into a reality after all.

"We're happy you got the opportunity," Ruby was saying. "And we want to send you in style."

Opal lifted a brow. "In style?"

"Yes," Amber said excitedly. "You'll be representing all of us and we want you to look good."

Opal glanced around the table at everyone. "Meaning?"

It was Ruby who answered. "Meaning, in the morning, we will be picking you up for a day of beauty."

Opal frowned. "A day of beauty?"

"Yes," Paige said, smiling. "You're getting the works."

Opal narrowed her eyes. "Define *the works*."

Ruby waved her hand. "You know, everything. New clothes, a new do, nails, pedicure, the works."

Opal leaned back in her chair. "And what if I don't want the works?"

Colleen chuckled. "Sorry, babe, you're outnumbered. The six of us will enjoy a wonderful dinner together tonight, and tomorrow we split up and take turns making sure you have the works, starting with me and Ruby tomorrow morning. We're taking you shopping. Then at noon we'll turn you over to Pearl and Amber. You have an appointment with a hair stylist. And then Paige will get you to the spa for a manicure and pedicure."

Opal glanced around the table at everyone. She had known her sisters and cousins long enough to know that, when they got together and made up their minds about something, there wasn't any changing them. "Okay, fine, but just as long as you know I'm not going to like it," she grumbled. "I'm going to be miserable."

Colleen smiled. "You might be miserable, sweetheart, but the five of us will have the time of our lives, and I have a feeling by Saturday afternoon you will be thanking us."

Opal doubted it.

Chapter 6

"You look simply beautiful, Opal."

Opal glanced over at Amber and saw the tears in her sister's eyes before she looked at herself in the mirror. She wasn't sure she looked beautiful, but she certainly looked different.

She noted her other two sisters and cousins staring at her, too, and she said jokingly, "Hey, what was I before? An ugly duckling?"

Ruby spoke up. "No, but I got so used to seeing that friggin' ball on your head that I'd forgotten what beautiful hair you have. This style certainly highlights it. It definitely becomes you."

Opal glanced back in the mirror. Yes, it certainly did, and the change in her hair would be the one thing she'd have to get used to the most. Long, luxurious medium-brown hair flowed down her shoulders in soft feathered waves. She even had bangs, something she'd never worn before. They stopped on her forehead just above her newly arched eyebrows.

But what really stood out was the makeup that had

been applied to her face. Light, yet at the same time dashing. Even the shade of lipstick seemed to have been made just for her skin color. Something could definitely be said for a makeover. She might not have been an ugly duckling before, but it was obvious she had never fully capitalized on the assets the good God had given to her. She looked like a totally different person, although she felt the same.

"The only thing left now is your nails and pedicure," Colleen broke the silence by saying. "And promise me, once you get your nails done, you will stop biting them."

Opal made a face at her cousin.

"And please," Pearl threw in, rolling her eyes, "no ugly faces. You're too beautiful now for that. I can't wait to see D'marcus Armstrong's expression when you show up at the airport on Monday morning."

Opal decided not to mention to her sisters that she and D'marcus wouldn't be meeting at the airport. He had called that morning to get her address. He would be picking her up at her apartment.

She glanced at her watch. "Okay, the five of you have dominated my entire day. I'm giving you another hour, and that's it." But Opal had to admit she'd had fun. This was the first time in a long while that she and her sisters and cousins had spent time together. Although she had been the victim, she felt it had been worth it and it reminded her of when they had been teenagers and almost inseparable. That was before death had claimed her mother and Colleen and Paige's within a year of each other. That had definitely put a gloom on the Lockhart and Richards households.

"Come on," Amber said. "We can't keep the spa wait-

ing. I had to work wonders to get you in. You're going
to love this place. A girlfriend of mine works there."

With her sisters' and cousins' help, Opal grabbed
her many bags. She had purchased a lot of new outfits
and she had to admit that, once she had gotten into the
swing of shopping, she was more than pleased with
her purchases.

As they left the beauty salon, she couldn't help but
ponder Pearl's statement. Exactly what *would* D'marcus
think when he saw her on Monday morning?

Later that same night, D'marcus sat across the table
from a woman, thinking he had made a grave mistake.
All week, anticipation had clawed at his insides, and
then there was that intense sexual desire that had almost
gotten the best of him, nearly driving him over the edge.

He had looked forward to tonight and hadn't been
disappointed when he had arrived at Priscilla's house.
She was a looker, and the outfit she wore did wonders
for her body. And he knew that had he pushed, they
would have ended up making love before leaving for
dinner. But he hadn't pushed.

Now he wished he had.

At least that would have given her something to talk
about other than herself…which seemed to be her favorite topic. The woman had been talking nonstop since he
had walked her out to his car. And she was still talking. The only time she had taken a break was when
they were eating, only because she had the decency
not to talk with food in her mouth. But now it seemed
she had gotten a second wind. He didn't remember her

being a talker of this magnitude before, and it was getting to him big-time.

"So will you be spending the night, D'marcus?" she asked in a sultry voice.

He was hard up, but apparently he wasn't as hard up as he'd thought. He refused to find sexual solace with this chatterbox. "No, I need to go home and start packing. I'm leaving town on Monday."

She leaned closer across the table, giving him a good look at her cleavage. "In that case, maybe I should go over to your place and help you pack."

Not hardly. "Thanks, Priscilla, but I can handle things."

Beneath the table he felt her rub her foot against his leg. "So can I," she all but purred.

He sighed and took a sip of his wine. Their date wouldn't come to an end fast enough to suit him. He had thought all he had to do was find a woman and relieve some of his sexual pressure, but this woman wouldn't do. In fact, there was only one woman who could probably do what he needed, and she was the same woman he blamed for this madness he was in—Opal Lockhart. Lately he had found himself comparing every woman to her, and none could size up.

"So what about it, D'marcus?"

"Not tonight, Priscilla. You'll be a distraction I don't need," he said, and that was putting it nicely. What he had stopped himself from saying was that she would get on his last nerve. At this point, any woman would… except for Opal.

He sighed inwardly, deciding to be totally honest with himself. The reason he was turned off by Priscilla had nothing to do with her being a chatterbox, and everything to do with her not being Opal. He could come up with any excuse he wanted to, but the bottom line was that he would find any woman other than his administrative assistant undesirable. More than ever, that realization didn't sit well with him, and it definitely didn't do anything to help his current sexual state.

He didn't fully understand how it had happened, but it had. Opal Lockhart had gotten under his skin.

Opal's cell phone rang at precisely seven o'clock on Monday morning. "Hello?"

"Ms. Lockhart, this is D'marcus Armstrong. I'm entering your apartment complex now."

She thought he had a very sexy phone voice. "I'm ready."

He ended the call, and she glanced around at her luggage. It was more than she'd planned to take, but her sisters had come by last night to help her pack and they'd claimed she needed everything she was taking with her.

She heard a car pull up outside and knew it was D'marcus. Inhaling deeply, she headed for the door when she heard the bell. She couldn't wait to see his reaction to her new look. Her tongue flicked over her lips in anticipation, reminding her of the beauty consultant's guarantee. *This brand will stay on all day— unless your man should lick, eat or kiss it off.*

She took another deep breath then slowly opened the door. "Good morning, Mr. Armstrong."

D'marcus stared at Opal. Speechless.

Gone was the knot of hair on top of her head. Instead, her hair hung loose, framing her shoulders with a mass of feathered waves that capitalized on her high cheekbones, straight nose and oval face. Her beautifully arched eyebrows emphasized her dark eyes and long lashes, something he hadn't noticed before. And she was wearing makeup that was so light you barely noticed it was there, but it seemed to make her features that much more striking.

He inhaled deeply. In his opinion, Opal Lockhart had always been an attractive woman, one who'd definitely gotten his attention at times when he'd wished otherwise. But now he found himself in really deep trouble. Whatever she'd done had only enhanced what had always been there. This new Opal had him totally mesmerized.

It didn't help matters that things hadn't worked out as he'd planned with Priscilla this past weekend. The real gist of his problem was that all of his sexual frustrations were centered on one woman. The one standing right in front of him.

"Ms. Lockhart," he said, clearing his throat. "You look different."

Opal tried not to frown. Was that all he was going to say? She nodded, thinking maybe she should be grateful. After all, he was her boss and not her boyfriend. She wouldn't want him checking her out too much. But she was dying to ask, "Different, how?" Instead, she took it as a compliment and said, "Thank you. My bags are over there."

She stepped aside when he entered her apartment. He glanced around before crossing the room to where her three bags sat. "Nice place."

"I'm moving in a few weeks."

He glanced back at her over his shoulder. "Why?"

"Too much noise. I'm sandwiched in by party animals and I'm not getting sufficient sleep at night."

"Oh." A vision suddenly flowed through D'marcus's mind. He would love having her sandwiched between him and his mattress, and she wouldn't get sufficient sleep then, either. He glanced down at her luggage. "You'll only be gone four days, Ms. Lockhart, not four months," he said jokingly.

She heard the teasing glint in his voice and relaxed. She hadn't been sure what type of mood he was in, although, since promising to improve his attitude, he had done a good job. "I know, but I'm not one to travel light. Besides, don't you know that a woman always takes more than she needs?"

"That's what I've heard. If you want to make sure everything is locked up, I'll start loading your luggage in my trunk. And if I suddenly develop back trouble," he said as a smile touched his lips, "I'll have my attorney sue you."

His smile almost made her heart miss a beat. "All right, you do that. But I may as well tell you that I have limited funds, so you won't be getting any money out of me."

She moved around the apartment and checked to make sure everything she needed turned off was and that a message was on her answering machine. Her family was fully aware that she was going to California on business, as were a couple of her church friends, including Reverend Kendrick. She didn't want anyone to panic when she didn't show up for prayer meeting on Wednesday night.

When she returned to the living room, she found he had taken out all of her luggage and was standing in the middle of the room holding a framed photograph of her and her sisters. She could go off on him as he'd done her that night in his office when she'd picked up the photograph off his desk, but she quickly recalled that he had apologized for his behavior.

"I gather these are your sisters with you," he said, studying the photograph.

"Yes."

"There's a strong family resemblance. The four of you have the same eyes."

She smiled as she crossed the room to where he stood. "Yes, we have our father's eyes."

D'marcus nodded. "Is he still living?"

She shook her head. "No. Both my parents are deceased. My father was a police officer and died in the line of duty when I was ten. And my mother died of cancer five years ago."

"I'm sorry."

"Thanks. So am I. My sisters and I were close to Mom. She did a good job of raising us after Dad died. She was our rock."

For a moment, neither said anything as he continued to look at the photograph that had been taken just last year. "Which one is the sister who thinks I'm a tyrant?" he asked, glancing over at her.

She chuckled. "That's Ruby, there," she said, pointing her out to him. "She's the eldest. And that's Pearl and Amber."

He glanced over at her and raised a brow and smiled. "Ruby, Opal, Pearl and Amber. Are you sure you're not a member of the Stone family?"

Opal released a startled laugh. He'd made the connection that her and her sisters' names were precious gemstones. Not everyone caught on to that. "It was my Dad's idea and Mom went along with it. It was because my mom's name was Emerald."

D'marcus nodded as he placed the photograph back down and checked his watch. "It's time for us to leave if we want to make it to the airport on time. I checked in with my pilot earlier and he'll be ready to take off when we get there."

"Will it be a straight flight?"

"No. We'll need to refuel in Dallas, but I can almost guarantee it will be a pleasant flight. Lee is good at what he does. You aren't afraid of flying, are you?"

She shook her head. "I haven't flown all that much. but when I did, it didn't bother me."

"Good. Ready to go?"

"Yes." Opal took a deep breath as she walked out of her apartment.

D'marcus clicked off his cell phone, ending the conversation he'd had with another of the Chargers owners and glanced at the woman sitting in the seat across from him on his private jet. She had fallen asleep reading some document he'd given to her. Evidently, it had been hard for her to remain awake, given the smoothness of the flight as well as the brevity of sleep the night before.

He leaned back comfortably in his seat, readjusting his seat belt as he continued to gaze at her. He liked what she'd done to her hair…a little too much. And he also liked—a little too much—how her makeup enhanced her features, although he'd thought she was a beautiful woman even when she hadn't worn any at all.

Even with their early start, traffic had been a bit hectic getting to the airport so thankfully, he'd been forced to place his full concentration on his driving and not on her. That had been the first time the two of them had ever shared car space, and he had found it hard to be so close to her and not let his mind fill with sexual thoughts. For some reason, she evoked those ideas in his head. He could have blamed it on her scent, but he knew her fragrance alone had not been a significant factor. It was the entire package.

In a way, he appreciated her sleeping now. It gave him time to regain his composure and take back control. Opal Lockhart had a way of making him lose both. She shifted in sleep and her skirt rose just a tad, showing a portion of her thigh. Surrendering to temptation, he assured himself that, since he was 100 percent male, it would be quite natural to stare. So he did. But there was no excuse for the lecherous thoughts that suddenly filled his mind.

He rubbed his hand down his face, wondering what the hell was wrong with him. He hadn't been this taken with a woman in six years. And then on Saturday night, he'd had every opportunity to take care of his needs but hadn't had the urge to do so. For some reason, only Opal filled him with red-hot desire.

And, for the time being, he wasn't sure how he planned to handle it.

His gaze left her thigh and went to her face when she

made a sound in her sleep. Then another. He quickly concluded from the moans emanating from her lips that she was having some dream. He leaned forward as, in her sleep, she suddenly moaned out his name.

Opal smiled in her sleep, dreaming about D'marcus. They were in his office and he was touching her all over, making her intensely hot. She wanted to fight the feelings, ignore the sensations, but they were too strong, too overpowering. So she surrendered and her insides began burning up with desire. She whispered his name moments before he leaned over and kissed her.

She felt a sudden jolt to her body and wrenched her eyes open. Then she stiffened all over when her gaze met that of D'marcus, who was sitting across from her. She blinked, remembering. They were in his company plane on their way to California. She wondered what had awakened her. As if he read her mind, he answered.

"We hit a little bit of turbulence. Excuse me for a moment while I check with Lee to see how much longer before we land."

She watched D'marcus undo his seat belt and head toward the cockpit. She decided to use the time he was gone to compose herself. She couldn't believe she had fallen asleep in front of her boss, and, to make matters worse, she had dreamed about him and had awakened to find him staring at her. When she thought of the dream, she couldn't help but blush.

She sighed deeply, thinking about her new look. Evidently, D'marcus hadn't been impressed. All he'd said was that she looked different. She didn't know whether to take that as a positive or a negative.

She glanced up when D'marcus returned. "Is everything all right?"

He smiled. "Yes, everything is fine," he said, sitting back in his seat.

She glanced down at the documents in her lap; papers she should have been reading. "I apologize for falling asleep," she said softly.

He buckled the seat belt around him. "No need to apologize. Evidently, you were tired. You have been working rather late at the office."

She thought it was kind of him to be so understanding.

"I'm going to have to make sure that some of your time in California is spent enjoying yourself."

She glanced up from the documents. "That's not necessary."

He held her gaze. "I think that it is."

Opal struggled to smile. There was something about the way he was looking at her that made intense heat slither through her body. It was the same feeling she'd gotten when he had touched her in her dream. Good grief! Her body was responding to him and all he was doing was sitting there staring at her.

She placed the papers on the seat beside her and unbuckled her seat belt. "Excuse me, I need to go to the ladies' room," she said, quickly getting out of her seat.

"Certainly," he said, his gaze still on her. "I'll be here when you return."

She nodded. That was what had her worried.

Chapter 7

Opal tried not to show her surprise when, instead of driving them to a hotel once they had landed in San Francisco, D'marcus had picked up a rental car and had driven them to a spacious home close to the bay. He evidently saw the question in her eyes and, after parking in the driveway and turning off the car, he said, "This is my uncle and aunt's home. I told them I was coming and they insisted I drop by before checking into the hotel."

She raised a brow. "Your uncle and aunt?"

"Yes, they're the ones who raised me after my parents were killed," he said as if she should know about his parents. She did, but he hadn't been the one to tell her. She'd found out through office gossip.

She was surprised when the door was suddenly flung open and a beautiful older woman with salt-and-pepper hair walked out. Opal could tell from the huge smile on her face that the woman was glad to see D'marcus. He immediately walked over to her and gave her a hug. "Aunt Marie, you get more beautiful every day."

And then a man appeared, who Opal assumed

was his uncle. He was tall and muscular and favored D'marcus somewhat. He gave his uncle a hug, as well. Another first. She'd never seen her boss display any type of affection with anyone, but it was easy to see that he was glad to see his family.

"Opal, I'd like you to meet my aunt Marie and my uncle Charles," he said, claiming her attention. "This is my administrative assistant, Opal Lockhart," he said to his relatives.

Both his uncle's and aunt's smiles were friendly. Instead of taking her hand, his aunt automatically embraced her. "Welcome to our home, Ms. Lockhart."

"Thank you."

"Come in. I knew the two of you were coming so I had Loretta prepare brunch."

D'marcus shook his head. "You still intend to fatten me up, Aunt Marie?"

She grinned. "You don't eat properly. I know you, D'marcus. Look, you're almost skin and bones."

Opal glanced over at her boss. He was far from being skin and bones. In fact, in her opinion, he was nicely built. She knew he worked out periodically at the gym, but she did agree with his aunt about his eating habits.

"Okay, I'll let you feed us a light lunch. But later tonight, Opal and I have a dinner date."

She raised her brow and glanced over at him. If they did, this was the first she'd heard of it.

His aunt locked Opal's arm into hers as they walked into the house. "Then come inside and get comfortable. Loretta is the best cook in the Bay area."

An hour later Opal was convinced that what Marie Armstrong said was true. Her cook and housekeeper,

Loretta, *was* the best cook in the Bay area. She had prepared them a tossed salad and grilled salmon that was
the best she'd ever eaten.

"Would you like anything else, Ms. Lockhart?"

Opal smiled over at Marie. "No, thanks, but brunch
was simply delicious."

D'marcus's aunt beamed. "Thank you. I enjoy seeing people with good appetites."

Opal grinned, thinking that she'd certainly had one.
She had skipped breakfast, and the muffin and juice
she'd eaten in Dallas hadn't quite done the job.

"It's time for me and Opal to be on our way."

"But the two of you will be back, right?"

Without looking at her, D'marcus said, "Of course
I'll be back, but Opal will be quite busy while we're
here."

His aunt's attention then went to Opal. "Promise me
that you won't let him work you too hard."

Instead of telling Marie that her nephew was paying
her well to work hard, Opal smiled. "Okay, I promise."

Ten minutes later, she and D'marcus were back on
the road and headed toward the hotel in downtown San
Francisco. D'marcus wasn't saying anything so Opal
took the time to study the beautiful San Francisco scen-
ery.

"This is your first time here?"

Opal glanced over at D'marcus, not believing he'd
spoken. He hadn't said much during the drive from the
airport to his uncle and aunt's home, nor had he had a
lot to say since leaving his relatives' house. "Yes, and
it's beautiful," she said.

"I have to agree. I once swore, when I was a teen,

that I would never leave this place. That I would live here forever."

"What happened?"

He chuckled and the sound sent shivers through her body. "Education happened. I left for Morehouse College in Atlanta and decided I liked the South. Then, when I attended Harvard for my master's degree, I made up my mind that I liked the North. But whenever I return home to Frisco, I know in my heart that the West is the best. There's nothing like the Bay area."

Opal nodded. Though she hadn't visited half the places he had, it was her personal opinion that, even with its sometimes harsh winters, Detroit was a nice place to live, as well.

"We'll be staying in the hotel only one night. Then we're going to my home, where we'll be for the rest of the week."

His home? Opal glanced over at him.

"We'll be working out of my office there, and I have several meetings set up."

She nodded. She knew about the meetings, but hadn't known they would be conducted from his home. In fact, she hadn't been aware of the fact that he owned a home here. Deciding what he did and what he owned was definitely none of her business, she didn't say anything.

When he pulled into the hotel's driveway for valet parking, he glanced over at her. "We're having dinner with Harold Phelps and his wife, Bernice. He's interested in opening several stores in Hawaii."

"That's wonderful," she said. She knew there wasn't a Sports Unlimited in that state. In fact, from the map D'marcus kept on the wall in his office, she was aware of each state his franchised stores had not yet invaded. She knew he was working hard to change that; he'd once mentioned that he wanted a store in every state in the union.

When they walked into the hotel, she was truly impressed. The lobby was a stunning atrium filled with young trees and flowering plants. For someone who loved flowers as much she did, it was a breathtaking sight. She admired it while D'marcus went to the check-in desk. He hadn't asked her to make the hotel reservations for this trip as he normally did. She had found that odd, but had not questioned him about it.

"Ready?"

She nodded at D'marcus, who handed her a key card and led her toward the elevator bank. A car was waiting and they stepped in.

"What time is dinner?" she asked.

"Seven. The restaurant's not far from the hotel, so I'll be to your room to get you around six-thirty."

"All right." Now she was grateful for those dressy outfits Ruby had insisted she purchase.

She stepped off the elevator onto the eighteenth floor, surprised when D'marcus did, too.

"I requested hotel rooms across the hall from each other. Things will be easier that way."

Easier? Having him so close certainly wouldn't be easier for her.

D'marcus stood in the hallway moments after Opal had gone inside her room. He had to force himself to get a grip. He wouldn't be surprised if his uncle and aunt had picked up on his attraction to her. He had a feeling his aunt Marie had, and that had been the reason she'd asked him to bring Opal back for a visit before he left the city.

Releasing a deep sigh, he opened the door to his room and went inside. As requested, his and Opal's rooms were spacious suites. Although they would only be staying for one night, he believed in comfort and convenience.

As he eased his jacket from his shoulders, he couldn't help but recall Opal's beautiful face when she'd sat across from him in the jet sleeping. And, when she had whispered his name, his gut had clenched and blood had rushed to every part of his body. Why would his administrative assistant be thinking about him while she slept?

Various reasons crossed his mind, but his brain was stuck on one of them—the possibility that she was as attracted to him as he was to her. He'd never had reason to think that she was…until now.

She didn't know how close she'd come to being awakened with a kiss. He couldn't help but smile at the thought. But he continued smiling when he thought of the changes she'd made. Although he hadn't given his opinion, he thought she looked good and liked what she'd done. He'd barely been able to keep his eyes off her.

He removed his tie, thinking he needed a shower—a very cold one. Then he would work on the report he had to complete for one of his meetings tomorrow. He had to remind himself that he wasn't a teenager noticing a female for the first time. He was a grown man.

A man who wanted to sleep with his administrative assistant.

* * *

At precisely 6:30 p.m. D'marcus was knocking on Opal's hotel room door. He had done all the things he had planned. First, he had taken a cold shower and then he had relaxed on the bed while completing the report for tomorrow's meeting. Now the only thing left was to maintain tight control of his desires while in Opal's presence for the rest of the evening. That, he knew, wouldn't be easy.

A part of him, a part that he hadn't known could be so persistent, dared him to turn his attention toward her as he would any woman. To forget she was his employee and see her for the desirable woman she was. That he never intended to settle down and get married had never stopped him from pursuing women when he was interested. Why was he letting the fact that the two of them worked together become a factor? He immediately knew the answer. Because things could get rather messy and awkward when he ended the affair.

Her door opened and D'marcus was taken aback. This morning, he'd been surprised at her makeover, but now he was rendered speechless. He knew it was a combination of her makeover and her outfit. Nevertheless, he was at a loss for words. Never before had a woman stirred his hormones to the extent that Opal did.

"I'm ready," she said, stepping in the hallway next to him.

Her smile was polite, but her outfit was hot. Nothing about her teal dinner dress was inappropriate for their dinner date, but on her it seemed sexy as sin. Maybe it was the way it seemed to drape around her curves or the way the color seemed to darken her eyes. Or the way the off-the-shoulder neckline emphasized a long, sleek neck and a pair of smooth arms. He'd never paid attention to a woman's arms before.

As they walked beside each other to the elevator, he tried not to stare over at her, but he couldn't resist. Her hair had so much body that it actually bounced around her shoulders when she walked. She glanced at him, catching him staring, and his breath hitched a bit when he said, "You look nice tonight, Opal."

"Thank you. So do you."

He wondered if her comment was sincere or automatic. He looked basically the same, but she didn't. She looked luscious. She looked ripe. She looked like a woman who was meant to be in a man's arms and in his bed.

When they reached the elevator, the doors swooshed open and he stepped back for her to step in ahead of him. That was when he saw her back. The majority of it was bare, which he concluded was the reason she carried the matching shawl. Though difficult, he resisted the temptation to reach out and caress the soft skin.

The ride in the elevator passed in silence. He decided not to say anything for fear he might say the wrong thing. He had to think. No matter what the testosterone in his body was saying, he knew an affair with Opal Lockhart was not an option.

They walked through the lobby to the valet station and D'marcus presented the man with his ticket. Within minutes, his rental car was brought to him. Instinctively, he took Opal's hand to walk her over to the car, and the moment they touched, an electrical charge seemed to vibrate through his entire body. He glanced up at her and knew she'd felt it, too. He quickly opened the car door and she settled in the seat.

She glanced up at him. "Thank you."

"You're welcome," he said, shutting the door.

He walked around the car. With just that simple touch, he became even more hotly aware of the predicament he was in, namely the temptation he had to resist. Desire curled up in his stomach. It wouldn't be easy.

He opened the door on the driver's side and slid behind the wheel. Glancing over, he saw her staring straight ahead while clutching her purse tightly in her lap. He was good at reading body language and hers said that she was nervous. "It's only a short drive," he said for lack of something witty.

"All right."

D'marcus knew she was fully aware of the chemistry between them. Would she try to ignore it like he'd been doing over the past few weeks, or would she want to act on it? Judging from the way she sat stiffly in the seat, he quickly concluded she intended to ignore it.

He returned his eyes to the road at the same exact moment he decided, for once in his life, he wanted to rebel. He intended to do the opposite and act on it.

Chapter 8

"The Phelpses are a nice couple," Opal said as she and D'marcus walked across the hotel lobby several hours later. "And he seems very interested in opening those stores in Hawaii."

"Yes, and I hope he's still interested when we have a conference call with him, his attorneys and his financial manager next week." He could tell the Phelpses had been impressed with Opal, as well. He had introduced her as his administrative assistant, but it quickly became evident that her knowledge of his company was quite extensive, which had made things easy when Harold Phelps had needed facts, figures and stats.

As they reached the elevators, the sound of jazz music could be heard coming from a nearby lounge. D'marcus glanced at his watch and then he turned to Opal. "It's still early. If you aren't tired, would you mind joining me in the lounge? I'd love to just sit and listen to some music awhile to unwind."

Opal swallowed deeply, surprised by D'marcus's request. She knew she should tell him that the plane trip had tired her out and that she wanted to rest. But deep down, she knew that would be a lie. She really wasn't tired and listening to jazz did seem like a good way to relax. Besides, she was enjoying his company. At dinner he had been like another person. In fact, since making that promise last week, his attitude had changed. He no longer frowned as much. So she bit back her rejections and instead said, "Yes, I'd love to."

Her uneasiness returned the moment he took her arm to lead her to the lounge. The moment he touched her, all kinds of sensations spread through her body. At dinner with the Phelpses, D'marcus had been utterly charming and talkative. She knew he had impressed the older couple, who seemed to have more money than they knew what to do with. According to Mr. Phelps, opening those stores would be an investment in their granddaughter's future. She was only four.

The first thing Opal noticed was that the lounge was crowded. She glanced at D'marcus and watched him scan the place for available seats. "Looks like this is our lucky night," he said, indicating a couple at a table near the front who were standing to leave.

Still holding her arm he led her over to the empty table. As soon as they sat down, she tried shifting her attention from D'marcus to the band that was performing.

"What would you like to drink, Opal?"

She glanced over at D'marcus and saw a waiter standing next to him to take their drink order. "An Opal cocktail."

D'marcus raised his brow and then gave the waiter his own drink order, a Bloody Mary. When the waiter walked off he looked over at her and smiled. "An Opal cocktail? I've never heard of it."

She couldn't help but grin. "Imagine how giddy I got one night when my cousin Colleen and I visited our first bar and the waiter, after finding out my name, suggested I try it. I did, and it's been my mixed drink of choice ever since."

He nodded. "What's in it?"

"Gin, triple sec, orange juice, powdered sugar and ice. It's fairly simple to make and I like the taste."

At that moment, the band began playing another number and they decided to listen to the group. That was fine with Opal, since she really didn't know what type of casual conversation the two of them could exchange. He was her boss, for heaven's sake!

With the band playing and the lights turned down some, she took the opportunity to study him. As usual, he was wearing a suit and looked good in it. But what had captured her attention during most of dinner were his features. They were the same features he'd always had, but, for some reason, tonight she'd been drawn to them. He had beautiful brown skin and long eyelashes that would make any woman envious. And now that he was smiling a lot more, his looks were more dashing than before. Then there were his lips. She had noticed them a lot during dinner. She wondered how they'd feel under hers. She blushed, not believing she'd actually thought that. In fact, she inwardly admitted, she'd been thinking a lot of sexual things about D'marcus lately.

"Enjoying the music?"

She blinked. He had caught her staring at him. She

quickly looked away at the band. "Yes. What about you?"

"I'm enjoying them. They sound good."

She had to agree with him. "Are you unwinding?"

He chuckled. "Pretty much. Even you have to admit it's been a rough couple of weeks."

She nodded. But she was sure it had been more so for him than for her. He'd been the one wheeling and dealing, getting richer by the minute. "So what happens when there're no more stores left to franchise?"

Amusement shone in his gaze. "There will always be stores to franchise. As long as Americans enjoy their favorite sports, we will be there to supply whatever they need to make them happy."

She knew it was more than just earning a dollar for him. He was also a big contributor to various worthwhile charities, especially those for children.

At that moment, the waiter returned with their drinks. D'marcus glanced over at the glass the waiter placed in front of her. "Mmm, that looks good. Maybe I should have ordered one of those."

"Would you like to try it?"

"Sure."

He was about to use the extra straw the waiter had left for his own drink but made a quick decision to use hers instead; the one already in her drink. He wondered how she would react if he was bold enough to do such a thing. He decided to find out by reaching for her glass and taking a sip.

Ever since she had whispered his name in her sleep, he'd been attentive, watching and waiting to see what it all meant. He was ready for any sign that indicated she wanted him as much as he wanted her.

He slid the glass back over to her. "You're right. It tastes good."

He watched her. Seeing what he'd done had definitely put her out of her comfort zone. She was beginning to act rattled, as if she wasn't sure what she should do. Should she use the same straw that he had? Should she take the straw out and sip the drink without it? He could envision all those questions going through her mind and was curious as to which solution she would take. He decided to make it easier for her.

"I guess it's only fair that now I let you take a sip of mine," he said, sliding his glass over to her. She glanced up at him and then, just as he'd done earlier, she took a sip of his drink using his straw. She slid the glass back to him.

"Well, what do you think?" he asked her.

She smiled nervously. "It's okay if you like tomatoes, but I like mine better because I love the taste of oranges."

He chuckled, and then, without thinking twice about it, he took a sip of his own drink, using the same straw she had. He wondered if she would follow his lead.

She did. For some reason, seeing her using the straw his lips had touched did something to him, as did knowing he was using the same straw her lips had touched. He felt a hard jolt in his gut and knew he was almost losing his battle for control. He quickly took another sip of his drink.

"You uncle and aunt are nice," Opal said.

She had told him that already, earlier that day. "Thanks. Aunt Marie likes you."

She raised a brow. "How do you know that?"

"Because she asked me to bring you back."

That made Opal smile. "Your uncle didn't have a lot to say," she noted.

He grinned. "As you saw, my aunt has a tendency to talk enough for both of them. Uncle Charles can never get a word in, so I guess he figures why bother."

Opal couldn't help but widen her smile at that. "What time will we check out of the hotel tomorrow?"

"Right after my meeting with Fred Johnson. I'll need you to be in my suite at nine. Will that be a problem?"

"Not at all."

"Then afterward, we'll check out and go to my home. It's on the beach."

Opal was looking forward to that, especially since the weather was so nice. Amber had encouraged her to bring a bathing suit to go swimming in the hotel's pool, but going to the beach was even better.

Assuming she went without D'marcus. No way would she wear a swimsuit in front of him. Her pulse was still racing since he'd sipped her drink through her straw. It was so…intimate. And when she did the same, goose bumps formed on her arm.

She glanced up and her gaze suddenly collided with his. She wanted to look away and couldn't. It didn't help matters that the band was now playing a slow tune. She was glad the lounge didn't have a dance floor.

"Do you know what I like about jazz music?" he asked in a mild voice.

She decided to take a guess. "It helps you to unwind?"

He smiled. "Yes, but also, you don't need lyrics to complement the music. You can add your own words."

She never thought of it that way.

"What type of music do you like listening to?" he asked her.

"All kinds, but lately because of my sister Pearl I've been exposed to a lot of gospel. She sings in the church choir and she finally decided to send off a demo to several gospel labels all over the country. We haven't heard anything back yet but we're hoping someone is interested. She has a beautiful voice."

"Then I hope things work out for her."

"Thanks."

Opal wasn't sure if it was the drink or the nice conversation and relaxing music, but she wasn't as nervous as she usually was around D'marcus.

To her surprise he then shared with her that he used to play the saxophone and still enjoyed playing it sometime. "I played in high school and then in college at Morehouse. I enjoyed those times."

"I play the piano," she decided to share with him. "All of us had to take piano lessons and I think I'm the one who enjoyed it the most. We used to own a piano, but one year when money got tight Mom had to sell it."

At that moment the waiter came up to see if they wanted refills on their drinks. She declined and so did D'marcus. After the waiter walked off, D'marcus glanced over to her and said, "I guess it's time for us to call it a night and go up to our rooms. Although I don't want to think about it, we have a lot of work to do tomorrow. Thanks for sharing this time with me, Opal."

She started. This was the first time he'd called her by her first name. "You're welcome, Mr. Armstrong."

He chuckled. "You've been working for me around four months now. I think it's time for us to stop being so formal and go on a first-name basis, unless you have a problem with me calling you Opal."

She shook her head. "No, I don't have a problem with it."

"Good. And from now on, you can call me D'marcus."

Opal nodded uncomfortably. "It's going to be hard."

He grinned. "Go ahead. Try it and see."

Opal gazed at D'marcus and saw he was dead serious. He was waiting for her to say his name. "I know how to pronounce it," she said softly.

"I know, but I want to hear you say it," he said in a low, throaty voice. Sensuous shivers moved down Opal's spine at the sound. "Go on," he said encouragingly.

Opal looked at him strangely. She wasn't sure why he wanted her to say his name, but she decided to do it and get it over with. "D'marcus."

He smiled as he leaned back in his chair. "I like the way you say it."

She definitely didn't know what to think of that. Why would it matter to him how she said his name?

"I'm ready to leave any time you are."

He had already stood up, so she got out of her seat. "I'm ready."

To Opal it seemed all the women watched the tall,

dark, handsome, muscular man walking beside her as they left the lounge. But none as much as she.

D'marcus walked her to her hotel room door and she nervously opened it before turning back to him. "Good night, Mr. Arms— I mean, D'marcus."

He chuckled. "Good night, Opal."

Deciding she wasn't going to give either of them a chance to say or do anything else, she quickly went into her room and closed the door behind her. She leaned against it, holding her breath, and didn't release it until she heard him enter his own room and close the door behind him.

She couldn't help wondering what had happened in the lounge. Why had he prompted her to say his name? And why, even now, was her heart beating furiously in her chest?

"D'marcus," she said, liking the sound of saying it. She would definitely have to get used to not calling him Mr. Armstrong. She was about to get undressed when the telephone in her room rang. Would D'marcus be calling her? Maybe he had forgotten to tell her something important about tomorrow. There was only one way to find out. She picked up the phone. "Hello."

"Where have you been?"

She relaxed upon hearing Ruby's voice.

"Yeah, Opal, we've been trying to call you."

She shook her head. Now that was Pearl's voice. She played her hunch and said. "I know Amber's in school tonight but, Colleen, are you on the line, too?"

She heard her best friend and cousin chuckle. "How did you guess?"

"Easily," she said.

"So where were you?" Pearl asked.

"D'marcus and I had a business dinner with one of his clients."

"And you're just getting back?" Ruby asked.

"Yes," she said, deciding not to tell them she and D'marcus had shared a drink after dinner in the hotel lounge. "Why are the three of you still up?" she asked, knowing with the difference in time zones it had to be almost two o'clock in the morning in Detroit.

"We wanted to talk to you to make sure you're okay," Pearl said.

Opal frowned. "Didn't the three of you get my messages? I left one on each of your cell phones."

"Yes, we got them," Colleen said. "But that was earlier. When Ruby tried to call you at a time that we figured you should be getting ready for bed and you didn't answer, we began to worry."

"Well, don't worry. I'm a big girl who can take care of herself."

"And what about the tyrant?" Ruby asked.

"He's not a tyrant, and what about him?"

"Has he been on his best behavior?"

"Why wouldn't he be?"

"Because of your makeover, Opal," Ruby said on a sigh. "You look gorgeous. Any man would notice. So, did he?"

Opal smiled. Her family was definitely nosy. "Yes, he noticed."

"What did he say?" Pearl asked excitedly.

"Nothing other than I looked different."

"That's all he said?" Colleen sounded downright disappointed.

Opal chuckled. "Yes, that's all he said. If all of you stayed up late hoping to hear some off-the-wall nasty stuff, then I hate to disappoint you. D'marcus Armstrong has been a perfect gentleman."

"So, in other words, he hasn't gotten you naked yet." Colleen laughed.

"And trust me, he won't," Opal countered. "Good night, ladies."

"Just watch yourself around him," Ruby warned.

"Good night, ladies," Opal repeated. "All of you have jobs to go to tomorrow so *please* go to bed. Love you all," she said, then sent a huge kissy-smack through the phone line before hanging up. She shook her head, grinning, as she crossed the room to the bathroom.

She thought about Colleen's question of D'marcus getting her naked. Boy, was her cousin way off the mark. She bet the thought of doing something like that hadn't even crossed the man's mind.

What would she look like naked?

D'marcus shook his head as if to rid his mind of the thought, and stepped into the shower. But he couldn't stop thinking of just how good Opal had looked tonight. She was sexy in an understated way, and the outfit she'd had on had definitely brought out that fact. At dinner, when she had excused herself to go to the ladies' room, he had watched her leave. So had every other male in the room. Her dress had been clinging to her body in several delectable places.

Tonight in the lounge when she had sipped his drink

through his straw and then he had drunk it himself, he had gotten a little taste of her. But a little taste wasn't enough.

He wanted it all.

He no longer wondered what the hell was wrong with him. He was too far-gone to be concerned any longer. He was attracted to her. She was the first woman since Tonya who got his hormones out of whack.

He then thought about what would or would not happen when he took her to his home. As he had told her earlier today he intended for her to have some fun before returning to Detroit.

It had been some years—six, to be precise—since he had so thoroughly enjoyed a woman's company, and that same length of time since he had invited a woman to his home. Although Opal's visit was for business, he thought of it as for pleasure, too. Like tonight. Around her he had a tendency to feel more relaxed.

Moments later, as D'marcus stepped out of the shower, he decided he was looking forward to taking Opal to his home. Maybe she would eventually say his name the same way she had said it in her dream. He liked hearing her moan, and he totally intended to hear her moan some more.

Chapter 9

Sitting in the rental car next to D'marcus, Opal glanced around as he drove down a hill that led to his home on Stinson Beach. Already she could see the Pacific Ocean and was getting excited at the thought that she would be staying in a house right on the beach. She wondered how on earth D'marcus could trade this for Detroit's often harsh winters.

She knew he had moved to Michigan after becoming the primary owner of the Chargers but still, she would be tempted to live 90 percent of the time here and just commute to Detroit when needed.

"The ocean is beautiful," she said, without glancing over at him. She wasn't used to so many hills and wanted to make sure he had no reason to take his eyes off the winding road.

"I think it's beautiful, too. Whenever I return it seems to have a way of beckoning me home, making me feel welcome and glad to be back."

Moments after stopping briefly at a gated entrance, they pulled into the driveway of a beautiful two-story home. Opal smiled and pulled in a lung-filling breath of the ocean. She didn't know of anyone other than D'marcus who actually had the ocean in their backyard.

And then there was the house itself. The huge stucco structure created in the Tuscan style was stunning, unlike anything she'd ever seen other than in magazines.

"Your home is gorgeous, D'marcus," she said, and meant every word.

"I'm glad you like it." And D'marcus meant every word, as well. He wasn't sure what was going on between him and Opal, but he was certain something was, although he seemed to be picking up on it more than she was. When she had arrived at his hotel room a few minutes before nine, she had been business as usual. Twice, she had reverted to calling him Mr. Armstrong and he had reminded her of their agreement.

"Can you swim?" he decided to ask her.

"Yes, that was one of the things Mom made sure we could all do," she replied when he turned off the car's ignition.

"Good." Tonya hadn't been able to swim and he'd never taken the time to teach her, though he had promised her several times. "We have a meeting at three and then later, if you'd like, we can take a walk on the beach and maybe tomorrow after all our work is done, we can go swimming." In his mind's eye he was already visualizing her in a bathing suit. One that revealed all her luscious curves.

"Just a moment and I'll open the car door for you," he said, coming around to her side.

That, in Opal's opinion, was a gentlemanly gesture, just one of several she'd noted that D'marcus automatically did. What she'd told her sisters and cousins last night was the truth. He was a complete gentleman.

When he opened her door, she unbuckled the seat belt and got out of the car. "Thanks."

"You're welcome."

She hadn't been aware of just how close they were standing until she suddenly realized she could feel the warmth of his breath on the side of her face. And when she glanced into his eyes, she could swear she saw them get even darker than they had been earlier. She took a step back to give him room to shut the door.

She glanced at the house when she saw a movement out of the corner of her eye. "Someone is at your door," she pointed out, her voice barely able to say the words since she hadn't quite recovered from having him standing so close.

He glanced over his shoulder at the older woman standing in the doorway. "That's Bertha, my housekeeper. I called her to come over and get things ready. Come on. I'll introduce you."

Opal inhaled a deep breath as she walked by his side up the walkway and then up the steps. The older lady gave her a friendly smile when they came face-to-face.

D'marcus made introductions, and although he introduced her as his employee, Opal could tell from the look in the housekeeper's eyes that she thought there was probably more to their relationship than that.

"Everything was done as you requested, Mr. Armstrong," Bertha said. "So I'll be leaving now. If you need me for anything else just give me a call."

"Thank you, Bertha."

He then turned to Opal. "I'll bring your bags in later. Let me show you around first."

"All right."

While touring his home, Opal became even more impressed. Downstairs, the house had a huge kitchen with all stainless-steel appliances, a large living room with a fireplace and a study with built-in bookcases and floor-to-ceiling windows that provided a majestic view of the dunes and ocean. The focal point, however, was the great room. It contained a huge plasma television, several leather sofas and, to her surprise, a grand piano. D'marcus explained it was one of the furnishings that had come with the house when he'd purchased it.

Upstairs, she only got a quick glance of the master bedroom that had a deck and a huge limestone bath with a Jacuzzi. There were four guest bedrooms, all with separate entrances and their own private baths.

"This will be your bedroom while you're here," he said, and she smiled upon seeing she had French doors that led down a wrought iron spiral staircase to a landscaped garden and patio. And the room was beautifully decorated. "Thank you. It's stunning."

"I'll go out and bring in your bags now."

Opal waited till he walked out of the room. She then turned and studied the huge bed. The prospect of sleeping in it was pleasant, since she could hear the sound of the ocean. She smiled, thinking she could definitely get used to this. However, knowing that would never happen, she left the room to see if she could help D'marcus with her luggage.

By five o'clock D'marcus had concluded his business meetings, all of which had gone rather well. However, a short while later he had received a telephone call that had sent his blood pressure rising.

He had talked to Grayson Meadows, head coach of the Chargers, who'd reported that Dashuan Kennedy hadn't shown up for the team's first game. D'marcus had made it clear to Kennedy that he was to report, although he would be sitting on the bench due to his ankle injury.

"I take it that Dashuan Kennedy didn't show up to the game."

D'marcus glanced up. He and Opal had finalized their last meeting for the day and she was still sitting in the chair not far from his desk. "No, he didn't," he said in a disgusted tone. "Although I shouldn't be surprised. That kid is trying me. He doesn't know the meaning of respect and obedience."

Opal nodded. She had to agree with him there. The few times she had seen Kennedy he'd walked around with his head in the air like he was all that.

"What are you going to do?" she couldn't help but ask.

D'marcus rubbed his hand down his face. "The only thing I can do and what I told Dashuan I would do if he didn't straighten up his act."

Opal raised a dark brow. "You're actually going to trade him?"

D'marcus shook his head. "I wish. The other two owners won't go along with anything that drastic, but I think they'll agree with my recommendation of a suspension without pay. That should teach him a lesson and make him think twice about not following orders. I'd like you to set up a conference call with Williams and Hennessy first thing in the morning."

"All right. Are you sure you don't want me to do it now?"

He nodded. "Yes, I'm sure. I promised you a walk on the beach and I plan on doing just that."

The thought of walking with him on the beach had her somewhat nervous. In fact, the more time they spent together, the more rattled she became. "I'll understand if you're busy."

"No, I need to unwind again. I'm booked with meetings all day tomorrow, as well." He studied her a moment, noticing she seemed somewhat tense. "Unless you have a problem with us taking a walk on the beach."

Well, it certainly wasn't something that a boss and his employee would normally do, but she was not about to tell him that. Especially since he'd said he needed to unwind. "No, I don't have a problem with it."

"You sure?"

"Yes, I'm sure."

"Good. I'll give you time to change and we'll meet back here in half an hour. And I thought it would be nice if we grilled a couple of steaks for dinner."

Opal sighed under her breath, thinking they sounded like a couple instead of employer and employee. "Sounds great," she said. "I'll meet you back here." She quickly left his study.

Walking up the stairs to the guest room that she was using, she noted it was the closest one to the master bedroom. Probably a coincidence, she thought, entering her room and closing the door behind her.

Although they were working out of D'marcus's home, she'd dressed in a skirt and blouse set that displayed a semblance of professionalism. Pearl had picked it out for her. Opal had to admit it had a way of making her feel sophisticated and feminine at the same time.

As she undressed, her thoughts went back to D'marcus. Her sisters and cousins thought she should be more assertive and dress more provocatively. She had refused to purchase outfits she'd felt were overkill, but she had to admit she liked all the items she had finally settled on. None of them were the type of clothing she would have selected on her own.

She slipped into a pair of latte-colored silk lounging pants that had a delicate, feminine-looking matching top with an embroidered hem. She was glad she wouldn't be going swimming until tomorrow and she hoped, when she did so, that D'marcus wasn't around.

Leaving her bedroom, she expected to find him ready and waiting for her, but discovered she had dressed more quickly than he had. She was about to leave the study and head toward the kitchen when she turned and accidentally bumped into him. "Oh, sorry."

D'marcus automatically reached out to keep both of them from losing their balance. His long fingers wrapped around her waist, splaying against her back. He looked down at her. "You okay?"

"Yes, I'm fine," she said, and, for the second time that day, they were standing close enough to kiss. She tried to take a step back, but his hand on her back prevented her from doing so. "Sorry, I wasn't looking where I was going," she muttered in a low breath.

"Neither was I, but no harm's been done," he told her with a brief smile.

When moments passed and he just stood there looking down at her with his hand at her back, she said softly, "I guess we should head on down to the beach now."

It seemed that he slid his hand the rest of the way around her waist before releasing her and saying, "Yes, we should."

They walked side by side out of the house and down the brick walkway that led out to the beach. She tried to remember how things had been with D'marcus when she'd first been hired. He had been anything but friendly and definitely was all business. It was as if he had deliberately placed a wall between them that neither of them could ever breach. He was the boss and she was his employee.

Now things had definitely changed. Ever since that night he had apologized for his rash behavior when he had awakened to find her in his office holding the framed photo he kept on his desk, he had started being less demanding and more polite. What had remained was the professional barrier he had erected between the two of them.

But, for some reason, now she had a feeling that barrier was slowly being torn down. By his hands, not hers. More than once she had caught him staring at her. And then, just now in his study, she'd had a feeling he had come close to actually kissing her. A few more inches and their lips would have touched.

Opal sighed deeply. She was way out of her league here. When it came to men, she had no experience. None. The thought that she was still a virgin at twenty-seven didn't bother her. No one knew of her sexual status but Colleen. She was sure her sisters assumed she had gotten intimate with Richard, the last guy she'd dated for six months about two years ago. For some reason, although Richard had wanted to move to that level in their relationship, she had not. His kisses hadn't stirred her to the point where she had wanted to sleep with him, and she couldn't see doing it just because it was something he wanted. It had to be something she wanted, as well. After Richard had quietly left the picture—when his old girlfriend had returned to town—Opal had been glad she'd made the decision that she had.

She paused in her thoughts when D'marcus stopped walking. He stood looking out at the ocean and she followed his gaze. It was simply beautiful. Then she decided to ask him the question that she had thought of upon first arriving in San Francisco. "How can you give this up to live in Detroit most of the year?"

He slowly turned to her and his dark eyes held hers. "For a long while the ocean lost its appeal to me," he said in a low tone. "The woman I was to marry lost her life in it."

"I'm sorry," Opal whispered, shaken by what he'd said. She had felt the pain in his words. She had forgotten that his fiancée had died two weeks before their wedding when the boat she was in capsized. Even after six years, it was evident that D'marcus Armstrong was still suffering from a broken heart.

"I'm okay now, but, for a long time, it was hard. In fact, she died before I bought the house, while I was still in college. I had figured buying a house on the ocean would be therapy to help me get over things, but it didn't work."

Opal nodded. She understood and part of her regretted he was reliving painful memories because of the question she had asked him. "We can go back inside if you'd like."

He surprised her by reaching out and taking her hand in his. "No, I'm fine. Come on and let's finish our walk."

He still held her hand as they walked slowly, side by side, along the sandy shores. She tried changing the subject by asking his permission to play something on his piano after they ate dinner.

He smiled over at her. "Sure you can. I'd love to hear you play."

She chuckled. "What about you? Do you still have your saxophone around?"

He grinned. "Yes, I do. I keep it in the closet in my bedroom. I enjoy playing it every once in a while. Maybe I'll play something later, as well."

They continued walking, and Opal couldn't help but wonder how she would make it through dinner with D'marcus. She was doing all she could not to show how much she was attracted to him, but it was taking a toll. When he had told her about his fiancée, her heart had gone out to him and she had wanted to reach out and hug him and let him know it was okay and that life went on.

But she hadn't reached out to hug him. Although she had a reason, she didn't have a right. Besides, she wasn't sure how he would react to such a gesture.

Suddenly he stopped walking, and she automatically stopped with him. He slowly turned and looked at her, gazed deep into her eyes. Then she felt it. Everything she had tried ignoring for the past month seemed to be tumbling down on her. And the look she saw in his eyes wasn't helping. They seemed to have gotten darker and were so seductive that she was beginning to feel dizzy. Evidently, she swayed a little because he quickly released her hand and captured her around the waist.

"D'marcus?"

She whispered his name because she didn't understand what was happening between them. That fact must have shown in her expression because he tightened his hold around her as he began lowering his mouth toward hers.

"Don't think right now, Opal," he whispered, just inches from her lips. "Just close your eyes and feel."

She did just as he asked and, the moment she felt his mouth take possession of hers, she released a moan from deep down in her throat. She felt the quiver that ran through her stomach when he folded her closer into his arms, closer to his muscular frame.

And then his mouth went farther as he took the kiss deeper in such a way that it almost overwhelmed her. The moment his tongue invaded her mouth, taking control of hers, something hot and fiery shot straight to every part of her body, but mainly to the area between her thighs. She couldn't help but moan again.

When he finally lifted his head, she opened her eyes and stared at him, trying to clear her mind, reset her pause button and slow down her heart rate. Then she was hit by the realization of what they'd done. They had actually shared a kiss.

She pulled out of his arms, feeling embarrassed all the way to the core. "I'm sorry," she managed to get out as she took a step back, almost stumbling in the process. "I should not have let that happen."

D'marcus saw the emotional turmoil in her eyes and decided to be honest with her. "I'm glad it happened, so there's no reason for you to apologize."

Opal shook her head, not believing what he said and not understanding it, either. She backed up a few more steps. "No, what we did was a mistake."

He begged to differ, but he decided that, logically, he could see why she assumed that. However, he was determined to prove her wrong. He was through trying to ignore his attraction to her. He wanted her. He had always wanted her. And now he was powerless to stop his emotions and desires.

Common sense had told him to take things slowly with her, but his desires were too strong, had gotten the best of him. There was no way he could not have kissed her when he had. And, from the way she had kissed him back, she had enjoyed it as much as he had. Okay, she was upset about it now, but he believed that beneath all that indignation was a woman who wanted him as much as he wanted her.

"I think we need to talk," he finally said, ending the silence that had ensued between them after her last statement. "I disagree about it being a mistake. I am attracted to you and have been for some time."

When he saw the expression on her face, he knew that whatever she was about to say was something he didn't want to hear right now. He held up his hand. "Let's wait and discuss things further after dinner. All right?"

Opal pulled in a deep breath and nodded. "Okay, but I want to go back to the house and rest up for dinner," she said, taking another step back. She turned to leave and he called out to her.

"Opal?"

She stopped and turned back around. "Yes?"

"Are you afraid of me?"

She stared at him for a moment before shaking her head. "No, D'marcus, I'm not afraid of you."

He inhaled deeply, relieved. "Then what are you afraid of?"

She glanced out at the ocean before looking back at him. "Of the unknown," she said in a soft voice. "I've always wanted to share something with a man that will last a lifetime. I take it you don't want that from a woman. You don't want to marry, nor do you want to have children. I'm not into casual relationships and you're the last type of man I should become involved with. And on top of that, you're my boss."

He nodded. "But?"

She stared at him wondering how he knew there was a *but*. "But I admit I'm attracted to you, as well." And, since it seemed they were going for honesty and admissions of the soul, she added, "And I have been for a long time."

With that said, she turned and began walking toward the house.

Chapter 10

Opal paced her bedroom, not knowing what she should do. It had been bad enough when she'd tried ignoring her attraction to D'marcus. Bad enough when her sisters had accused her of having a crush on him, and she had denied their allegations with a passion. But now, after the kiss they'd shared on the beach, she had to admit a few things to herself. What she was feeling was worse than a crush. She had fallen heads over heels in love with him.

"That's just great, Opal," she said aloud to herself, throwing up her hands. "Why are you setting yourself up for failure and heartbreak?"

She knew the answer. Falling in love with him was something she hadn't planned on. In fact, she had been prepared not to like him, and, initially, he had made it quite easy to do just that. But, at times, she had seen beyond his overbearing demeanor, his demanding ways. It was there in his voice whenever he had spoken to the coordinators of his various charities and, twice a month, when he served as mentor for a group of high school students who were interested in getting into business one day. The totally different attitude, the caring, was obvious.

Falling in love with him was her problem, one she would have to deal with while doing everything she could to maintain her dignity. D'marcus was a handsome man who could arouse her silly with just a kiss. She couldn't let her emotions overwhelm her. And, no matter what, she had to consider the consequences of loving a man who didn't love her back.

Disappointment filled her heart at the thought that she might have to find employment elsewhere. She liked her job, but the fact that she loved her boss was a major issue. She tried not to think about how she had felt in his arms or how his mouth had taken her with a mastery that, even now, had her breathless. The chemistry between them was obvious although she wished it wasn't. In Detroit, they had downplayed it, ignored it, bottled it. But now it seemed it couldn't be avoided any longer.

She sighed deeply when she heard him moving around downstairs, probably in the kitchen preparing the steaks to be grilled. Somehow, she had to go down there and act as though nothing had happened. Had to pretend his kiss hadn't rocked her world or that, even now, she wanted him to kiss her again.

As she headed for her bedroom door, she promised herself that, no matter what, she would get through the evening and later, when they did sit down to talk, she would try to be open-minded about things. But if she had to resign from her job, she would do it.

* * *

D'marcus glanced up from what he was doing when Opal walked into the kitchen. Although he was wondering if she was still uptight about the kiss they'd shared, he wouldn't ask her. As he'd told her, they would talk later.

The kiss had been a surprise not only to her but to him, as well. But nothing had affected him as strongly as her standing there with the ocean breeze flowing through her hair and the look of total serenity on her face. That vision had touched him deeply, made him yearn for her profoundly. Leaning down to kiss her had been as natural to him as breathing.

"I'm about to put the steaks on the grill," he said when she walked over to him at the sink, pausing at what she evidently thought was a safe distance.

She nodded. "Then what do you need me to do?"

He used his head to point out the white potatoes sitting on the table. "I've washed them already. You can get them ready to be baked."

"Okay."

He watched as she crossed the room to the table. "Everything you need is either in the refrigerator or the second cabinet on the left. Aluminum foil is in the pantry."

"What else will we have besides meat and potatoes?" she asked, and he could detect a semblance of a smile on her lips.

He couldn't help the smile that also touched his. "I thought a tossed salad would work, which is what I'm putting together. And I think a glass of wine would be nice."

As they worked, he turned and glanced over his

shoulder at her. She was quiet, busy getting the potatoes ready for the oven. She was wearing the same outfit she'd worn when they'd gone walking on the beach.
He hadn't gotten the chance to tell her how good she
looked in it. And what he dared not tell her was how
much he would love taking it off her. But that wasn't
all he wanted to do. He wanted to kiss her again, hear
her moan and feel her come apart in his arms. But more
than anything, he wanted to make love to her. All night
long.

He heard her open and close the oven door and knew
she was finished with the potatoes. Perfect timing, since
he was through preparing the salad. He covered the
bowl in plastic wrap to place it in the refrigerator. "I'd
better go back on the patio and check on the steaks.
Would you like to sit out there with me?"

He watched the indecisiveness in her features and
knew the exact moment she reached a decision. She
crossed the room to him. "Yes, I'll sit out there with
you."

Relief had him swallowing thickly. "All right." He
fought the urge to take her hand as they walked side
by side from the kitchen, through the dining room and
out the French doors. The patio faced the ocean and a
welcoming breeze touched their faces the moment they
placed their feet on the brick surface.

"So what's your secret recipe for the steaks?" she
asked him as she sat in one of the wicker chairs.

"My secret?"

"Yes, my dad once said every man who cooks has
a few."

He chuckled. "In that case, if I told you then it

wouldn't be a secret anymore, now would it? Besides, I don't cook a lot. While I was growing up, Aunt Marie enjoyed cooking and rarely allowed me or Uncle Charles in her kitchen. Then, when I went to college, if it wasn't for a few of the Spellman girls feeling sorry for me and rescuing me with timely dinners, I would have starved to death."

Opal couldn't help but smile. She could just envision those Spellman girls quickly coming to D'marcus's aid.

"By the time I entered Harvard," he continued, "I had learned to fend for myself. Tonya helped by clipping out simple recipes and sending them to me."

Probably to make sure he wasn't rescued by any Harvard girls, Opal quickly thought. She had watched how he'd smiled when he'd said his fiancée's name. She then remembered the pain and anguish that had been on his face earlier when he'd spoken of her death. It was evident that he had loved his Tonya very much.

She studied him while he gave his full concentration to grilling the steaks. His features were perfect in every way, from the deep set of his dark eyes to those incredibly sexy lips. Lips that had devoured hers earlier. The memory of them doing so caused an ache in her midsection.

"I think these are going to be very tasty."

She jerked until she realized he was talking about the cooking steaks and not his lips. Never had a man kissed her the way he had. He had caught her off guard and, even when she'd seen his mouth descending toward hers, she hadn't known what to expect. She hadn't been quite ready for the desperation she had tasted in his mouth, the hunger. But then, she definitely hadn't been ready for the response she had given him. It was as if she hadn't been able to get enough of his mouth, especially his tongue. It hadn't taken her long to realize that he was a gifted kisser.

"So what do you think, Opal?"

She glanced up at him and tried not to focus on his lips when she said, "Yes, I think they're going to be very tasty, indeed."

They both had been right. The meat, the potatoes, the salad, everything, had been tasty. Instead of eating in the kitchen, they had sat on the patio to enjoy the view of the ocean. They hadn't done a lot of talking and, when they had talked, it had been about their families. He shared more tidbits about his aunt and uncle, and she told him about her sisters and cousins and how close they were. She also told him about her church and how she considered the church members her family, as well.

"Our new minister is a former gangster," she said.

D'marcus raised his brow. "And he went from being a gangster to a minister?"

"Yes, after a personal tragedy that involved his brother. God was able to turn Reverend Kendrick's life completely around. He has such a great testimony to share."

D'marcus nodded. "I'll bet he has. An old high school friend of mine went through a similar situation. Doug was pretty smart, but his family couldn't afford to send him to college. He started hanging out with the wrong people and the next thing I knew, I got a call from Tonya telling me Doug had gotten arrested and had been sent off to jail for breaking and entering. He served two years of a five-year sentence, got off and changed his life around. He runs a boys' club in downtown Oakland and works hard to make sure others don't make the same mistakes he did."

He decided not to mention the fact that Doug had been Tonya's brother and the two of them were still close friends today. "I talked to Doug a few months ago and he wanted to let me know he had gotten called into the ministry. I am very proud of him and all he has accomplished in his life. He's a good man."

D'marcus and Opal shared the duty of washing dishes; he washed and she dried. In a way, Opal began feeling a little nervous. Dinner was over, the dishes were being washed and the next thing on the agenda was for them to talk. Now she was wondering if talking was such a good idea. They had kissed just once. Maybe they should move on and let bygones be bygones. But then, if they were to move on, which way would they move? No matter how much she was enjoying his company, he was still her boss and today they had broken the rule of work etiquette by indulging in a kiss.

"Okay, are you ready for some music now?"

D'marcus's question interrupted Opal's thoughts. "Music?"

"Yes. You play the piano and, afterward, I'll play the saxophone."

The fact that she had forgotten all about that must have shown in her face since D'marcus said, "Hey, don't try to get out of it. I want to see what you can do on that piano." A challenging, teasing grin touched his lips.

Tossing the dish towel aside, she couldn't help but

smile back. "Just remember I never said I was an accomplished pianist."

"As long as you remember that I'm not an accomplished saxophonist, either."

A few moments later Opal was sitting on the bench in front of the piano. It was nothing like the one she and her sisters used to have. That had been used and as plain as a piano could get, but it had served their needs and purpose. The one she was sitting at was a Steinway grand piano in flawless mahogany.

She glanced across the room. D'marcus was sitting in a chair watching her. Part of her wondered if he actually thought she couldn't play. Well, she would just show him that she could do more in life than keep his business matters straight.

"My first piece is simple, traditional and short. And it happens to be one of my favorites and was the one I did at my first recital."

"How old were you?"

"Nine. It was the year before my father died," she said, remembering. "It was during the Christmas holidays and he was there that night and I could tell how proud he was of me by the smile in his eyes."

Thinking she had said enough, probably too much, she looked down at the keys and lifted her hand and began stroking them, eliciting a tune. She glanced over and saw him smile and knew it was a song he recognized: "Joy to the World."

She closed her eyes as her hands continued to stroke

the keys and she remembered that night so long ago
and, just as she had then, she felt she was giving her
best performance.

D'marcus sat still. He didn't dare move. He watched
how Opal's fingers were stroking the piano keys and
part of him wished she could stroke parts of his body the
same way. And then he noticed her posture, straight and
upright, showing the beauty of her long neck, the bone
structure of her face and the firmness of her chin. And
then there was the tempting shape of her mouth, how her
lips, full and luscious, were curved in a smile. It was a
smile that tempted him to cross the room and kiss her.

This was the first time anyone had taken the time to
play his piano and she was filling the room with beautiful music. He could envision her as a little girl sitting at
a piano and playing that same song for her family and
others. He bet the room had gotten quiet and all eyes
had been on her. She had held everyone's attention just
as she was holding his now. Whether she would ever
admit it, he would admit it for her—she was a gifted
pianist.

Too soon, the music ended and she opened her eyes
and looked over at him. He smiled. "That was beautiful. Can I request one more?"

She smiled back. "Yes, just one more."

He watched as a teasing grin touched her lips and she
began playing. Again he recognized the tune immediately. It was the theme from the movie *Against All Odds*.

He leaned back in his chair, thinking he could sit
there all night and appreciate the music she was playing.
When she ended the number, she glanced over at him.

For a suspended moment, their gazes held and locked. Then he felt something—heat—escalate through all parts of his body. Sensations stroked him just the way she had stroked the piano keys. As he continued to gaze into her eyes, he wondered if she felt it, too, or was he alone in this madness?

"Now it's your turn, D'marcus. To play your sax."

He heard her voice, watched her lips move. He wanted to kiss those lips, devour them again. Instead, he nodded and got his saxophone off the table. He put it to his lips and began playing one of his favorite tunes. For the first time for him it held a special meaning. It was a classic from Roberta Flack—"The First Time Ever I Saw Your Face."

Chapter 11

By the time D'marcus lowered the saxophone from his lips, Opal had been moved nearly to tears. He had kept his eyes glued to her the entire time, making her feel as if the song had truly been dedicated to her. She knew that wasn't true, but, still, it had felt that way. She wondered how anyone so gifted in music could choose a career in business, instead.

As if he could read her mind, he said, "My father was a musician. In fact, he played the sax. I remember him being gone a lot, but I also remember the times when he came home and how happy my mother was to see him. They loved each other very much. Even as a child, I could feel it. And I could also feel their love for me. Whenever Dad was home he would play for me, and I always wanted to one day master the sax, just like him."

For a moment, he didn't say anything and then he continued, "When I was six, Mom decided to travel with Dad to see him play. He was performing at a real classy place in Los Angeles and he wanted my mom there. I stayed here with Aunt Marie and Uncle Charles. On the way back from the airport my parents were involved in the accident that took their lives."

Opal's heart went out to the little six-year-old boy who had lost his parents. The boy who had grown into a man and had mastered the sax, but whose father hadn't lived long enough to hear his son play. She then recalled how, years later, just two weeks before he was to marry, that same man had suffered another loss—this time of the woman he loved.

A sharp pain settled in her chest at all D'marcus had lost in his thirty years. But then she thought about how much he'd gained. Although nothing could ever replace what he'd lost, he had grown up to be a very successful man. And she knew his parents, as well as his fiancée, would have been proud of him. There was no way they could not have been.

"Now we can talk about what happened this afternoon, Opal."

She glanced up and saw he was standing next to her by the piano bench. She hadn't heard him move. Their eyes held and undeniable sensations swept through her. In a way, she knew they really didn't need to talk about it, since she was beginning to understand things a little clearer now, especially her emotions. But then she knew that they *did* need to talk about it.

He reached out his hand and she took it as he assisted her from the bench. "Where do you want to go?" he asked her quietly.

She knew it had to be somewhere with a lot of light, so the patio wouldn't do. Neither would the living room. And she preferred they not remain in this room, either. "We can sit in your office," she said, thinking in there they would be reminded of their roles in each other's lives.

"Okay, let's go to my office."

When he touched her arm, something stirred deep inside her. She knew she loved him, but she also knew that, in this situation, love would not be enough, and that was sad news for an optimist like herself. She would have to be realistic. Nothing could be sugarcoated.

When they reached his office, she went to sit in the chair across from his desk and he took the chair behind his desk. She felt comfortable since these were positions they were used to.

"All right, D'marcus, tell me," she requested quietly, "why the kiss?"

He met her gaze. "I think the reason should be obvious."

She locked into his gaze and said, "It's not obvious, so please explain."

She watched him build a steeple with his fingers under his chin as he continued to hold her gaze. "I'm attracted to you and I have been since the day I hired you. And, against my better judgment, I brought you into the company anyway, thinking as long as I kept things professional between us that would suffice. It worked for a while, but not for long. The sexual chemistry was too strong. Every time I saw you, there was this deep tug of desire that wanted to rule my mind, my thoughts and my very being. Since coming to San Francisco and being around you more, I've finally accepted something about myself."

"What?"

"I'm male, human and have an incredible degree of

desire for you. In other words, Opal Lockhart, I want you with a desperation that is almost killing me."

Opal didn't know what to say, so she sat there speechless, incapable of uttering a single sound. However, her heart rate increased tenfold and sensations she only encountered around D'marcus began rushing fast and furious through her veins. No man had ever told her he wanted her that much before. Richard had let it be known he wanted to sleep with her, and she guessed, in a way, it meant the same thing. But D'marcus's delivery touched her in a way Richard's statement had not.

Okay, so he wanted her and, deep down, if she was completely honest, she would admit that she wanted him, too. But what if they were to cross over the boundaries that had been established when he had hired her? What would happen to their business relationship, the one she depended on for her livelihood? She knew the only thing he was interested in was an affair and she was smart enough to know that affairs didn't last. What would happen when theirs ended? Things at work would become awkward, unbearable. What would she do then?

She decided to let him answer that. Ask him questions that would start him to thinking, and then he would realize just what he was saying, what he was asking of her. In this life, we don't always get what we want. Unfortunately for both of them, this would be one of those times.

She moved past the lump in her throat to ask, "Are you saying that you're in love with me, D'marcus?"

"No."

His response, quick and easy, had cleared that up fast. "Then are you saying you want to marry me?"

"No."

"All right then, what are you saying?"

He didn't reply at first and then he slowly leaned forward in his chair. "First of all, I want you to understand that love and marriage are not in my future. The possibility of both were destroyed the day Tonya drowned. The only thing I can offer you or any woman is an affair they won't forget or regret."

Her heart actually ached at his words. "For how long?" she asked. "How long will the affair last?"

"For as long as it's mutually acceptable. All either of us has to say is that we want out and things will end."

"Without any drama?"

"Yes, without any drama."

Opal thought on his words and then wondered out loud, "But I'm your administrative assistant. You employ over eight hundred people at the Detroit office. What do you think their reaction will be? They'll think I'm sleeping my way to the top."

"Our affair would be private. In the office, things between us would remain the same. But after-hours—"

"So you want us to sneak around?"

"No, that's not what I want, but I'll do whatever you need me to do to uphold your reputation. I don't want you to be hurt in any way, Opal."

But didn't he see that she would be hurt? When he finally got enough of her and moved on, was she supposed to be able to pick up the pieces to her life and just move on without looking back?

"I know I'm asking a lot of you," he said softly. "And

you probably think I'm nothing but a selfish bastard for doing so. But if things had been different and if I had met you any other way, I would still want to have an affair with you. You working for me did not make me attracted to you. I would have been attracted to you if we would have met on different terms. You are a very beautiful and desirable woman, Opal. And your make-over has nothing to do with it. I wanted you long before then."

She averted her gaze and absently studied one of the paintings he had on the wall. He was making it hard. "I need to think about this," she finally said.

"I understand, and I want you to think about it. You know what I want, but I will respect what you want. However, part of me remembers our kiss earlier today and I have a feeling that, deep down, you want me, too. If you do, Opal, we can make this work. What we do is nobody's business but ours. We're adults who don't have to answer to anyone."

A smile touched her lips. In his circles it might not be anyone's business but theirs, but he didn't have three nosy sisters and two cousins who felt it their God-given right to know what was going on with them.

She sighed as she stood up. Today had been quite a day, physically and emotionally. "I'm going to bed now," she said. "I'm going to sleep on it and let you know tomorrow."

"Okay."

She turned to leave but stopped at the door and looked back. He had stood and was staring at her. Deep, hard, unwavering. She swallowed, actually feeling the intensity of his desire for her. It touched her in a way it should not have. It had every bone in her body aching. She came close to crossing the room back to him to take the both of them out of their misery. But she couldn't. As she'd told him, she had to think things through because she knew that, whatever decision she made, there was no going back.

Inhaling a deep breath, she turned around and walked out of his office, closing the door behind her.

Opal glanced at the clock on the nightstand. It was almost two in the morning and she couldn't sleep. Nor had she been able to think rationally. Every time she closed her eyes, she envisioned D'marcus, as handsome as he could be, ready for her, letting her know the depth of his desire for her.

Part of her ached to tell him she craved what he wanted and that she didn't care about their working relationship, nor what others would think. But she held back because she did care.

She got out of bed and walked over to the window and looked out at the ocean. Now would be the perfect time to walk beside it. Alone. Maybe out there she would find answers she couldn't find in this bedroom, especially knowing that D'marcus was sleeping just one room away. And that he wanted her.

Pulling off her nightgown, she slipped into a pair of jogging pants and matching top. She had discovered that, at night, the temperature near the Bay area seemed to drop, producing cool nights.

Leaving her room, she quietly made her way down the stairs, opened the French doors and slipped out onto the patio. The night breeze touched her face and the scent of the sea teased her nostrils. It was a beautiful night and she felt lucky to be out in it.

Opal found a nice boulder and sat down and looked out at the ocean. In the light from the stars and moon, it seemed she could see for miles. She thought about D'marcus and how much she loved him. But he had made things clear in his office today. He didn't want love and he had no intention ever to marry. The love she felt was one-sided. Their relationship would strictly be for sex. Could she handle such a relationship, one in which they shared only their bodies and not their emotions? And, if she couldn't, could she find the strength to walk away and not look back?

She heard a sound behind her and turned to stare into familiar dark eyes. D'marcus evidently hadn't been able to sleep either, and, like her, had decided to walk on the beach.

He didn't say anything. He stood leaning against a tree staring at her with such a penetrating gaze, it made her breath catch. In a pair of jeans and a T-shirt, he looked handsome, muscular and virile. Only one thought kept racing through her mind: this magnificent specimen of a man wanted her.

That was when she knew she was fighting a losing battle.

As she looked at him, love swelled her heart. She felt incapable of doing anything but loving this man, sharing love with him in any way that she could. She thought about the questions she had asked herself earlier. Yes, somehow she would handle a relationship with D'marcus and, when the time came for them to part, she would somehow find the strength to walk away. It would be better to share something special with him than not to share it at all. And, yes, she was willing to accept whatever consequences resulted. She could no longer be satisfied by dreaming about how it would be in his arms. She needed to find out for herself. There was this thing flowing between them, something that was so volatile, so explosive that even now she felt it—combustible energy, sexual awareness, blatant desire.

She tipped her chin when she saw him move and begin walking toward her slowly. She heard his heavy breathing and wondered if he heard hers. She didn't want to think about all the sensations he was able to evoke within her. It was enough for her to feel them in her most intimate places.

He came to a stop in front of her and she continued to gaze into his dark eyes. Even with the coolness of the night, she felt his heat.

"Earlier you said you wanted me. Show me how much," she said in a whispered tone.

She watched his eyes darken even more and watched his sensuous lips move when he spoke. "Please, don't ask me to do anything you don't mean," he warned quietly while at the same time shifting his stance to bring his lips, as well as his body, close to hers.

"I'm not asking for anything I don't mean, D'marcus. I accept your terms." Then, repeating his earlier words, she said, "I want you with a desperation that is almost killing me."

No sooner had the words left her mouth than he captured that same mouth in one sensual onslaught that rattled every sense Opal possessed. Somehow he locked her mouth tightly to his while his tongue did all kinds of erotic things. Desire was rushing rampant all through her and she knew in her heart that her decision wasn't a mistake. She would have this for as long as it lasted.

She would have him.

And then she felt herself being swept into his arms without him breaking the kiss. He finally released her mouth when he turned on his heels and carried her back toward his house. Opal knew that, once they were inside, their relationship would never be the same.

Chapter 12

D'marcus lowered Opal onto her feet by his bed and stared down at her. The look he saw in her eyes let him know she wanted him as much as he wanted her and that knowledge, that reassurance, sent his pulse escalating. He had to kiss her again, something he would never get tired of doing.

He lowered his mouth to hers, pleased when she lifted hers up to meet his. He captured her lips at the same time his hands wrapped around her waist, bringing her body closer to the fit of him, showing her just what she was doing to him, how she was making him feel and how much he desired her.

The moment his tongue entered her mouth and he deepened the kiss, he felt the shiver that touched her body, heard the moan that rumbled in her throat and felt her arms wrap around his neck. He wasn't a novice when it came to kissing women, but something about Opal's taste had him wanting to come back time and time again.

Her nipples hardened, pressing against his T-shirt,

making his heart pound more furiously in his chest. She was robbing him of control, driving his desire to a level it had never reached before and sending all kinds of sensations ripping through him.

Unable to take any more, he pulled his mouth free when she pressed her curvaceous body more intimately against him, setting off a groan that came from deep within his throat.

He had to undress her because he wanted her now. He couldn't wait a moment longer. First, he took off her top and then, after removing her walking shoes, he took off her jogging pants. In between the removal of each piece, he leaned over and kissed her deeply. When she stood before him wearing only a bra and panties, he straightened and let his eyes rake over her from top to bottom. The sight of her nakedness nearly made him lose it, but he was determined to remain in control. He wanted to make this moment as special for her as it was for him.

"I'll finish undressing you later. Now I want you to undress me," he whispered in her ear.

He pulled back and stared into her face. The expression he saw there was exquisite, totally priceless. He knew immediately that she had never undressed a man before. For some reason, that knowledge sent heat escalating through every part of him.

She looked into his eyes and he could see a nervous glitter in their dark depths. "What if I don't do it right?" she whispered back.

He smiled. "Trust me. There is no wrong way. Do it your way. Any way you like."

For a moment, she seemed to consider what he said,

then she reached out and gently pulled his T-shirt from the waistband of his jeans. She lifted the shirt over his head and threw it atop her clothes on the floor. When he stood before her, bare chested, he saw her studying the contours of his muscular frame. The breath she drew was ragged.

And then her trembling fingers undid the snap at his waist and slowly eased down his zipper. He didn't have the heart to encourage her to hurry, but her touch was killing him. To survive the torture, he summoned more strength and willpower. It seemed she was having a hard time pulling the jeans from his body so he asked, "Need my help?"

She lifted her eyes to his. "Yes, please."

He smiled as he reached down to remove his shoes, something she hadn't thought of doing. His smile widened at the embarrassment that immediately shone on her face when she realized that fact.

"I guess you can tell I'm not good at this," she whispered after he kicked off his shoes and began easing his jeans down his thighs.

"You're doing just fine," he assured her. In nothing but a pair of black briefs, he sat down on the side of the bed. "Come here, sweetheart."

She came to him and he pulled her down into his lap and cradled her close. "Why are you so nervous, Opal? You do trust me, don't you?"

She gazed at him and nodded. "Yes."

"Are you having doubts?"

She quickly shook her head. "No, I'm not having doubts."

"Then what is it?"

Opal knew now was the time to tell him she had never done anything like this before. In fact, she'd never come close. He had a right to know that, if he was expecting an experienced woman to share his bed, he would be sadly disappointed.

"I—I should tell you something," she said, breaking eye contact with him and looking down at her trembling fingers.

"Tell me what?" he asked gently.

When she didn't answer right away, he reached out and touched his finger to her chin, lifting her face so their eyes could meet. "Tell me what, Opal?"

She swallowed past the lump in her throat before saying, "I've never made love to a man before."

He stared down at her as the full impact of her admission hit him. She had just admitted to being a virgin. A twenty-seven-year-old virgin, at that.

"D'marcus, does that make a difference?"

He heard her question and, deep down, he knew that, yes, it did make a difference. He would be her first, and now, more than anything, he wanted it to be special for her. As special as he knew it would be for him. That had been his intent all along, but now it was doubly so. She deserved that and more.

"If you're asking if knowing you're a virgin makes me want you less, the answer is no. It makes me want you more because I'm the one who will introduce you to pleasure so profound just thinking about it takes my breath away. I just hope I'm worthy of what you're about to let me do."

She smiled up at him. "You are. I wouldn't be here in this room with you if you weren't." She wrapped her arms around his neck and held on to him the way he was holding on to her. For a moment they just sat on the edge of the bed that way, needing this time to be in each other's arms.

Moments later, he glanced down when he felt the tip of her fingers tracing a line down his chest. She smiled at him. "You have a beautiful chest."

His breath caught when she leaned forward and placed a kiss on it, just beneath his heart. At that moment, something touched him, deep. The woman in his arms, whom he desired with a passion, totally fascinated him in an innocent sort of way. Everything she did was born not of experience but of desire. He suddenly wanted to teach her everything he knew about pleasure, the kind a man and woman shared.

He leaned down and shifted her body in his arms so he could kiss her again. And then he stood and brought her to her feet, as well.

"I need to make love to you, Opal. I can't hold out any longer," he said in a tormented voice, reaching out and undoing her bra. He slid the thin straps off her shoulders, down her arms to remove the garment from her body, tossing it on the pile to join their other pieces of clothing. His breath caught when he gazed at her bare breasts. They were just the right size, the perfect shape and the dark nipples were erect, hard tips.

He couldn't resist reaching out and touching them, hearing her sharp intake of breath when his fingertips caressed them gently. Lowering his head, he took one between his lips. Her taste delighted him, filled him with pure enjoyment, and when he shifted his attention to her other breast, she was moaning out his name.

It sounded just as it had in his jet when she had been asleep and dreaming.

He pulled back, getting his own breathing under control, and then he got on his knees to pull her panties down her legs. Up close, he saw just what gorgeous legs she had. Her hips were curvy, her thighs firm, her stomach flat. She was beautifully built. As he eased her panties down her legs, his breath caught when he gazed at the area it had hidden.

He wanted to lean forward and taste her, but he didn't want to shock her. He would introduce her to other things first, but he would keep that in the back of his mind as something he definitely had to do later.

He leaned back on his haunches and his gaze raked over her naked body. Thrilled by what he saw, he felt his own body harden. "Now you can finish up on me," he said as he stood.

She only had his briefs to remove and, like him, she got on her knees and began pulling them down his legs. Her breath caught when his shaft was exposed, hard and erect, fully aroused.

D'marcus drew in a deep breath when, in a surprising move, she reached out and took his shaft into her hands, letting her fingers caress its firmness. "Opal," he said through clenched teeth. Reaching out, he pulled her up off her knees and held her close to him, letting her feel the heat of him against her stomach.

He then picked her up and placed her on the huge bed, right in the center, and she gazed at him intently, her eyes glued to the mass of dark curls surrounding the instrument that would bring her pleasure.

He reached into a nightstand and pulled out a condom packet. The condoms had been there awhile and he had never used them; Opal was the first woman he had invited to this house to share his bed. He knew she watched curiously as he tore into the packet and put one on.

With that done, he eased onto the bed to join her there. But instead of placing his body over hers, he wanted to introduce her to foreplay of the most erotic kind. When he entered her body, he wanted her totally ready for him.

He kissed her, more desperately than he had the other times, and he could feel her responding, actually melting in his arms. Her breasts were pressed against his bare chest, making him crave her that much more.

The tempo of his kiss changed and his mouth and hands began traveling everywhere over her. She shuddered uncontrollably beneath his lips and fingertips, so much so that, by the time he slipped his hands between her legs, her feminine core felt like wet heat, and she released a deep, startling moan.

"D'marcus!"

"Yes, sweetheart?"

"Please."

He met her gaze and saw the deep desire in them. He knew she really didn't know what she was pleading for, but he would definitely show her. He eased his body over hers, loving the feel of her naked flesh against his. He held on to her gaze as he braced his elbows on each side of her, as he situated himself between her quaking thighs. When he saw her close her eyes, he asked her to keep them open. He wanted her to watch him give her pleasure.

He leaned the lower part of his body down and his erection immediately touched her womanly core. Again she moaned.

He smiled at her. "You like that?"

Instead of speaking, she nodded.

"Hold on, there's more of me to give. You might feel a little pain."

He eased his shaft into her. The pain came and went so quickly, she barely felt it. What she was feeling now was pleasure. But she noticed he had stopped moving. "What's wrong?" she asked in a voice filled with panic.

He leaned down to kiss her to assure her everything was all right. There was no way he could explain the magnitude of the emotions he felt being inside of her. But he was only halfway. "You're tight and I don't want to hurt you. Relax."

She smiled up at him. "I am relaxed."

He chuckled. "Then relax some more."

She thought if she got any more relaxed, she would fall asleep. He eased into her deeper and she felt more pain than she had before.

"You okay?"

She nodded, feeling him deeply embedded within her to the hilt. She wrapped her arms around his neck and smiled up at him. "I'm fine."

Holding her gaze, he began moving, in and out, setting a pace that had her moaning. Her body became wrapped up in pleasure so intense she could barely stand it. All the while, their gazes were locked, and then her body seemed to explode in tiny pieces. She screamed out his name and her body shuddered uncontrollably.

"D'marcus!"

And then she was floating…. When she heard him call out her name, another erotic spasm tore through her as his body thrust continuously into hers and her hips automatically rose to receive him. The rhythm he established showed once again what a gifted musician he was. Each stroke into her body was precise, well tuned and unerringly perfect. He finally broke eye contact with her when he threw his head back and called out her name again. The sound seemed to echo off the walls.

Once their breathing was under control, he kissed her again. Opal knew this was what they would share for the rest of their time together. She loved him and, although he didn't love her, she believed she had made the right decision in having an affair with him.

Her love would be enough to get her through.

Chapter 13

Opal awoke the next morning in D'marcus's bed alone. She glanced over at the clock on the nightstand and saw the time was past nine. She jerked upright. She'd never slept this late before, and technically it was a workday. In fact, D'marcus had had a conference call with the other owners of the Chargers team at eight.

She swung her feet over the side of the bed and moaned when she felt a distinct soreness between her legs—a blatant reminder of her activities last night and in the predawn hours. Under D'marcus's masculine powers she'd been unable to think, only to feel. When he touched her, she'd been filled with pure sensual sensations that had flowed through every vein and invaded every nerve of her body.

The mere memory quickened her pulse, a testament to his sexual prowess. But now her lover was absent, gone to work. Exactly where she should be.

She left his room and went into hers, wondering why D'marcus hadn't awakened her when he knew she had work to do. She quickly showered and dressed and, in less than thirty minutes, she was rushing down the stairs.

From behind his desk, D'marcus looked up when she walked into his office. The moment Opal saw him she had to fight back a ragged moan. Just seeing him instantly reminded her of everything they had done the night before. Unable to move, she stood there staring at him.

He did the same and she could see his eyes darken. She wondered if he, too, was reliving their lovemaking in his memory. She couldn't help feeling a little embarrassed. There wasn't a part of her body that he hadn't kissed, touched, tasted. The mere thought sent heat flowing all through her and she felt flushed.

Somehow, she found her voice. "Why didn't you wake me?"

"You needed your rest," he said, as if that settled everything.

For her, it didn't. "But I have a job to do."

"Nothing that couldn't wait until you were ready to get up."

In a way, she was shocked by his statement. How many bosses waited to start their day until their staff was ready to come to work? For him to give her that kind of leverage was not only unfair but ridiculous. "What about the conference call with Williams and Hennessy?"

D'marcus leaned back in his chair. "They called, we talked and made decisions. We'll be placing Dashuan on suspension without pay. However, they're going to let me deliver the news to him personally when I return to Detroit next week."

Opal didn't like the sound of that. She'd noticed more than once that the other two owners left unpleasant matters for D'marcus to handle, especially when they concerned Dashuan Kennedy.

She shook her head, deciding to go back to their earlier topic of conversation. "I should have been present for that conference call, D'marcus."

He tossed a pen on his desk. "And I preferred letting you sleep, Opal. End of conversation."

She glared at him and turned to leave the room.

"Opal?" She kept walking away, but quickly remembering that he was still her boss, she stopped and turned around. "Yes?"

He had come around his desk and was sitting on the edge of it. "Will you come here for a moment, please?"

She wished she could say no, but knew that would be total disrespect. "Yes, sir."

He lifted a brow. "'Yes, sir'?"

She nodded when she came to a stop in front of him. "Yes, sir."

At first, she thought she had made him angry by being so formal with him until she took a good look into the dark depths of his eyes. What she saw almost took her breath away. It wasn't anger but male hunger. The same look that had been in his eyes most of last night. She had discovered over the past eight hours that D'marcus had a sexual appetite unlike anyone she'd ever met. But then he not only took, he gave. She was almost too embarrassed to think about all the orgasms she'd had. Her body had been receptive to his lovemaking over and over again. He probably had more passion in his little finger than some men had in their entire bodies. Even now her body was beginning to feel hot and bothered just standing this close to him.

"First of all," he said, reclaiming her attention as he reached out and caressed the bare part of her arms, "I prefer you not calling me *sir*. Second, if I feel you need more rest and decide to let you sleep, then I'd rather you not question it."

"But what about my work?"

"What about it?"

She rolled her eyes, deciding to try another angle. "Will we be working today, D'marcus?"

"Not until later today. Much later. I'm going to enjoy the morning."

She lifted a brow, not really liking the sound of that. "And do what?"

"This, for starters."

He pulled her to him and his mouth captured hers. The moment he did so, more memories invaded her and her body automatically responded. She was helpless not to kiss him back with the same hunger with which he was kissing her. He released her mouth only long enough to sweep her off her feet and into his arms. He began moving out of the room.

"Where are you taking me?" she asked in a whisper.

"Back to my bed where we're going to stay for a while."

"But what about—"

He didn't let her finish what she was about to say. Instead, he stopped walking and kissed her again to silence her. When he finally released her mouth, she was too drunk on desire to think straight, let alone speak.

When they made it up the stairs to his room, he

quickly dispensed with her clothing, as well as his own, then laid her down on the bed. Smiling down at her, he put a condom on just as he'd done the night before, but, unlike last night, she was no longer embarrassed to watch him.

Moments later he eased his powerful body down on the bed and kissed her, making her moan deep in her throat when his tongue plunged into her mouth. He joined his body with hers, driving into her deeply then pulling out, over and over again.

"D'marcus!"

He smiled as he thrust into her once more. "Now, that's what I want to hear. My name on your lips." And then he kissed her again when he felt his own orgasm charging through his body.

She wrapped her arms tightly around him to hold him close and locked her legs around his back to pull him deeper into her. How he was making her feel now, as well as last night, was beyond any sensation she'd ever experienced. When D'marcus released a raw groan and called out her name, everything within her shattered and she felt the most wonderful, explosive sensations all the way to her toes.

Long after the orgasm ended, they lay in each other's arms with their gazes locked and their bodies still connected. "Now, tell me," D'marcus said in a low and husky voice, "why you were in such a bad mood this morning?"

Opal frowned. "I wasn't in a bad mood. But…"

"But what?"

"But I still don't understand why you didn't wake me up."

He shook his head. He appreciated her dedication, however, he just didn't understand what the big deal was. "Would you believe me if I told you that I like how you look when you're asleep?"

"That shouldn't matter. I have a job to do. And I just don't want you to forget that."

D'marcus felt there was a deeper meaning behind her words. "And why would I forget you have a job to do, Opal?"

"Because of *this*," she said quietly, shifting her body slightly.

He released a deep groan. "You keep that up and *this* will become *that*," he said, shifting his own body, letting her know that he'd gotten aroused again. "Now, back to the issue of your job. Us sleeping together will not make me forget that you work for me. They are separate concerns."

"Then why are we here in bed and not in your office working?"

He leaned down and placed a quick kiss on her lips. "Mainly because Henry Gregory called and asked if he could change his appointment to this afternoon. His wife has a doctor's appointment this morning and he wants to be there with her. She had breast cancer a year ago and today is the day for her recheck."

"Oh."

"And since there was nothing else on our schedule, I thought you and I would do something to relax." He leaned down and kissed her on the lips again. "You do find making love with me relaxing, don't you?" he asked with a quick smile.

Relaxing? She didn't want to inflate his ego by say-

ing she found making love to him more like mind-
blowing. If they kept it up on a frequent basis, it might
become outright habit-forming. "Yes, it's relaxing," she
said instead. "But so are a number of other things," she
quickly added.

"But would you prefer doing those other things to
this?"

She knew the answer to that question right away.
She didn't prefer doing anything to this. "No," she said
simply.

Another smile touched the corner of his lips. "I'm
definitely glad to hear that." He leaned forward to kiss
her neck, then her shoulder. "I guess I should be a good
host and at least feed you breakfast," he said, kissing
her lips once again.

Opal's heartbeat increased every time he used his
tongue that way. "Right now food is the last thing on
my mind," she said in a shuddering voice.

"Really? And what's the first thing on your mind?"
he asked, pulling her closer to the fit of him, making
sure she felt how and where their bodies were connected.

Opal instinctively flexed her hips, making him go
deeper inside of her. "This is the first thing on my
mind," she answered with a fragmented moan.

D'marcus shifted their bodies so she lay directly beneath him. "I'm very glad to hear that." He then proceeded to show her how much.

For the first time in three years, D'marcus decided
to jog along the beach. Jogging was something he did a
lot in Detroit, even when the weather wasn't at its best.

Usually, though, when he returned to the Bay, he never stayed in his home long enough to indulge in this pastime. Besides, he had avoided the ocean for years, failing at accomplishing what he had originally purchased the home for, which was to make peace with the sea.

His lips curved slightly into a smile when he thought about the woman he had left sleeping in his bed. This time, he intended to wake her up so she could have time to prepare for their meeting later today with Henry Gregory. She had gotten upset because she'd assumed because they had become lovers he had seen her duties to him as changing.

If only she knew how much he had come to depend on her efficiency and her expertise. Although she didn't know it, several of his department managers had approached him with positions they thought she would more than adequately fill once her internship ended. He would hate losing her as his administrative assistant, but he was not one to stand in the way of her opportunities.

What he'd told her earlier today was true. Once he had made up his mind not to avoid having a relationship with her, he had decided that her working for him and their affair were two separate entities, having nothing to do with each other.

He slowed down and inhaled a deep breath. It was time to head back to the house. His aunt had called and again had insisted that he bring Opal back for a visit before she left on Friday.

He smiled. It seemed that his aunt had really been taken with Opal. But then, he was quite taken with her, as well.

Chapter 14

Opal smiled at D'marcus's announcement the next morning at breakfast. They would be joining his aunt and uncle for dinner later that day. She really liked his relatives and was looking forward to the visit.

Yesterday, they had met with Henry Gregory to discuss plans to open the new stores in California. After that, D'marcus had taken her to downtown San Francisco for her first cable-car ride. They rode from Union Square to Fisherman's Wharf, where they dined at a seafood restaurant. Then, holding hands, they strolled through the various shops on the wharf, where she picked up souvenirs for her sisters and cousins.

It had been late when they'd returned home and, after taking a shower together, they had gone to bed. It was as if they couldn't get enough of each other and they had made love most of the night.

"What time is your aunt expecting us?" Opal asked, after taking a sip of her coffee.

"She wanted us for noon, but I explained that we had several projects to complete today, since you'll be leaving tomorrow. I told her the best we could do was around four."

Opal was fully aware of the projects they needed to complete and was anxious to get started. They had several conference calls scheduled, including one from his suppliers in Tokyo. Doing all the legwork for the successful opening of D'marcus's stores always excited her.

"Eat up. You and I will be quite busy until at least one o'clock today."

"Yes, sir," she said, grinning.

The look he gave wasn't one of amusement, so she said, "Sorry."

"I've told you I don't like you calling me *sir*. I never did."

"Then why didn't you say something about it long ago?"

"Because it made things a lot easier to keep distance between us."

She nodded, understanding his reasoning for that. "And now?"

"And now I find it quite annoying since I don't want distance between us anymore."

She didn't say anything as she took another sip of her coffee. He wasn't interested in love or marriage, but he wanted to make sure the two of them got as close as they could get. He had done a good job of proving that, she thought, remembering how they'd slept pressed against each other, barely an inch separating them.

"Will we be staying overnight at your aunt's?" Opal asked as she stood to place her coffee cup and cereal bowl in the sink. If they were, she needed to pack an overnight bag.

out it. Chances were his aunt would think that if Op
ly believed that, why were the two of them lovers
"Of course he is," Marie countered. "The boy can
ep his eyes off you. And he has never taken a woma
his home before. Trust me, he loves you."

Opal would stand her ground and argue with th
man if she thought it would do any good, but sh
w it wouldn't. The woman was steadfast in her b
Unfortunately, she was getting love mixed up wi

I want to make a request of you," Marie said, i
ing Opal's thoughts.

Yes?"

thought he would never get over Tonya. Her dea
him. It's taken him a long time."

al was a split second from saying that he st
gotten over it. D'marcus was still suffering fro
e heartbreak and pain to the point where he wou
ove another woman and he would never comm
to one, either.

d then when he found out that Tonya had be
nt, he—"

ya was pregnant?" Opal asked, almost in shoc
unt nodded. "He didn't tell you that part?"

was tempted to say that he really hadn't to
hing, other than how his fiancée had died a
I had an aversion to the ocean as a result of
she said, "No, he didn't tell me."

nt inhaled a deep breath. "I'm not surprise
im to talk about it, especially since he blam
r Tonya's death."

r surprise revelation. Opal stared at the old

"Aunt Marie requested that we do, but I declined. I want to sleep in my own bed tonight with you in it with me."

Opal turned to him. "I hope that's not the reason you gave her."

When he didn't say anything, she raised an arched brow as she held his gaze. "D'marcus, what reason did you give your aunt?"

After putting his dishes in the sink, he stood in front of her and smiled. "Don't get uptight on me. I merely told her that with you flying out tomorrow we had a lot of work yet to do that could take us well into the night to finish."

Opal rolled her eyes. "I can just imagine what kind of work you're referring to."

"I'll never tell."

"But I'm sure you're going to show me later, right?" she said, pressing her body against his and wrapping her arms around his neck.

"That's a very strong possibility." He drew in a quick breath when she freed one of her hands and reached down and caressed the front of his zipper, as if testing the state of his arousal.

"Mmm, nice and big," she whispered into his ear.

"You're asking for it, aren't you?" he said, wrapping his arms around her, as well.

She laughed. "I'm sure if I was, you would be more than happy to oblige."

"Without a moment's hesitation. How about right now?"

She shook her head as she removed her arms from around his neck and took a step back. "Sorry. I believe you told your aunt that we had several projects to complete this morning since I'm leaving tomorrow. I suggest we get a head start on them. Tokyo is expecting a call from you in less than an hour." With that said, she turned and sashayed out of the kitchen.

D'marcus watched her leave, thinking that she had one hell of a sexy walk. He rubbed his hand down his face in frustration. His administrative assistant was turning into one seductive temptress.

"I'm glad D'marcus agreed to bring you to dinner this evening," Marie was saying as she and Opal walked out onto the patio through a set of French doors. The backyard boasted a lovely garden and huge swimming pool. D'marcus and his uncle had walked next door to take a look at their neighbor's new boat.

"Thanks for inviting me. Dinner was great. You're a wonderful cook."

Marie beamed at the compliment as they sat down together at a patio table. "I had to be, especially when Charles and I suddenly found ourselves as guardian to a very active and hungry little boy. I swear, when D'marcus was little, he ate everything and anything he could get his hands on. There wasn't anything he didn't like," she said with fondness.

Opal smiled as the older woman poured her a glass of iced tea from the pitcher on the table. She could just imagine D'marcus as a kid. But, unlike the kid then, he rarely ate now. His aunt would probably be surprised if she knew just how many meals he routinely skipped due to working so hard. She decided that she wouldn't be the one to tell her.

"So did you and D'marcus finish up a ects today?"

Opal smiled over at Marie after takir "Yes, we got all of them completed. Th should open without any problems."

"And later this evening, I understand have work to do that will take you wel

Opal hoped the older woman didn' her face. "Yes, that's what I understa

"Well, don't let my nephew work wants to be a workaholic, then that' don't let his overzealous work habit

"I won't," Opal said with a smil

"And another thing," the older w know you and D'marcus want to ing going on between the two of ter. I may be old but I'm not blin

Opal almost choked on her te gazed at her with concern. "Are

Opal nodded since she wasr that moment.

"Well, like I was saying," going to get into you and D just wanted you to know tha happy that he has found lo extremely happy."

Opal knew D'marcus's au tions. He was not in love w

"Marie, please."

Opal smiled. "Marie, me," she said. In a way

woman for a few moments before asking, "Why would he blame himself?"

"Because he was supposed to go with Tonya on that boating trip. He had flown home for a few days to see her, but had skipped the boating trip in order to study for an exam."

Opal's heart immediately went out to D'marcus. No wonder he was still hurting, even after six years.

"Now, with you in his life, his uncle and I are hoping that he will move on."

Opal sighed. She hoped he would move on, as well, but his aunt was wrong in assuming she was in his life for the long haul. She was more in his bed than in his life.

She took another sip of her tea and thought about all that Marie Armstrong had shared with her. She understood D'marcus a little better now because of it, and although she still knew he didn't love her, her love for him had increased at that moment. She would never be able to take Tonya's place and she wouldn't think of trying. But just for a little while she would try to make him the extremely happy man that his aunt assumed he was. The extremely happy man he deserved to be.

And, most important, she wanted to make him the extremely happy man she loved with all her heart.

"You didn't say much on the drive back. Are you okay?"

Opal turned toward D'marcus when they entered his home and smiled at him. "Yes, I'm fine."

A smile touched the corners of his lips. "Then I guess

your reason for not saying much is that my aunt probably talked you to death. I told you she was a talker."

Yes, she was, but Opal appreciated her tendency to chatter. Otherwise she would not have known as much about D'marcus as she did now. "I'm going to my room to pack."

Even as she said the words, a sharp pain speared her heart. Getting on that plane and leaving him tomorrow would be hard on her. She knew her emotions were more caught up in this relationship than his, but at the moment, she couldn't help herself. Whoever said when you were in love you had the tendency not to think straight certainly knew what they were talking about.

"Do you need my help?" he asked her in a deep, sexy voice. He stood leaning against the living room doorway staring at her with those intense dark eyes of his. He looked like the perfect male specimen.

Their gazes held and at that moment, something inside of her seemed to break free. Tomorrow at noon she would be flying back to Detroit on D'marcus's jet without him. It would be the middle of next week before she saw him again. Five days without looking at his handsome face, tasting his succulent lips, lying in the warmth of his arms. She began to miss him already.

She would think of him every waking moment. She would think of him even when she slept. In other words, every minute of every day. Would he think of her at all?

"Come here, Opal."

She heard the deep urgency in his voice. She heard the depth of desire in it, as well. Tonight was their last night together for a while and she wanted it to be one that he remembered as much as she did. She was still a novice when it came to making love with a man, but over the past couple of days, D'marcus had taught her a lot, and she intended to use some of those saucy lessons on him now.

She kicked off her shoes as she slowly walked across the room to him, not breaking eye contact. When she got halfway she pulled her blouse over her head and tossed it to the floor. She undid the waistband of her skirt and let it shimmy down her hips to the floor. She smiled when she stood in front of him wearing her black high-cut panties and matching bra.

Opal took a few more steps and then she stopped to remove her bra, tossing it aside, as well. Then, as gracefully as she could, she removed her panties. Instead of dropping them to the floor, she tossed them to D'marcus. He caught them with the proficiency of a skilled football player on the field and held them in his grasp.

She watched as he slipped them into his back pocket. "I think I'll keep them as a souvenir," he said in a deep, throaty voice. And then he moved away from the door, slowly walking toward her.

As he moved closer, Opal felt heat flood her entire body, especially the area between her legs. But she stood immobile. Immobile and naked. Naked and hot. Hot and ready.

When he was halfway across the room to her, he stopped and tugged his shirt from the waistband of his jeans. He pulled it over his head and threw it aside. He then kicked his shoes off and Opal watched as his hands went to his fly. Her body tensed with anticipation as he eased it down.

"Do you know you're the most beautiful woman I've ever known?" he whispered, his gaze still on her.

She knew his words weren't the full truth, but decided she would accept his compliment anyway, as well as provide one of her own. "Thank you, and I think you're the most handsome man I've ever met." Her words were the full truth.

"If that's true," he said, kicking his jeans aside, "you and I make one hell of a couple, don't we?"

Not a couple, really. More like bed partners. She started to correct him but his briefs caught her attention. Well, not exactly the briefs but definitely the size of his erection. He was undeniably aroused. And when he removed his briefs, she saw that her eyes hadn't lied. She smiled, knowing she had been the one to bring him to such a state.

"What are you smiling about?" he asked when he finally stood right in front of her.

She wrapped her arms around his neck. "I was thinking about something I would really like to do to you."

He lifted a dark, sensuous brow. "What?"

"It's something I've never done before," she said, reaching down and encircling her fingers around his large, thick shaft. When she heard his sharp intake of breath, she proceeded to stroke him, the same way she had stroked the keys on the piano that night. Meticulously and precisely. Her smile widened when he released a groan from deep within his throat.

She met his passionate gaze and asked sweetly while she continued to stroke him, "You okay?"

He shook his head. "No, I think I'm dying."

"Umm, not before you get to experience this."

And, before D'marcus realized what she was doing, she slowly dropped to her knees and took him into her mouth.

The next groan he released was one of profound pleasure, not that of a dying man.

Chapter 15

"Well, did you enjoy your time in California?"

Opal smiled over at her sisters and cousins. She'd been back in town less than a day and they had arrived at her apartment, bringing bottles of wine and boxes of pizza. Now that their stomachs were filled and the wine had loosened their moods, she was ready for the questions to begin.

"Yes, I enjoyed it. San Francisco was simply beautiful."

"And what about the tyrant?" Ruby didn't hesitate to ask. "Did he give you a hard time?"

"Did anything happen between the two of you?" Pearl asked almost before Ruby had finished her question.

Opal tried to hide her smile. D'marcus had given her something hard, all right, but it hadn't been a hard time. And yes, something had happened between the two of them, something she wanted to keep private for now. The time she'd spent with him had been simply wonderful and the memories would be etched in her mind, as well as her heart, forever. He had brought out her sensuous side and she had enjoyed sharing it with him.

"No, he didn't give me a hard time and, no, nothing happened."

To steer her sisters and cousins away from asking any more questions about her and D'marcus, she presented them with the souvenirs she had purchased for them at Fisherman's Wharf. Then, after bringing her up-to-date on Reverend Kendrick's sermon the Sunday before, her family decided to call it a night. However, before they left they all promised to be there to help her move the following weekend. Everyone left except for Colleen, who claimed she needed Opal's help on a report she had to present to her employer on Monday.

It took Opal a few seconds after closing the door to know Colleen did not have any report she needed help with. From the way her cousin was standing in the middle of the room with her arms folded across her chest, Opal knew Colleen had not accepted her rendition of how things had gone in California as easily as the others.

"Okay, Opal, what's the real deal with you and D'marcus Armstrong?"

Opal shrugged. "I don't know what you mean."

"Don't you?" Colleen countered. "Then explain that glow that's all over your face. And how about that funny-looking smile, the one you have on your face even now?"

Opal shook her head. She could fool her sisters some of the time, but never Colleen.

She couldn't help but smile. She was bursting with so much love for D'marcus that she wanted to share it with someone, and she could think of no one better than the person she considered her very best friend. "Okay, I'll be honest with you," she said, walking across the room to sit down on her sofa.

Colleen curled up on the sofa facing Opal. The inquisitive expression on her face, Opal thought, was priceless. She reached out and took her cousin's hand in hers.

"The most wonderful thing happened to me while I was in San Francisco with D'marcus," she whispered.

Colleen's eyes filled with even more curiosity. "What?"

"I realized that I loved him."

Colleen nodded. "And what was the reason for this big eye-opener?"

Opal smiled. "Spending time with him, getting to know him better...and being with him."

Colleen lifted a brow. "Being with him how?"

Opal chuckled. "Being with him intimately. D'marcus and I became lovers."

She could tell from the expression on Colleen's face that her cousin was trying to absorb what she was saying and also trying to determine if she thought her announcement was a good thing or a bad thing.

"It's a good thing, Colleen," she decided to say. "I love him."

Colleen nodded slowly. "Okay, and how does he feel about you?"

Now, that was the million-dollar question, Opal thought. And truthfully, it was one that could be answered rather easily. "D'marcus hasn't gotten over his fiancée's death and, because of it, he has no intentions of ever falling in love again or committing himself to anyone."

"So you're saying the two of you are having an affair?"

Hearing Colleen say it so blatantly hit home for Opal, made her again realize that *was* the only thing she and D'marcus were sharing—an affair that would lead nowhere. She loved him but he did not love her. But she would depend on her love being enough. And when things ended, she would have memories of a special time in her life, a time she would rather have with him than anyone else.

For that reason she felt no remorse or regret when she met Colleen's gaze and said, "Yes, we're having an affair."

For a long moment Colleen was silent. Then she quietly asked, "And are you okay with that, Opal? Are you okay with knowing that one day he might get tired of what the two of you are sharing and just walk away and not look back?"

Colleen had never been a person to sugarcoat anything. She called it as she saw it. But what her cousin didn't know, Opal concluded, was that she was seeing something totally different. She was seeing a man who'd had a lot of hurt and pain in his life, first losing his parents and then losing the woman he loved. He was a special man, a gifted man, a man who had the ability to make her smile, laugh, feel feminine and sexy and make her experience things she'd never had before, both in and out of bed. She couldn't help but blush when she thought about all the things he had done to her, all the things she had done to him, all the things they had done to each other.

"Opal?"

She blinked. Colleen was saying something to her. "Yes? Did you say something?"

"I don't want him to hurt you."

Opal reached for Colleen's hand again. "And he won't. I know the score. I know D'marcus's feelings. I'd be a fool not to say I'm hoping that one day he'll grow to love me as much as I love him, but I'm not holding out for miracles. I just want to live one day at a time, with him in my life. And when the time comes for him to go his way and for me to go mine, I will find the strength to do just that."

"And what about your job? Have you forgotten that he's your boss?"

Opal shook her head. "No, I haven't forgotten, but he has assured me that one has nothing to do with the other. We plan to be discreet, but I won't sneak around and I doubt he will, either."

Colleen's hold on her hand tightened. "If you're satisfied and happy with the situation, then so am I. And no matter what, I'll always be here for you if you ever need me."

Smiling, Opal reached out and the two of them hugged. Deep down she knew what Colleen said was true. She would be there for her when and if the time came. Part of Opal was hoping that it never would.

On Wednesday Opal anxiously sat at her desk. D'marcus was to return to the office today. She had spoken to him on Monday but the conversation had been all business since he'd been in a meeting with others around. But later that night he had called her, taking the role of the lover she had left in San Francisco. He had told her how much he missed her, how he wished he could have talked her into staying over the week-end. He had been invited to several social functions and had wished she'd gone with him instead of him having gone alone.

Lost in thought, she nevertheless heard the door to the office open and saw D'marcus walk in. Opal had to immediately downplay the smile she had for him when she saw he wasn't alone. Three of his department heads were following in his wake.

"Good morning, Opal," he said in a businesslike tone.

Following his lead, she replied, "Good morning, D'marcus. Welcome back."

He smiled. "Thank you, and it's good to be back. Please hold all my calls until my meeting is over."

"Yes, sir."

She almost laughed out loud when he glared at her. Keeping a straight face, she then said, "Yes, D'marcus, I will do that."

The meeting lasted all of three hours. When the department heads left, D'marcus remained in his office because he had several important phone calls to return.

Opal went to lunch and, when she returned, the phone system on her desk indicated that D'marcus was still on the phone. Since he had skipped lunch as usual, she had picked him up a sandwich and soda at the deli downstairs.

Easing his door open, she stepped into his office to

place his lunch on his desk. He glanced up at her and smiled as he continued his phone conversation. She then slipped back out the door as noiselessly as she had entered.

It was approximately thirty minutes later when he came on the intercom and said, "Opal, will you step into my office for a minute, please?"

She had been in the middle of typing a report. She saved the data and closed down the screen, noticing her hands were shaking. This would be the first time she would face him alone since returning to town after they had become intimate.

Taking a deep breath, she opened the door and walked into his office with her notepad in her hand as professionally as she could manage. "Yes, D'marcus?"

She saw that he had finished his lunch and was leaning against the front of his desk. He stared at her for a moment before saying, "Come here for a moment, but please lock the door first."

Her heart began pounding furiously in her chest as she did as he asked, then crossed the room, coming to a stop in front of him. "Yes?"

"Thanks for lunch."

"You're welcome."

He took the notepad from her hand and tossed it on his desk. He then reached out and cupped her chin in his hand. "I missed you," he said huskily. "Probably more than I really should have."

She smiled because he actually looked confused at that. "Poor baby," she said, wrapping her arms around his neck. "Would it make you feel better if I told you that I missed you just as much?"

"A little. But I'd really feel a lot better if you give me a kiss to show me just how much you missed me."

"Umm, I can handle that."

She leaned forward and brought her lips just inches from his, and then she darted her tongue out of her mouth for a quick sweep of his lips. She felt him shudder, heard his quick intake of breath and felt the hardness of his erection pressed against her middle. She smiled and then went in for the kill.

She captured his mouth with hers, hungrily, aggressively, choosing her moves carefully, one stroke at a time, opening herself up to all the emotions she felt. They were emotions she was transferring to her kiss. She knew he felt it when he began responding, proving that, when it came to sexual matters, he was a master.

His tongue captured hers, sucked on it, held it tight, stroked it, did all kinds of erotic things to it. This kiss was what fantasies were based on. It was what dreams were made of. And he was giving both to her. Blood hadn't flowed this freely in her veins since she'd left California.

Knowing it was time to come up for air, she pulled her mouth away. But not before tracing the outline of his lips with her tongue.

"Come to my place later," he whispered against her moist lips.

"It has to be later," she said quietly. "I'm going to a prayer meeting at church tonight."

He nodded. "Then afterward?"

"Yes."

She took a step back. "I need to get back to work."

He chuckled. "So do I, but I don't know how I will after that kiss."

She gave him a saucy look. "But I'm sure you'll manage."

When she got to the door he said, "Oh, by the way, Dashuan Kennedy is supposed to show up within the hour."

She knew the reason D'marcus was meeting with the young man. "All right. I'll send him in when he gets here."

"Yes, you do that."

She smiled over her shoulder as she left his office.

Dashuan arrived an hour late and walked in as though he expected her to get up from her desk and bow at his feet. "Your boss is supposed to see me," he said cockily, leaning a hip against her desk. "Let him know I'm here."

Opal gave him a crisp glance. "Certainly." She then punched a button on the intercom on her desk and said, "D'marcus, Dashuan Kennedy is here to see you."

"All right, please send him in."

She glanced back up at Dashuan. "You can go in now."

Instead of moving, he continued to stand there. He had his arms crossed and a smirk on his face.

She lifted a brow. "Is anything wrong?"

He chuckled in a way that actually grated on her nerves. "No, nothing is wrong. I just noted you call him D'marcus. It's not Mr. Armstrong anymore?"

"What?"

"That Saturday I was here for that meeting, every

time you addressed him it was Mr. Armstrong. What happened?"

His question as well as his observation annoyed her. "Nothing happened. D'marcus decided he wanted us to operate on a first-name basis."

An all-knowing, cocky smile touched the corners of Dashuan's lips. "Oh, that's how it is, huh?"

Opal refused to give him the benefit of an answer to that. "D'marcus is waiting. I suggest you go on in, *Mr. Kennedy.*"

His cocky smile turned into a frown. "Whatever." He then turned away from her desk and opened the door to D'marcus's office.

In less than twenty minutes, he was storming out of it, saying in a raised voice, "You've made a huge mistake, Armstrong, and I'm going to make sure it's something you live to regret."

Chapter 16

"I thought you would never get here," D'marcus said, opening the door and gently pulling Opal inside his home.

His mouth quickly captured hers and she responded immediately, not resisting when he lowered her to the carpeted floor.

"Aren't you going to give me a tour of your home?" she asked when he began removing their clothes.

He smiled at her. "Later. Right now I want to concentrate on giving you something else."

When he had her completely naked, he leaned back on his haunches and looked at her. Unable to help himself, he reached out and began touching her. First, he went straight for her breasts to give them his full attention. Moments later, his mouth joined his hands as he cherished that part of her. Then he hungrily moved to her stomach. It was flat, smooth, soft. He drew circles around her navel with both his fingers and his tongue. Then he eagerly moved lower, to the part of her he desperately needed to taste. Reaching down, he cupped her thighs and lifted her up to meet his mouth in a very intimate kiss.

"D'marcus!"

He held her tight when she began squirming beneath his mouth. But when his tongue went deeper, she held on to him for dear life, holding his head to her, refusing to let him go anywhere, which he had no intention of doing until he'd gotten enough of her. Something he doubted he could do in this lifetime.

When he felt her shuddering beneath his mouth, he continued to hold her until the last tremor had left her body. Then he stood and reached for the condom in his pants pocket and put it on.

"Now I'm going to show you just how much I missed you," he said, rejoining her on the floor.

"I thought you already did." She held out her arms to him. "Show me again."

And he did.

Emotions rammed through Opal with every stroke he made into her body. Sensations she knew she could only feel with him were seeping through her pores and her pulse rate was increasing at an alarming rate. And all because of D'marcus and what he was doing to her, what he was sharing with her.

"D'marcus!"

"Opal!"

They came simultaneously, reaching the pinnacle of sexual height together as they clung to each other. Something had snapped, making them shudder uncontrollably, making them shatter into tiny pieces.

It was on the tip of Opal's tongue to tell him how much she loved him, but she held back. Those were words she could never share with him no matter what. So she thought them to herself, pressed the feelings deeper into her heart and when, moments later, he pulled her into her arms and held her close, she held him in hers, as well. If she could never tell him she loved him, then she was determined always to show it. Maybe one day he would accept the love she had to offer.

"Dashuan was pretty upset when he left the office today," she said as they sat at his kitchen table drinking hot tea. After making love they had gotten dressed and he had given her a tour of his home. It was decorated beautifully, but it lacked warmth.

"Yes, and I wish I could say he'll get over it, but I can't. There is something about him that I can't put my finger on."

Opal smiled. "You mean besides him being just outright rude, obnoxious and conceited?"

D'marcus grinned. "Yes, besides that. I'm hoping the suspension without pay will give him something to think about. He's used to spending money, so I think we hit him where he lives, so to speak."

"I don't like that threat he made against you today," she said softly.

D'marcus shrugged. "Don't worry about it, because I'm not. Kennedy's all mouth."

Then, as if wanting to change the subject, he said, "So how's the packing coming along?"

She grinned. "It's coming. I still have a lot to do."

"You've contacted movers?"

"No, I'm basically using my family and some friends."

He nodded. "Will they be able to handle everything?"

"Just about. You've seen my place. I don't have a lot."

"You have a nice place. I could tell it's where you've made your home. This, on the other hand, is just a place where I eat and sleep."

His words touched Opal deeply. He had his home in California, which he'd said he really didn't consider home, either. She wondered if he would ever live somewhere that he'd think of as home.

"Don't do that."

She glanced over at him. "What?"

"Bunch up your forehead like that. It means you're in deep thought about something."

She tilted her head. "And how do you know that?"

"I used to watch you a lot in our meetings. I could always tell when you were about to come up with an idea or a suggestion."

His comment surprised Opal. She'd never realized he had been studying her that closely.

"And then there are the times you have a tendency to tap your fingers. That lets me know when you're annoyed about something."

"Really?"

"Yes."

"Umm, so you think you can read me well?"

"I think so."

"So what do you think this means?" she asked, standing up and slowly removing her blouse.

He leaned back in his chair and smiled. "That's easy. It means you want some more of what I gave you earlier."

"And this?" she said, stepping away from the table and shimmying out of her skirt.

"Same thing." He looked her up and down. "You are one brazen woman."

"If I am then it's your fault. Before you came into my life I was the tamest person you could ever meet. And now I'm doing things I've never done before."

"But you're doing them with me," he pointed out, getting up from the table to remove his shirt.

"Yes, and that's why I said it's all your fault."

"Okay, if you have to place the blame somewhere…" he said, coming around the table toward her.

"I do."

"Then I don't mind being it," he whispered softly, before pulling her into his arms. "Have I ever told you how much I enjoy seeing you naked?"

"No, I don't think you have."

"Then, let me go on record here and now. Opal, I enjoy seeing you naked."

"Thanks."

And then he kissed her and she felt it all the way to her toes. He released her mouth and, before she could catch her breath, he swept her up into his arms and headed toward the bedroom.

Saturday, midmorning, Opal stood with her hands on her hips as she stared at all the boxes that cluttered her living room. D'marcus had encouraged her to take yesterday off work so today wouldn't be too hectic. She had taken the day off, but the day was still hectic. Her sisters and cousins had shown up bright and early, bringing breakfast with them. Amber had convinced her that no one could possibly do any work on an empty stomach, which was the reason they had brought so much food.

At least they also brought reinforcements in the way of family friend Luther Biggens. Even Reverend Kendrick surprised Opal and came by, saying he was available to help out until noon, and then he had to leave to counsel a couple planning to get married.

Not surprisingly, that announcement set off a heated debate between Pearl and the minister as to whether or not such a thing was still needed in this day and age. Opal rolled her eyes. It seemed Pearl would pick the least little thing to do or say to get on Reverend Kendrick's last nerve.

"It was nice of the reverend to drop by to give us a hand," Opal heard Ruby say behind her.

She turned to her sister in time to hear Pearl say, "Well, I'm glad he's gone. Listening to him on Sundays is bad enough."

Opal shook her head. "What do you have against Reverend Kendrick, Pearl? You seem to deliberately argue with him about something whenever he's around."

She shrugged. "Can I help it if we don't see eye to eye on a lot of things? Besides, the man is too traditional. Even our former minister, God rest his soul, wasn't always shoving family values down your throat. Reverend Kendrick makes it seem like it's a sin and a shame to have fun. I bet he wouldn't give a party girl a second look."

Ruby rolled her eyes. "Of course he wouldn't. He's a minister. I certainly wouldn't want some floozy as the first lady of our church. I hope, if and when he does find a wife, she's someone to complement him."

"You would think that way," Pearl said, glaring at her sister.

Opal knew it was time for her to intervene. Before she could open her mouth to do so, the sound of a masculine voice stopped her. "Need any more help?"

She jerked around to find D'marcus standing in her doorway, looking at her with a very sexy smile on his face.

"I like your family," D'marcus said later that day after Opal had finally gotten moved into her new home. "Even the one who thinks I'm a tyrant seems nice."

Opal couldn't help but laugh. If he liked her family then she felt comfortable telling him they liked him, as well. After finding a private moment to rake her over the coals for not leveling with them about her relationship with D'marcus, they'd told her that they thought he was even more handsome up close and that he seemed like real people. She figured they thought that way because Luther liked him. Luther had been a close friend to the family for so long her sisters trusted his judgment in most things. They probably figured if Luther hit it off with D'marcus, then they should like him, as well.

D'marcus looked around. "Where did everybody go?"

Opal smiled. "They left to bring back food. One thing you'll discover about my family is that they like to eat."

He chuckled. "I noticed."

She knew he was recalling how at lunchtime Luther had gone to a chicken place and brought back an entire bucket of chicken with all the trimmings. Everyone had stopped to eat and only once their stomachs were full did they get back to work.

"I will say this about your family," D'marcus said, "they know how to work together."

"Yes, once they stopped disagreeing about where I should place my plants. It really doesn't matter since I have so much more space here."

Opal was glad she had made the move. She had met a couple of her neighbors already and they seemed to be older, settled couples, not like the party animals from her last place. "I appreciate you coming over to help. You really didn't have to do it."

"Not help my best girl? Are you kidding?" he said, grinning.

Opal smiled, wishing he thought of her as his *only* girl. But she knew that was too much to hope for. "Are you going to hang around for dinner? They should be back soon."

He shook his head. "No, I need to head out. Williams and Hennessy are coming over and we're looking at video footage of a college basketball game. There's a kid who has really caught our eye."

He pulled her closer into his arms. "What's on your agenda for tomorrow?"

"I'm going to church and then I'll be having dinner with my family. Would you like to attend church with me?"

"No, I don't think so."

She could tell from his expression that going to church was a touchy subject, but she refused to let it go. "When was the last time you went to church?" she asked him.

He answered right away. "Six years ago."

Not since his fiancée had died. She'd bet the last time he'd set foot in a church had been when he'd attended Tonya's funeral. "Okay, but if you change your mind, call me. But you have to catch me early because I also attend Sunday school."

"I won't be changing my mind." He glanced at his watch. "I've got to go. If it's okay, how about if I drop by tomorrow just in case there're some framed portraits or pictures you want hung on the walls."

She grinned, knowing his interest in coming over to her place tomorrow had nothing to do with hanging pictures on her wall. "By all means, please do so. And, since you're willing to be so handy, I'm sure there're a number of other things I can get you to put together."

"Okay, let's not get cute," he said, leaning over and brushing a kiss on her lips.

She melted against him and D'marcus liked the way her body fitted against his. "My bed is going to feel lonely without you in it."

She had spent Thursday night over at his place because she hadn't had to go into the office Friday morning. In fact, he had made love to her before leaving her there in his home to go to work. She wondered if that was how things would be if she was married to him. Would he wake her up before leaving for work just to make love to her? She quickly snatched the thought back when she vividly remembered that marriage was not in their future.

"You haven't been in my bed yet," she said, leaning back in his arms and gazing up at him.

"Thanks for reminding me. I will definitely make that my top priority the next time I come to visit."

And then he pulled her into his arms—to make doubly sure she understood he was deadly serious.

D'marcus sighed deeply as he stepped into the church. The realization of where he was sank in and he glanced around. Yesterday Opal had invited him to come, and he had turned her down. Now here he was, still not sure how it had happened. What compulsion had brought him here? All he knew was that after thinking about her all night, even within the depths of his dreams, he had awoken that morning with an intense desire to see her. He wanted to be with her and spend time with her, and he knew she would be here.

Her cousin Colleen was the first to see him, since she was standing at the door as an usher. Smiling brightly, she walked him down the aisle toward where Opal was sitting. The choir was singing and the congregation was alive, actively participating and reminding him of the last time he had been inside a church. It had been for Tonya's funeral. The minister had referred to it as a happy occasion instead of a sad one. D'marcus hadn't agreed with the man's assessment, especially when his heart had been grieving the way it had. And for that reason he'd sworn he would not set foot inside another church. He shook his head. Opal was certainly making a liar out of him.

When Colleen walked him to the row of seats where Opal was sitting, Opal glanced over at him as he crossed in front of several people to reach her. "You're here," she whispered in utter shock, moving to make room for him beside her on the pew.

A slight smile touched his lips. "Yes, I'm here," he whispered back while sliding into the empty spot next to her. After someone he assumed was the church's clerk got up to read the announcements and acknowledge visitors, the choir began singing again. Opal joined in, and D'marcus listened. She came to church often, so she knew the words. He didn't have a clue.

"Thanks for coming, D'marcus."

His lungs tightened at the sincerity he read in her gaze, and he could only nod. After the choir finished, a man he figured was her pastor stood and went up to the podium. D'marcus leaned toward Opal. "That's your minister?" he asked, whispering.

She smiled over at him. "Yes, that's him. And like I told you, he's a dynamic speaker."

D'marcus nodded. He leaned back in the chair, wondering what this particular preacher had to say and if it would be any different from what he'd heard before.

After church, everyone went to Ruby's house, and D'marcus was invited to join them. Just like yesterday at Opal's new apartment, there was plenty of food. She hadn't been exaggerating when she'd said her family loved to eat. Luther was there, and again they hit it off. The women didn't seem to mind that he and Luther spent time in the living room watching the football game on television.

Later, he was surprised when Opal's minister walked in, and D'marcus got the chance to meet him, as well. Reverend Kendrick was a likable guy, and when he and Opal's sister Pearl began a heated debate about something the minister had said during his sermon, Luther interrupted the two and teasingly asked if they could take the discussion outside, since he was trying to watch the game.

"Did you enjoy the church service today, D'marcus?" Reverend Kendrick inquired a short while later when they were sitting at the table, eating. The ladies had all brought covered dishes, and D'marcus thought the food was to die for. The fried chicken was *actually* finger-lickin' good.

D'marcus nodded. "Yes, I did," he said truthfully. The sermon was something he had heard before, but he had to give it to the minister for delivering it in such a way that it had held everyone's attention and interest, including his. Opal was right. The man was a dynamic speaker.

After dinner someone suggested a game, and D'marcus couldn't help but notice again how Pearl seemed destined to find a reason to disagree with Reverend Kendrick over any little thing.

"Your sister really doesn't like Reverend Kendrick, does she?" D'marcus asked Opal later that night when they were sitting together on her sofa.

She smiled at his comment. "They're like oil and water. But if you notice, it's Pearl who always starts things."

D'marcus nodded. Yes, he had noticed that. He grinned, thinking maybe Pearl had the right idea about starting things.

"What are you grinning about?" Opal asked him, raising a dark brow.

He chuckled as he reached over and pulled her into his arms. "Starting things," he said, brushing a kiss across her lips. "I decided I want to start something right here and now with you."

Chapter 17

D'marcus stood at the window in his office and watched Opal walk across the parking lot. The day promised to be a chilly, windy one and the long leather coat she wore wrapped around her legs when she walked. He'd hoped to get a better glimpse of those shapely, gorgeous legs.

He shook his head. It wasn't like he hadn't seen them a number of times up close and personal. He'd even taken his tongue and traced a path up her legs to the center of her, where he had found her wet, hot and tasty.

He inhaled deeply, wondering what was wrong with him. It was as if he couldn't get enough of her. They had made love Sunday night, Monday night, and here it was Tuesday and he wanted her with an intensity that was mind-boggling. He felt as if they hadn't slept together in months.

There was something about the feelings he always experienced in her arms. Even when they weren't making love, when he was just lying beside her and holding her while listening to her sleep, he felt it. A warmth, a con-

tentment, a sense of being home. He doubted he would
ever get used to it. He hadn't gone to those extremes
with any other woman. Usually after they'd shared a
bed he was quick to go back to his place or to send her
to hers. But there was something about Opal that made
part of him crave to stay after each sensual encounter.

He crossed the room to check his calendar. He had
two meetings this morning and his calendar was basically clear after lunch, although there were a number
of things he needed to do. But important things came
first, and his physical needs were of the utmost importance. He wondered what Opal's response would be if
he were to suggest they go to his place to indulge in a
little playtime. The more he thought about it, the more
he liked the idea.

As soon as he heard her enter her office, he made
up his mind. An afternoon delight with Opal was just
what he needed. He shouldn't have a problem getting
her to go along with him on it.

He punched the intercom. His body got aroused just
from hearing the sound of her voice when she said,
"Yes, D'marcus?"

"Opal, would you step into my office for just a minute? There's something I'd like to ask you."

"Certainly. I'm on my way."

He smiled as he released the intercom button. The
day might look chilly outside, but by this afternoon he
planned to be wrapped up in sensuous heat.

D'marcus blinked, certain he hadn't heard Opal
right. "No?"

"No," she said for clarification. "I can't play hooky
from work with you today."

He really hadn't expected her to turn him down. "And why not?"

She crossed her arms over her chest. "The same reason you don't need to play hooky, either. We have a lot of work to do."

He laughed at that. He, of all people, knew what they had to do, since he owned the company. "I don't have any appointments after lunch."

"No, but you do have several reports to complete. And have you forgotten your conference call with Harold Phelps and his attorneys and financial adviser in the morning? Mr. Phelps wants to open at least five stores in Hawaii. That means I'll be busy the rest of the day getting all the information you need to make a strong presentation since I'm sure his attorneys and financial adviser will be asking a lot of questions. And they're questions I'm going to make sure you're prepared to answer."

"I know my company, Opal."

"Yes, but I'm sure you also know that stats, facts and figures change from day to day. Now, if you will excuse me, I have work to do."

He clenched his jaw, and she had the audacity to smile sweetly at him when she turned and walked out of his office.

By the end of the day D'marcus was walking around his office feeling like a lustful caged animal. His chance for a little afternoon delight had been dashed by a very beautiful woman who had basically told him she wasn't interested, that her work was more important than spending an afternoon with him.

He inhaled, deciding the last thing he needed to indulge in was a pity party. In a way, he couldn't help but appreciate Opal for standing up to him just to make sure he had his ducks in a row when he had that conference call with Phelps tomorrow.

Damn, he had actually forgotten all about that. The man had attorneys who were sharks and a financial adviser who probably ate numbers for breakfast. The possibility of adding five new stores was at stake. They would advise Phelps against it if D'marcus didn't have his act together. It was going to be a very important meeting and Opal had remembered that.

Still, that didn't stop the ache he felt below the belt nor the rush of desire that flowed through his veins. Nor did it help the memories that had been clogging his mind all day; memories of times when he had been inside her as she came, her inner muscles milking him for more.

What he was going through would have been understandable if he'd spent the past few days or weeks separated from her. But he hadn't. So what was this intense desire to have her today? In fact, to have her right now?

He glanced over at the clock on the wall. She would be getting off work in ten minutes. He had asked her to go home with him, or let him go home with her, but she'd told him that she and her cousin Colleen had made plans to go see a chick flick right after work, but that he could stop by later. The way he was feeling now he might be dead later. Dying of a sexual ache really wasn't the way be wanted to go. He'd rather settle for a heart attack.

He recalled earlier that day when he had walked out

of his office to return a report for her to correct for him; she hadn't heard him approach and had been sitting at her desk eating a sandwich. He had stood there— aroused as any one man could get—and watched while she took a bite of her sandwich. He had observed how that delicious mouth of hers had widened just enough to fit the bread and meat. Immediately he had been reminded of the times she had done the exact thing to a certain part of him.

Instead of leaving the papers with her, he had quickly returned to his office. That had been the first time he'd regretted that he hadn't supported the practice of keeping a stash of alcohol somewhere in his office like a few of his colleagues. They claimed such a practice made very hectic days go faster. He'd always thought that, although having a bottle of booze within your reach might shorten your workday, it would kill your liver. Now, though, he felt the need for a huge stiff drink. Straight from the bottle.

Her voice over the intercom interrupted his crazy thoughts. "I'm leaving for the day, D'marcus. Is there anything you need me to do before I go?"

That was the one question she should not have asked me, he thought as scintillating scenes played out in his head. "Actually, there is something," he said, unable to hold out any longer.

"Okay, I'll be right in," she said in her professional voice.

He stood up from his desk, thinking the last thing he wanted her to be right now was professional.

* * *

"Yes? What do you need me to do?" Opal asked, walking into his office. D'marcus was standing by the window looking out, and turned toward her when she asked the question.

Even before he provided a response, Opal knew the answer. It was there in the dark eyes staring back at her. It was there in the way he was standing. It was there in the huge erection pressed against his zipper that he wasn't trying to hide. And it was there in every part of him. Desire so rich and thick you could cut it with a knife.

"I would like you to release me from my misery before you leave, Opal," he said in a somewhat tortured voice.

Opal stood there and studied the man she loved. He wanted her with an intensity that sent blood rushing through her veins. Never in her lifetime had she thought that any man would ever want her this way. His stark desire seemed to trigger hers, and she breathed in deeply, picking up the potent scent of a deeply aroused man.

"It will be my pleasure," she said turning to lock the door. And then she began removing her clothes as he watched. Her fingers were trembling and she blamed it on nerves more than on modesty, since she had undressed before him many times. But never here in his office. Although they had shared a heated kiss in here once or twice, they had never gone beyond that. But it seemed that things were about to change.

As D'marcus watched Opal undress, he almost found it difficult to breathe. And when she had removed every stitch of clothing except for a pair of panties, he moved from the window, closing the blinds before doing so. That made the interior of his office seem dark and intimate. The perfect setting.

Like a moth to a flame, he seemed drawn to her and, slowly, he began crossing the room to her. When he stood in front of her, he took a whiff of her scent. It was overpowering and he found himself nearly drowning in the depths of her luscious fragrance.

At that moment, something within him snapped and he quickly began removing all his clothing, almost tearing off the buttons on his shirt when he couldn't take it off fast enough. And when he stood in front of her, he got down on his knees to remove the last scrap of thin lace covering the part of her he so desperately wanted.

He eased her panties down her legs and then leaned back, almost at eye level with her womanly core. He leaned forward and placed a kiss there, then another before coming to his feet.

The tender thread that had been holding his control together all day broke and he pulled her into his arms and kissed her with all the hunger he felt. When he finally let go of her mouth, she moaned his name in a breathless sigh. It was then that he totally lost it.

Reaching behind him, he knocked everything off his desk onto the floor, not caring if anything got broken or damaged. He then swept Opal into his arms and placed her on top of his desk, spreading her out. Seeing her that way flared his desire to another height.

"Opal."

He whispered her name as a number of sensations gripped him. The feel of his heart beating unmercifully fast in his chest made him groan. The need to connect to her, be inside her, was so strong he couldn't think straight. He decided not to think at all. Just to act.

He reached out and opened her thighs and came to stand between them. Her hips arched slightly off the desk and he leaned forward, his erection hard, firm and aimed precisely at the intended mark. When she wrapped her legs around him, he inched closer and then, unable to take any more, he thrust inside her to the hilt. He released a guttural groan at the feel of her wet flesh gripping tightly to his engorged hardness.

He drew in a sharp breath at the feel of being inside her, the feel of her muscles clenching him, pulling everything out of him, milking him. He threw his head back as he continued to move in and out of her, stroke after stroke, thrust after thrust, taking her hard and fast while releasing one ragged groan after another.

Sensations assailed him. Sensations he'd only felt with Opal. He could feel his mind shutting down as his body took over. But he wasn't ready to let go yet so he fought back the orgasm that tried to rip through him. He wanted to stay inside her longer, for the rest of the day. Hell, he'd even stay for the night. He wanted to take over her mind the way she had taken over his.

"Doing this is all I've been thinking about today," he whispered huskily as he leaned down closer to her lips. "I had to have you like this. I don't understand it, but I couldn't fight it any longer." And then he put his hands at the center of her back to lift her so their mouths could touch. The moment his tongue delved between her lips, he captured hers and began a mating rhythm that matched the activities going on below.

He released her mouth to whisper one single word.

A word he had never said to a woman before. "Mine." And, with the release of that word, a satisfied sensation settled in his chest.

Opal's body began shaking violently and D'marcus held tightly to her as an orgasm of gigantic proportion rammed through her and then through him. He felt his body explode within her, felt his release shoot to every part of her, and the feeling was incredible. Earth-shattering and amazing.

He froze when he suddenly realized what he hadn't done. But when her body continued to clench him, pull even more out of him, he released a deep groan and another orgasm tore through him. He was too caught up in the sensations to do anything but let it rip.

He pulled her closer to him and moaned out her name the same moment she moaned out his. And then he leaned down and kissed her again, needing his mouth on hers just as his body was connected to hers.

"Mine," he repeated again. As he leaned down to kiss her once more, he knew how it felt not only to give in to temptation, but to let it take over your very existence, as well.

Opal began getting dressed, wishing there was a connecting bathroom in D'marcus's office. He had gotten dressed before her since it had taken her a while to get enough energy to move.

She glanced over to where he stood at the window looking out. He was quiet and had been for a while. She wondered if he'd regretted what they had done in his office. It would be hard for her ever to come in here without thinking about it, remembering it.

She glanced at the clock on the wall. "I need to call Colleen and let her know I'll be a little late. I don't want her to worry about—"

"I didn't use anything."

Since he hadn't turned around she didn't fully hear his interruption. "I'm sorry, D'marcus, what did you say?"

He turned to her then, the expression on his face unreadable. "I said, I was careless and didn't use anything. You could be pregnant."

His words hit her and she shook her head to clear her mind. She had gotten just as caught up in what they'd been doing and hadn't given any thought to birth control, either.

She quickly calculated in her mind and then let out a relieved sigh. "I don't think so because—"

"But you don't know for sure, do you?" he snapped.

Opal swallowed, not liking his tone and not understanding it. "No, I don't know for sure, but according to my calculations, it's the wrong time of the month."

"And when will you know for sure?" he demanded.

Opal placed her hands on her hips and her eyes flared in anger. "In a couple of weeks. Why are you so uptight about it? If there's a baby, then there's a baby. I can deal with it."

He slowly crossed the room to her. A degree of anger she had never seen before was etched on his face. "Well, I can't deal with it. I promised myself I would never be that careless again."

Opal didn't have to ask what he meant by that. His aunt had shared with her the fact that Tonya had been pregnant at the time of the boating accident. "Don't worry about it, D'marcus. More than likely, I'm not pregnant," she said as calmly as she could.

"And if you are, I don't want a child."

His words seemed to reach in and slap her heart. She lifted her chin and glared angrily at him. "It really doesn't matter what you want. If I am pregnant—and that's a big if—having an abortion isn't an option, so don't even think it. And how dare you suggest such a thing?"

He rubbed his hand down his face. "Opal, I wasn't suggesting that you—"

"Weren't you? I think it's best that I go now." Without giving him a chance to say anything else, she stormed out of his office, slamming the door behind her.

It was only after she'd left that he glanced around at the mess he'd made on the floor when he'd knocked everything off his desk in his haste to put Opal on top of it. His gaze suddenly latched on to one particular thing and he crossed the room to pick it up. It was the framed photo of Tonya. The glass was broken.

His heart twisted in pain as he stared down at the woman he had once loved to distraction. The only woman he had ever wanted to have his child. As he began picking up the pieces of the broken glass, he thought about Opal. He could still hear the hurt and disappointment in her voice.

Today he had lost it. Even now, he couldn't believe that he had made love to her unprotected. He had to make sure such a thing never happened again. His relationship with her was getting too deep. He was getting too obsessed. He could never allow himself to lose his self-control again. Things between them had definitely gotten out of hand.

That meant there was only one thing for him to do. Tonight he would drop by to see her when she returned from the movie with her cousin.

It was time things ended between them.

"Opal, are you sure you're okay?" Colleen leaned over to whisper, momentarily taking her eyes off the huge movie screen in front of her.

"Shh," Opal hissed to her cousin. "I've already told you once that I'm okay, so let's finish watching the movie."

In a way, she was glad they were in the darkened movie theater. That way Colleen couldn't see the tears staining her cheeks. D'marcus had really become upset at the possibility that he had gotten her pregnant. She had tried assuring him, but he hadn't wanted to hear it. But the worst thing he had said was that he didn't want a child because, in essence, he was telling her that he didn't want *her* to have his child. Her heart hurt at the thought.

When she felt her phone vibrate in her purse next to her, she pulled it out. Seeing it was D'marcus calling, she whispered to Colleen. "I need to step out to take this call. I'll be back in a minute."

As soon as stepped out of the theater and into the lobby, she clicked on the line. "Yes?"

There was a pause. Then a masculine voice she clearly recognized said, "Sorry, I didn't think you had your phone on. I was prepared to leave a message."

"That's fine. What do you want?" she asked, frowning. Hadn't he said enough?

"I think you and I should talk."

"Okay, I'll see you at the office tomorrow."

"No. I need to talk to you tonight. Please. What time do you think you'll be home?"

Opal glanced at her watch. "In an hour. The movie is almost over."

"All right. I'll be there then. Goodbye."

She didn't bother saying goodbye to him. Instead, she clicked off the phone and slid it back into her purse. A chill of foreboding ran up her spine and, unlike the other nights, she wasn't looking forward to D'marcus's visit tonight.

D'marcus was ringing the doorbell within minutes after Opal got home. She opened the door and stood back to let him enter. "Would you like something to drink?" she asked him.

"No, I don't plan on staying but a minute. I thought it would be more appropriate saying this in person than over the phone."

She raised an eyebrow. "Saying what?"

His eyes met and held hers. "I think we should end things between us and let them go back to the way they were."

She swallowed hard, knowing, in a way, she should have expected this. "And that decision was made just because you think I may have gotten pregnant today?"

"That's not the only reason. I can't control my actions around you. You make me crazy."

Anger consumed Opal, propelling her forward. "And that's supposed to be *my* problem?"

"No, I admit it's mine and I'm going to deal with it the best way I know how."

Opal inhaled deeply, fighting back the anger, refusing to give in to any drama. They had agreed in the beginning that the affair would last only as long as either of them wanted it to, and he had come to say that he no longer wanted her.

She considered questioning him further, but her pride kept her from doing so. "Okay, fine. Things will go back to being as they were before. Good night, D'marcus."

He turned to leave, and when he got to the door he paused for a second, but then, without turning back around or having anything further to say, he opened the door and left.

Opal stormed into her bedroom, warning herself that she'd better not cry.

A few moments later she was doing that very thing anyway.

Chapter 18

A week later, Opal sat at her computer finalizing her resignation. She and D'marcus had tried putting things back as they had been before and it wasn't working. He knew it and she knew it, so there was only one thing left for her to do.

Although she didn't want to leave the company, she knew doing so was for the best. She just hoped she could find another job that would let her finish up her internship, but that was a chance she would have to take. Her peace of mind meant more to her than anything.

It wasn't that D'marcus was rude to her; in fact, whenever they encountered each other, he was respectful. But those times were few and far between since he'd gone out of his way to avoid her. She knew that a lot of the documents she used to handle for him were now being handled by the typing pool just so he wouldn't have to be bothered with her. In that case, he could do very well without her, she concluded, as she pulled her resignation letter from the printer to sign it. With that done, she stood, crossed the room and knocked on his office door.

"Come in."

Taking a deep breath, she opened the door and walked in. He was sitting at his desk with files spread everywhere, his sleeves rolled up to his elbows. He gave her only a cursory glance before looking back down at the file he'd been working on.

"Yes, Opal?"

"I just want to give this to you, sir," she said, knowing her use of the word *sir* grated on his nerves. She handed him the paper she held in her hand.

He took it from her and for the longest time he didn't say anything, didn't even look up. Finally he met her gaze. "Is this what you really want to do, Opal?" he asked in a quiet tone.

She decided to be honest with him. "No, but I think it will be for the best."

"You may not have to do this," he said, still holding her gaze. "I received a call this morning from Laura Hancock in the marketing department. She's very interested in you becoming a member of her team."

Opal raised a surprised brow. "She is?"

"Yes. It's not the first time she's spoken to me about you. The first time was a few months ago. At the time I wasn't ready to let you go anywhere. I had considered you irreplaceable."

But not now, Opal quickly concluded. But then, she wasn't surprised. A lot had changed between them since then.

"Moving to that department is a wonderful opportunity for you, Opal. In addition to a salary increase of ten thousand a year, it will place you in an even greater leadership role. And you'll be utilizing a skill that I believe you're good at. Personally, I think you should take it."

She sighed deeply. It was a wonderful opportunity and she had been eying that position for some time. Something flashed through her mind then. "And you didn't have anything to do with it, did you?" She couldn't help but wonder if he had.

His eyes blazed into hers. "No, I had nothing to do with it, Opal. You earned the recognition for this promotion on your own. I only confirmed what an outstanding employee you are."

Opal nodded. "Thanks."

"Will you consider it?"

"When would I have to start?"

"In two weeks."

She nodded again. That was the same time her resignation was to become effective. The marketing department was on another floor, so chances were slim that her and D'marcus's paths would cross often. "Yes, I'll consider it. Can I think about it over the weekend and give you my answer on Monday?"

"Yes, and while you're doing so I'll hold off doing anything with this," he said, slipping her resignation letter into his desk.

Without saying anything else, she turned and walked out of his office.

"A promotion! Opal, that's wonderful," her sisters were saying when she met them for dinner later that evening.

"That should make things a lot easier for you and D'marcus. With you in another department, that means the two of you won't have to be so discreet," Ruby was saying.

Opal hadn't told them she and D'marcus had ended their affair and she wasn't ready to do so, either. "We'll see."

"So this calls for a celebration," Pearl eagerly suggested. "And, no matter what, please don't invite Reverend Kendrick."

Opal shook her head. "I'm really not up for a party. Besides, I haven't accepted the offer yet."

"Why wouldn't you accept it?" Ruby asked. Everyone knew that when it came to advancing on a job, she was a strong advocate of doing so.

"I'm looking at all my options. I told D'marcus I'd let him know my decision next week."

"Well, it sounds like a good job and a ten thousand dollar increase in salary isn't something to decline. You'd be crazy not to take it," Amber said, adding her two cents.

"We'll see."

Ruby leaned back in her chair and studied Opal. "Is there something going on that you're not telling us, Opal?"

Leave it to Ruby to be so suspicious, Opal thought. "Why would you think that?" she asked, knowing there was a lot she wasn't telling them.

"No reason. Just a hunch."

Opal continued to eat her food, knowing her three sisters' eyes were on her, but she refused to tell them anything now about her breakup with D'marcus. She was still trying to deal with it herself. And the last thing she wanted to do was to break down and cry in front of them. She had agreed to the affair knowing that one day it would end. Now it had ended and she needed to move on. It was that simple.

But then, she had discovered that loving a man was never simple.

"How about a movie tomorrow night?" she asked her sisters.

Pearl raised a brow. "Saturday night? I would think you'd have a date with D'marcus."

Opal shrugged. "Well, I don't, so how about it?"

"Sounds like a good idea to me," Amber said, ready to dig into the meal the waiter had placed on their table. "Just as long as we go early. I want to hit the clubs at a decent time."

Ruby made a comment to Amber about her clubbing ways and then Pearl got into the conversation. Opal was grateful that for a little while the topic of conversation had shifted from her to her little sister.

"I've decided to take the job, D'marcus."

Pain he tried to ignore clutched at D'marcus's heart. He was going to lose her, but deep down he knew he already had. It was for the best, but still, he ached for what they used to have. She was a woman who would one day want to marry. She would want children. She wanted the very things he didn't.

"All right," he said, tossing aside the papers he'd been looking over. "I'll give Laura a call and let her know your decision." He leaned back in his chair and added,

"I think you're making the right decision, Opal. You're an excellent employee who's going places."

"Thank you."

When she turned to leave, he couldn't help but ask, "How have you been?"

"I've been fine, D'marcus," she answered somewhat irritably. She was getting the promotion of a lifetime and instead of being really happy about it, it was almost a downer for her. The only good thing was that she wouldn't be spending her time around D'marcus. The hurt and pain was too much to bear.

"And how is your apartment coming along? Do you have everything arranged the way you want?"

"Yes." And deciding she couldn't handle the small talk another minute, she said, "If you don't need me for anything else, D'marcus, I need to finish up that report."

He nodded. "No, there's nothing else. However, I would like to ask you something."

She lifted a brow. "What?"

"It's been almost two weeks. Do you know if you're pregnant?"

Opal winced inside, and part of her actually felt physically ill that he was asking for what she considered to be all the wrong reasons. He didn't want a baby, and definitely not one from her. "No, I don't know yet."

"Aren't there ways a woman can find out before—"

She held up her hand to stop him from saying anything else. "Look, D'marcus. I really don't want to discuss this now. I told you the day it happened that I'm probably not pregnant. When I know for sure, you'll be the first to know. And to answer your question about if there's a way for me to find out early, yes, there is, but

I have no intention of doing so just to lighten whatever load of guilt you're hauling on your back." She turned and walked out of his office.

D'marcus threw the pen he was holding onto his desk, angry that lately he always seemed to say the wrong things around her. Part of him wished he could take back everything that had happened that day between them in his office, but another part didn't want to even consider it. Although he had lost control, there was never a time he had made love to her that he regretted.

He got up from his desk and walked over to the window to look outside, thinking he had certainly made a huge mess of things.

Opal sat at her computer, trying to compose herself, though a sob was caught in her throat. She refused to cry another tear for D'marcus Armstrong. Trying to concentrate on the report she was typing, she determined moments later that it was no use. She needed to leave.

She glanced at the clock and saw it was a few minutes before three. She had two more hours to work, but there was no way she could. She pressed the intercom on her desk.

"Yes, Opal?"

"D'marcus, would it be all right if I left a little early today? I'll be in tomorrow to finish the report, and I'll make sure it's on your desk before nine."

"Are you okay?"

"Yes, I'm fine. You've asked me that already."

"I'm just concerned because you want to leave early."

"There's no need for you to be. May I leave?"

"Yes, of course."

"Thank you." She quickly closed the connection and gathered her belongings, feeling battered inside.

D'marcus stood at his window, watching as Opal made her way across the parking lot to her car. The wind was rather brisk, and she bent over slightly to ward off the whirling breeze, clutching her coat tight. He heard his cell phone ring but didn't move from where he was standing to pick it up. He was glued to the spot, needing to watch and make sure that Opal made it to her car okay. He would call to see if she made it home, but he doubted she would welcome such concern from him. He couldn't blame her too much for that.

He sighed deeply as he watched her car pull out of the parking lot. Moments later, the vehicle could no longer be seen. It was only then that he went back to his desk and sat down. He picked up his cell phone and checked the caller ID. It had been Priscilla. He hadn't seen or talked to the woman since the night weeks ago when he'd taken her out as a way to get his mind and attraction off Opal. He really hadn't wanted to bother with her then, and he most certainly didn't want to bother with her now. The only woman he wanted hated his guts.

When Opal came into the office the next morning, she saw the handwritten note on her desk. It was from D'marcus, advising her that he'd had to fly to San Francisco. His aunt had rushed his uncle to the emergency room last night.

Opal's breath caught. She could just imagine how D'marcus felt. His aunt and uncle were the only family he had and he was incredibly close to them. She bowed her head and said a prayer that his uncle Charles would be okay. She could imagine how upset his aunt was right now.

It was late afternoon before she heard from D'marcus. She could hear the strain in his voice. "How is your uncle?" she asked him.

"He's doing fine, but it was a rough night, especially for Aunt Marie. Uncle Charles had never been sick a day in his life. He was having chest pains and she thought it was a heart attack. Luckily it wasn't anything but a bad case of indigestion."

Opal nodded. "And how is Marie?"

"She's doing better now that she knows Uncle Charles is all right."

"I'm glad." She then assured him that everything was under control at the office and that she'd gotten that report they had been working on off to Mr. Phelps and his group.

"I'm not worried about anything, Opal. I know you have everything under control."

"Thank you, sir."

He didn't say anything for a moment, and then he said, "I'll let you get back to things now. Since Uncle Charles is okay, I'll be returning in a few days."

"All right. I'll see you then. Goodbye."

"Goodbye, Opal."

D'marcus hung up the phone feeling frustrated and angry with himself. Part of him had wanted to tell Opal that he missed her and wished she was there with him, but he had stopped himself from doing so. He wondered if she could hear the longing in his voice. The desire. Even now, when he knew ending things between them had been for the best, he still wanted her. He still needed her.

Today, he had witnessed the love his aunt and uncle shared. Their love was a strong love. The kind meant to endure a lifetime. That was what true love was about, and for the first time in six years he actually felt a tug of regret in his heart at what he had decided never to have and share with a woman.

Two days later Opal's breath caught when she walked into the office to find that D'marcus had returned. "Welcome back, D'marcus."

He glanced up and smiled. "Thanks. How are you doing?"

She knew why he was asking. "I'm fine."

"And how is your family?"

"Everyone is fine. I'd better get to work." She quickly left his office.

When she sat down at her desk she glanced at the calendar. She had only one week left to work for D'marcus. Tomorrow she would start training her replacement. That would keep her busy, and she wouldn't have time to think about him. And more than anything that was what she needed—something else to occupy her time so she wouldn't think about her boss so much.

Her strength was wearing thin, and whenever she looked at D'marcus, she remembered happier times, especially the times he had given her so much pleasure. Just thinking about it made warm sensations fill her.

She tilted her head back and inhaled deeply. She would get through this period of her life. She had to.

* * *

A few nights later, D'marcus finished the soup he'd heated for dinner and placed his bowl in the sink. He turned and looked at his kitchen table, remembering the last time he had sat at it to eat a meal. It had been over two weeks ago, the night Opal had been there and had stripped off her clothes right there in the middle of his kitchen.

A smile touched his lips when he thought about all the other times they had spent together, both in California and here. They had been special times for him and his memory was full of them.

And then he thought about the last time they had made love—right in his office. He had lost control bigtime and had taken her with an obsession he hadn't known he was capable of. As a result, now she could be having his baby.

His baby.

The thought of a little boy or girl with Opal's smile and features didn't bother him now as it had that day, mainly because he'd had time to think over the past two weeks and put a few things in perspective. Deep down, part of him actually liked the possibility.

He felt bad because she'd actually thought he had insinuated that she get an abortion. That had not been what he'd meant, although he could see why she would think such a thing when he replayed that scene in his mind.

D'marcus thought about how his life had been for the past two weeks. He had tried to hold himself together and not think about Opal, but he'd found himself thinking about her anyway. Seeing her around the office hadn't helped.

Today some of the workers on the floor had given her a party during lunch to celebrate her promotion. Knowing it would be for the best if he wasn't there, he'd left the office early. With nothing to do, he'd decided to come home.

He left the kitchen now and walked into the living room. But glancing around, he realized that there were memories of her here, as well. They had made love on the carpeted floor in front of the fireplace twice and, even now, he could vividly remember every detail of those nights.

Once he had let his guard down and allowed her into his life, it hadn't taken long to discover that Opal Lockhart was quite a woman, and he liked everything about her. He liked her boldness, her courage, the way she wouldn't hesitate to speak her mind and the way she took pride in both herself and her work.

He chuckled when he remembered how she had ignored his boorish behavior and brought him food from her family party anyway, and how, when he'd wanted to play hooky from work one afternoon, she had stood up to him and turned him down flat. Yes, Opal Lockhart was quite a woman.

But what he'd always liked about her was her sensuality, even when it had been hidden. He could vividly recall each and every time they'd made love, even the first time when they had shared her first experience together. That night had been very special for him and she'd said that he had made it special to her, as well.

He walked into his study to open the desk drawer.

That was where he had placed Tonya's picture with the broken frame. He had intended to take it to a shop to get a new frame but hadn't gotten around to doing so. In fact, Tonya hadn't crossed his mind since the day the frame had broken. The only person who had constantly been on his mind was Opal.

On his mind and in his heart.

He slammed the desk drawer and drew a deep breath through clenched teeth. He closed his eyes in an attempt to fight what his mind was trying to tell him. Tonya was a loving memory he would cherish forever. Opal was the woman he now loved, although he'd subconsciously been trying like hell to fight it.

And he did love her. He loved everything about her—even the baby she might be carrying in her womb. His baby. Their baby.

For the first time in six years, he'd come face-to-face with his inner feelings, and he no longer felt weighed down by guilt. His aunt had been right. Whether he felt somewhat responsible for Tonya's death or not, he needed to move on with his life. With Opal's help and without actually realizing it, over the past several weeks, he had done just that.

Now here it was the last week in October and he was about to let the best thing ever to happen to him walk out of his life just because he hadn't been strong enough to get his act together. He hadn't been strong enough to refocus and move on. He hadn't been strong enough to accept what his heart had already known.

Emotions clogged his throat when he thought about how he had hurt her. He knew he had to make it up to her and only hoped she would forgive him. He loved her and wanted her to know it. He wanted her to feel it. And he needed her to believe it.

He picked up the phone. Considering he was the last person Opal would want calling her, he placed the phone back down. He then walked back to his study and picked up a business card that he had placed on his desk weeks ago. It was the business card for Luther Biggens's auto dealership.

He had liked Luther from the first, and he knew Opal and her sisters considered him as a big brother. He was someone they trusted.

D'marcus had a plan and he hoped and prayed that, with Luther's help, it would work.

Opal spoke to Luther on her cell phone. "Luther, are you sure I'm supposed to meet all of you at this supper club?" she asked, looking around the parking lot. It was a very nice establishment in an affluent area of town. She'd never known any of her sisters or cousins to ever patronize the place.

"Okay, okay, I'll come on inside," she replied when Luther confirmed the place. Then she clicked off the phone.

Earlier that day, she'd gotten a call from Luther, who'd said that he was throwing a party to celebrate his end-of-the-month sales and wanted everyone to be at this particular place at seven o'clock. He said he would contact all her other family members, as well.

"Are you with the Biggens party, ma'am?" a well-groomed waiter asked her when she entered.

"Yes."

"This way, please."

She followed the man while admiring just how classy the place was. She could tell whoever owned it had money, as did its clientele. She saw her sisters and cousins wave at her, and she quickly joined them at their table.

"Luther is definitely celebrating in a big way," she said. "He must have had a banner month at the dealership." She glanced around. "And where is Luther? I just got off my cell phone with him." She automatically looked at Ruby.

"Hey, don't look at me," her eldest sister said. "I got the same phone call you got earlier today to be here at seven. We all did."

"Well, at least he didn't invite Reverend Kendrick," Pearl said, smiling.

"Uh, I think you spoke too soon, sis," Amber said, laughing. "Look who just walked in."

Pearl glanced across the room and let out a disappointed groan. It seemed Reverend Kendrick had been invited after all. "I wonder what the church members would think if they knew our esteemed pastor went clubbing?" she said with a sneer in her voice.

"This isn't really a club," Amber said. "Trust me. I, of all people, should know. It's too upscale for that. Basically it's a restaurant with live music. I wonder how Luther found out about this place."

At that moment, Luther stepped up to the table. After greeting everyone, he said, "Dinner will be served later. First, I have a special surprise for everyone in the way of entertainment."

"What?" they asked simultaneously.

He smiled. "You'll see."

As if on cue, the lights in the entire room dimmed.

Everyone at the other tables got to their feet when a lone figure emerged from behind the stage. Opal blinked, sure she was seeing things. But she wasn't. The man who stepped on stage with a saxophone in his hand was D'marcus.

"Hey, isn't that your tyrant?" Ruby asked.

Opal frowned. "He's not my anything, and I have no idea what he's doing here."

Colleen smiled. "I have a feeling that we're about to find out."

Everyone got quiet when D'marcus went up to the microphone. "Good evening. It's been a long time since I've paid you all a visit and I always appreciate my good friend and the owner of this esteemed establishment, Todd Roberts, inviting me back. I'm here tonight for a very special occasion. And that is to win back the heart of the woman I love. I've been a very foolish man in thinking I didn't need anyone, but now I realize just how much I need her and how much I love her. She's here tonight in the audience and I'm hoping this special number will let her know how I feel. It's a Stevie Wonder classic titled 'You Are the Sunshine of My Life,' and I want her to know that she's both the sunshine and the love of my life and I pray she will forgive me for being such a fool." He sat down on the stool and began playing, and all the while his gaze held steadfast to Opal.

Tears filled her eyes at D'marcus's public announcement proclaiming his love. She could tell he was putting his heart and soul into his performance and she was touched by it. She could actually feel the love flowing from him to her. Her heart rate increased and so did her love for him.

"Boy, he can sure play that instrument," she heard someone say.

"He certainly has talent," someone else added.

"This is so romantic," a third person threw in.

She agreed with everything being said, but her focus was on the man sitting onstage playing his heart and soul out for her. When the number was over, he stood and looked out in the audience. "If you forgive me, Opal, and are willing to give me another chance, please nod your head."

Opal quickly nodded her head and a huge smile touched D'marcus's lips. The entire room came to their feet clapping, but D'marcus was too busy making his way across the room to the woman he loved. When he reached the table, he pulled her into his arms and kissed her with all the love in his heart. And she kissed him with all the love in hers.

He released her mouth and took her hand and hurriedly led her to a room backstage, away from prying eyes.

Opal knew they had a lot to talk about, a lot to straighten out, but in her heart, she knew everything was going to be all right.

"You're wonderful," she whispered to him.

"No, you're the one who's wonderful, and I thank God for bringing you into my life and for giving me a reason to love and to live again. I love you, and if you are having my baby I want it as much as I want you."

He framed her face in his hands and kissed her again. He knew in his heart that this was the only woman he would ever need, want and love, and the kiss they were sharing promised a lifetime of love and happiness.

Later that night, Opal was in bed with her boss. A huge smile touched her lips when D'marcus gathered her into his arms after they had made love. Before doing so, they'd had a long talk and decided to bring their relationship fully out in the open and begin dating like a normal couple. They wanted to spend time together with the full intent of taking their relationship to the next level when the two of them felt they were ready. They had admitted to loving each other, and that was a very good beginning. And they'd decided that, if she was pregnant, they would be extremely happy about it. And, if she wasn't, there would always be a next time because they wanted a baby. Tears had filled her eyes when D'marcus had said that, more than anything, he wanted her to be the mother of his child.

Since she had a few days left before starting her new position, he had asked if she would fly to San Francisco with him this weekend, and she'd agreed to do so, looking forward to walks on the beach with him. He was the man she loved and the man who loved her. A man she could count on to fulfill her every desire and need.

"What are you thinking about, sweetheart?" he asked, pulling her closer.

She glanced at his eyes, smiling. "I was thinking about what a wonderful night this has been and how very happy you've made me."

His face broke into a broad smile. "And you've made me happy, as well. After I lost Tonya, I didn't think I could ever love again. I didn't want to. But I can't think of sharing anything with you other than love. I love you, Opal—very much. And I will always love you."

Opal blinked back her tears, never imagining such happiness could come into her life. "And I love you, D'marcus."

Joy touched her heart, which overflowed with love. Tonight, D'marcus had shown her just how much she meant to him, and she intended to spend the rest of her life showing her love to him, as well.

* * * * *

Dear Reader,

What a thrill to celebrate the print reissue of the launch book featuring one of my favorite families! The Landis Brothers series begins with *Rich Man's Fake Fiancée,* followed by stories for the rest of the brothers—*His Expectant Ex, Millionaire in Command* and *Tycoon Takes a Wife.* All the books have been reissued in ebook form and are available for download through your regular online stores. Since I adore family sagas and have a tough time saying goodbye to characters I've grown to love, many of my characters cross over into other series, as well. My website, www.catherinemann.com, contains info on where you can find the characters reappearing for peeks at their happily ever after years later.

On a personal note, I especially enjoyed the opportunity to set these stories in South Carolina, where I grew up. Also, while my sisters and I attended the College of Charleston, we all met our future husbands at The Citadel, where they were cadets. The South Carolina coast will always be a place of romance for me. I hope you find the area as enchanting as I still do!

Welcome to the Landis Brothers family!

Happy reading,

Cathy

Catherine Mann

P.S. I enjoy hearing from readers and can be found online regularly at

www.CatherineMann.com
www.Facebook.com/CatherineMannAuthor
www.Twitter.com/#!/CatherineMann1
www.Pinterest.com/CatherineMann/

RICH MAN'S FAKE FIANCÉE

USA TODAY Bestselling Author

Catherine Mann

To my sisters, Julie Morrison and Beth Reaves, and to their husbands, Todd Morrison and Jerry Reaves. Much love to you all!

"Family is the most important thing in the world."
—Princess Diana

Chapter 1

Only one thing sucked worse than wearing boring white cotton underwear on the night she finally landed in bed with her secret fantasy man.

Having him walk out on her before daylight.

Ashley Carson tensed under her down comforter. Through the veil of her eyelashes, she watched her new lover quietly zip his custom-fit pants. She'd taken a bold step—unusual for her—by falling into bed with Matthew Landis the night before. Her still-tingly sated body cheered the risk. Her good sense, however, told her she'd made a whopper mistake with none other than South Carolina's most high-profile senatorial candidate.

Moonlight streaked through the dormer window, glinting off his dark hair trimmed short but still mussed from her fingers. Broad shoulders showcased his beacon white shirt, crisp even though she'd stripped it from him just hours ago when their planning session for his fund-raiser dinner at her restaurant/home had taken an unexpected turn down the hall to her bedroom.

Matthew may have been dream material, but safely

so since she'd always thought there wasn't a chance they could actually end up together. *She* preferred a sedentary, quiet life running her business, with simple pleasures she never took for granted after her foster-child upbringing. *He* worked in the spotlight as a powerful member of the House of Representatives just as adept at negotiating high-profile legislation as swinging a hammer at a Habitat for Humanity site. People gravitated to his natural charisma and sense of purpose.

Matthew reached for his suit jacket, draped over the back of a corner chair. Would he say goodbye or simply walk away? She wanted to think he would speak to her, but couldn't bear to find out otherwise so she sat up, floral sheet clutched to her chest.

"That floorboard by the door creaks, Matthew. You might want to sidestep it or I'll hear you sneaking out."

He stopped, wide shoulders stiffening before he turned slowly. He hadn't shaved, his five-o'clock shadow having thickened into something much darker—just below the guilty glint in his jewel-green eyes that had helped win him a seat in the U.S. House of Representatives. Five months from now, come November, he could well be the handsome sexy-eyed *Senator* Landis if he won the seat to be vacated by his mother.

With one quick blink, Matthew masked the hint of emotion. "Excuse me? I haven't snuck anywhere since I was twelve, trying to steal my cousin's magazines from under his mattress." He stuffed his tie in his pocket. "I was getting dressed."

"Oh, my mistake." She slid from the bed, keeping the sheet tucked around her naked body. The room smelled of potpourri and musk, but she wouldn't let either distract her. "Since yesterday, you've developed a light step and a penchant for walking around in your socks."

Ashley nodded toward his Gucci loafers dangling from two fingers.

"You were sleeping soundly," he stated simply.

A lot of great sex tends to wear a woman out. Apparently she hadn't accomplished the same for him, not that she intended to voice her vulnerability to him. "How polite of you."

He dropped the shoes to the floor and toed them on one after the other. Seeing his expensive loafers on her worn hardwood floors with a cotton rag rug, she couldn't miss the hints that this polished, soon-to-be senator wasn't at home in her world. Too bad those reminders didn't stop her from wanting to drag him back onto her bed.

"Ashley, last night was amazing—"

"Stop right there. I don't need platitudes or explanations. We're both single adults, not dating each other or anyone else." She snagged a terry-cloth robe off a brass hook by the bathroom door and ducked inside to swap the sheet for the robe. "We're not even really friends for that matter. More like business acquaintances who happened to indulge in a momentary attraction."

Okay, momentary for him, maybe. But she'd been salivating over him during the few times they'd met to plan social functions at her Beachcombers Restaurant and Bar.

Ashley stepped back into the bedroom, tugging the robe tie tight around her waist.

"Right, we're on the same page, then." He braced a hand on the door frame, his gold cuff links glinting.

"You should get going if you plan to make it home in time to change."

He hesitated for three long thumps of her heart before pivoting away on his heel. Ashley followed him down the hall of her Southern antebellum home-turned-restaurant she ran with her two foster sisters. She'd recently taken up residence in the back room off her office, watching over the accounting books as well as the building since her recently married sisters had moved out.

Sure enough, more than one floorboard creaked under his confident strides as they made their way past the gift shop and into the lobby. She unlocked the towering front door, avoiding his eyes. "I'll send copies of the signed contract for the fund-raising dinner to your campaign manager."

The night before, Matthew had stayed late after the business dinner to pass along some last-minute paperwork. She never could have guessed how combustible a simple brush of their bodies against each other could become. Her fantasies about this man had always revolved around far more exotic scenarios.

But they were just that. Fantasies. As much as he tried to hide his emotions, she couldn't miss how fast he'd made tracks out of her room. She'd been rejected often enough as a kid by her parents, and even classmates. These days, pride starched her spine far better than any back brace she'd been forced to wear to combat scoliosis.

Matthew flattened a palm to the mahogany door. "I will call you later."

Sure. Right. "No calls." She didn't even want the

possibility of waiting by the phone, or worse yet, succumbing to the humiliating urge to dial him up, only to get stuck in voice jail as she navigated his answering service. "Let's end this encounter on the same note it started. Business."

She extended her hand. He eyed her warily. She pasted her poise in place through pride alone. Matthew enfolded her hand in his, not shaking after all, rather holding as he leaned forward to press a kiss...

On her cheek.

Damn.

He slipped out into the muggy summer night. "It's still dark. You should go back to sleep."

Sleep? He had to be freaking kidding.

Thank goodness she had plenty to keep her busy now that Matthew had left, because she was fairly certain she wouldn't be sleeping again. She watched his brisk pace down the steps and into the shadowy parking lot, which held only his Lexus sedan and her tiny Kia Rio. What was she doing, staring after him? She shoved the door closed with a heavy click.

All her poise melted. She still had her pride, but her ability to stand was sorely in question. Ashley sagged against the counter by the antique cash register in the foyer.

She couldn't even blame him. She'd been a willing participant all night long. They'd been in the kitchen, where she'd planned to give him a taste of the dessert pastries her sister added to the menu for his fund-raiser. Standing near each other in the close confines of the open refrigerator, they had brushed against each other, once, twice.

His hand had slowly raised to thumb away cream filling at the corner of her mouth....

She'd forgotten all about her white cotton underwear until he'd peeled it from her body on the way back to her bedroom. Then she hadn't been able to think of much else for hours to come.

Her bruised emotions needed some serious indulging. She gazed into the gift shop, her eyes locking on a rack of vintage-style lingerie. She padded on bare feet straight toward the pale pink satin nightgown dangling on the end. Her fingers gravitated to the wide bands of peekaboo lace crisscrossing over the bodice, rimming the hem, outlining the V slit in the front of the 1920s-looking garment.

How she'd ached for whispery soft underthings during her childhood, but had always been forced to opt for the more practical cotton, a sturdier fabric not so easily snagged by her back brace. She didn't need the brace any longer. Just a slight lift to her left shoulder remained, only noticeable if someone knew to check. But while she'd ditched the brace once it had finished the job, she still felt each striation on her heart.

Ashley snatched the hanger from the rack and dashed past the shelved volumes of poetry, around a bubble-bath display to the public powder room. Too bad she hadn't worn this yesterday. Her night with Matthew might not have ended any differently, but at least she would have had the satisfaction of stamping a helluva sexier imprint on his memory.

A quick shrug landed her robe on the floor around her feet.

Ashley avoided the mirror, a habit long ingrained.

She focused instead on the nightgown's beauty. One bridal shower after another, she'd gifted her two foster sisters with the same style.

Satin slid along her skin like a cool shower over a body still flushed from the joys of heated sex with Matthew. She sunk onto the tapestry chaise, a French Restoration piece she'd bargained for at an estate auction. She lit the candle next to her to complete the sensory saturation. The flame flickered shadows across the faded wallpaper, wafting relaxing hints of lavender.

One deep breath at a time, she willed her anger to roll free as she drifted into the pillowy cloud of sensation. She tugged a decorative afghan over her. Maybe she could snag a nano nap after all.

Timeless relaxing moments later, Ashley inhaled again, deeper. And coughed. She sat bolt upright, sniffing not lavender, but...

Smoke.

Staring out at the summer sunrise just peeking up from the ocean, Matthew Landis worked like hell to get his head together before he powered back up those steps to retrieve the briefcase he'd left behind at Beachcombers.

He slid his car into Park for the second time that day, back where he'd started—with Ashley Carson. He prided himself on never making a misstep thanks to diligent planning. His impulsive tumble with her definitely hadn't been planned.

As a public servant he'd vowed to look out for the best interests of the people, protect and help others, especially the vulnerable. Yet last night he'd taken advantage of one of the most vulnerable women he knew.

He'd always been careful in choosing bed partners, because while he never intended to marry, he damn well couldn't live his life as a monk. He'd already had his one shot at forever in college, only to lose her to heart failure from a rare birth defect. He'd never even gotten the chance to introduce Dana to his family. No one knew about their engagement to this day. The notion of sharing that information with anyone had always felt like he would be giving up a part of their short time together.

After that, he'd focused on finishing his MBA at Duke University and entering the family business of politics. His inheritance afforded him the option of serving others without concerns about his bank balance. His life was full.

So what the hell was he doing here?

Ashley Carson was sexy, no question, her prettiness increased all the more by the way she didn't seem to realize her own appeal. Still, he worked around beautiful women all the time and held himself in check. Something he would continue to do when he retrieved his briefcase—and no, damn it, leaving it there hadn't been a subconscious slip on his part. Matthew opened the sedan door—

And heard the smoke alarm *beep, beep, beeping* from inside the restaurant.

An even louder alert sounded in his head as a whiff of smoke brushed his nose. He scoured the lot. Her small blue sedan sat in the same spot it had when he'd left.

"Ashley?" he shouted, hoping she'd already come outside.

No answer.

His muscles contracted and he sprinted toward the porch while dialing 9-1-1 on his cell to call the fire department. He gripped the front doorknob, the metal hot in his hand. In spite of its scorching heat, he twisted the knob. Thank God she'd left it unlocked after he'd gone. The leash snapped on Matthew's restraint and he shoved into the lobby. Heat swamped him, but he saw no flames in the old mansion's foyer.

Through the shadowy glow, the fire seemed contained to the gift shop, and his feet beat a path in that direction. Flames licked upward from the racks of clothing in the small store. Paint bubbled, popped and peeled on aged wood.

"Ashley?" Matthew shouted. "Ashley!"

Bottles of perfume exploded. Glass spewed through the archway onto the wooden floor. Colognes ignited, feeding the blaze inside the gift shop.

He pressed deeper inside. Boards creaked and shifted, plaster falling nearby, all leading him to wonder about the structural integrity of the 170-year-old house. How much time did he have to find her?

As long as it took.

His leather loafers crunched broken glass. "Ashley, answer me, damn it."

Smoke rolled through the hallway. He ducked lower, his arm in front of his face as he called out for her again and again.

Then he heard her.

"Help!" A thud sounded against the wall. "Anybody, I'm in here."

Relief made him dizzier than the acrid smoke.

"Hold on, Ashley, I'm coming," he yelled.

The pounding stopped. "Matthew?"

Her husky drawl of his name blindsided him. A gust of heat at his back snapped him back to the moment. "Keep talking."

"I'm over here, in the powder room."

Her hoarse tones drove Matthew the last few feet. The door rattled, then stopped. A handle lay on the ground. "Get as far away from the door as you can. I'm coming in."

"Okay," Ashley said, her raspy voice softer. "I'm out of the way."

Straightening, he slid his body into the suffocating cloud. He didn't have much time left. If the blaze snaked down the hall, it would tunnel out of control.

Matthew shoved with his shoulder, again, harder, but the door didn't budge, the old wood apparently sturdier than the handle. He took three steps back for a running start.

And rammed a final time. The force shuddered through him as finally the panel gave way and crashed inward.

He scanned the dim cubicle and found Ashley— thank God—sitting wedged in a corner by the sink, wrapped in a wet blanket. Smart woman.

Matthew wove around the fallen door toward her. He sidestepped a broken chair, the whole room in shambles. She'd obviously fought to free herself. This subdued woman apparently packed the wallop of a pocket-size warrior.

"Thanks for coming back," she gasped out, thrusting out a hand with a dripping wet hand towel. "Wrap this around your face."

Very smart woman. He looped the cloth around his face, scarf-style, to filter the air.

Ashley rose to her feet, coughed, gasped. Damn. She needed air, but she wouldn't be able to walk over the shards of glass and sparking embers with her bare feet.

He hunkered down, dipping his shoulder into her midsection and swooping her up. "Hang on."

"Just get us out of here." She hacked through another rasping cough.

Matthew charged through the shop, now more of a kiln. Greedy flames crawled along a counter. Packs of stationery blackened, disintegrated.

Move faster. Don't stop. Don't think.

A bookshelf wobbled. Matthew rocked on his heels. Instinctively, he curved himself over Ashley. The towering shelves crashed forward, exploding into a pyre, stinging his face. Blocking his exit.

His fist convulsed around the blanket. A burning wood chip sizzled through his leather shoe.

"The other entrance, through the kitchen," Ashley hollered through wrenching coughs and her fireproof cocoon. "To the left."

"Got it." Backtracking, he rounded the corner into the narrow hall. The smoke thinned enough for light to seep through the glass door.

Ashley jostled against him, a slight weight. Relief slammed him with at least twice the force. Too damn much relief for someone he barely knew.

Suddenly the air outside felt as thick and heavy as the smoldering atmosphere back inside.

* * *

Ashley gulped fresh air by the Dumpster behind her store. Hysteria hummed inside her.

At least the humid air out here was fresher than the alternative inside her ruined restaurant. Soon to be her entirely ruined home if firefighters didn't show up ASAP and knock back the flames spitting through two kitchen windows.

The distant siren brought some relief, which only freed her mind to fill with other concerns. How could the blaze have started? Had one of the candles been to blame? How much damage waited back inside?

Matthew's shoulder dug into her stomach. Each loping step punched precious gasps from her and brought a painful reminder of her undignified position. "You can put me down now."

"No need to thank me," he answered, his drawl raspier. "Save your breath."

How could he be both a hero and an insensitive jerk in the space of a few hours?

Her teeth chattered. Delayed reaction, no doubt. The fine stitching along the bottom of his Brooks Brothers suit coat bobbed in front of her eyes. The graveled parking lot passed below. Now that the imminent danger of burning to death had ended, she could distract herself with an almost equally daunting problem.

Earlier she'd bemoaned the fact Matthew hadn't seen her in the pink satin nightgown—and now she wished he could see her in anything but that scrap of lingerie underneath her soggy blanket.

"Matthew," Ashley squeaked. "I can walk. Let me go, please."

"Not a chance." He shifted her more securely in place. The move nudged the blanket aside, baring her shoulder. His feet pounded the narrow strip of pavement at a fast jog. "You're going straight to the hospital to be checked over."

"You don't need to carry me. I'm fine." She gagged on a dry cough, gripping the edges of the slipping blanket. "Really."

"And stubborn."

"Not at all. I just hate for you to wear yourself out." Except after last night she knew just how much stamina his honed body possessed.

She grappled with the edges of the wet afghan, succeeding only in loosening the folds further and nearly flipping herself sideways off Matthew's shoulder.

"Quit wiggling, Ashley." He cupped her bottom.

Oh, my.

His touch tingled clear to the roots of her long red hair swishing as she hung upside down.

Two firefighters rounded the corner, dragging a hose as they sprinted past, reminding her of bigger concerns than the impact of Matthew's touch and her lack of clothing. Her restaurant was burning down, her business started with her two foster sisters in the only real home she'd ever known. The place had been willed to them by dear "Aunt" Libby, who'd taken them in.

Tears clogged her nose until another coughing jag ripped through her. Matthew broke into a run. She gripped the hem of his jacket.

A second rig jerked to a halt in front. With unmistakable synergy, the additional firefighters shot into action. Oh, God. What if the fire spread? A wasted minute could carry the blaze to the other historic wooden structures lining the beachfront property. Her foster sister Starr even lived next door with her new husband.

The fire chief shouted clipped orders. A small crowd of neighbors swelled forward, backlit by the ocean sunrise.

"Ashley?"

She heard her name through the mishmash of noises. Turning her head, Ashley peeked through her curtain of hair to find her foster sister Starr pushing forward.

Ashley wanted to warn Starr to get back, but dizziness swirled. From hanging upside down, too much gasping or too much Matthew, she couldn't tell. Lights from fire trucks and an EMS vehicle strobed over the crowd, making Ashley queasy. She needed to lie down.

She wanted out of Matthew's arms before their warmth destroyed more than any fire.

He halted by the gurney, cradling Ashley's head as he leaned forward. She should look away. And she would, soon. But right now with her head fuzzy from smoke inhalation, she couldn't help reliving the moment when he'd laid her on her bed. His deep emerald eyes had held her then as firmly as they did now. His lean face ended in a stubborn jaw almost too prominent, but saved from harshness by a dent dimpling the end.

In her world filled with things appealing to the eye, he still took the prize.

"Please, let me go," she whispered, her voice hoarse from hacking, smoke and emotion.

Matthew finished lowering her to the stretcher. "The EMS folks will take care of you now."

His hands slid from beneath her, a long, slow caress scorching her skin through the blanket. He stepped back, the vibrant June sunrise shimmering behind his shoulders.

Already edgy, she looked away, needing distance. Her burning business provided ample distraction. Smoke swelled through her shattered front window, belching clouds toward the shoreline. Soot tinged her wooden sign, staining the painstakingly stenciled *Beachcombers*.

What was left inside their beautiful home inherited from their foster mother? She and her two sisters had invested all their heart and funds to start Beachcombers. She raised herself on her elbows for a better view, sadness and loss weighting her already labored breathing.

"Ashley." Her sister—Starr—elbowed through to her side. She wrapped her in a hug, an awkward hug Ashley couldn't quite settle into and suddenly she realized why.

Starr was tugging the wet blanket back up. Damn. The satin nighty. Maybe no one else had seen.

Who was she kidding? She only hoped Matthew had been looking the other way.

Her eyes shot straight to him and… His hot gaze said it all. The jerk who'd walked out on her had suddenly experienced a change of heart because of her lingerie, not because of her.

Damn. She wanted her white cotton back.

Chapter 2

"Ashley?" Matthew blinked, half-certain smoke inhalation must have messed with his head.

He blinked again to get a better view in the morning sun. Ashley was now covered back up in the blanket. Except one creamy shoulder peeked free with a pink satin strap that told him he'd seen exactly what he thought when the soggy covering had slipped. Ashley Carson had a secret side.

Something he didn't want anyone else seeing. He angled his body between Ashley and the small gathering behind them.

A burly EMS worker waved him aside. "Back up, please, Congressman. The technician over there will check on you while I see to this lady." The EMS worker secured an oxygen mask over Ashley's face, his beefy, scarred hands surprisingly gentle. "Breathe. That's right, ma'am. Again. Just relax."

Vaguely Matthew registered someone taking his vitals, hands cleaning his temple and applying a bandage. He willed his breathing to regulate, as if that could help

Ashley. She needed to be in the hospital. He should be thinking of that, not last night.

A light touch on his sooty sleeve cut through his focus. Ashley's foster sister stood beside him—Starr Reis. He remembered her name from other political events hosted at Beachcombers. Long dark hair tumbled over her shoulders, her eyes crinkled with worry.

"Congressman? What happened in there?"

"I wish I knew." How had the place caught on fire so quickly? He hadn't been gone that long.

"If only I hadn't overslept this morning, maybe I would have heard the smoke alarm." Starr shifted from one bare foot to another, her paint-splattered shirt and baggy sleep pants all but swallowing the petite woman. "I just called David. He's on his way home from an assignment in Europe."

"I'm glad you could reach him." He recalled her air force husband worked assignments around the world. A photographic memory for faces and names came in handy on the campaign trail.

This had to be hell for the woman, seeing her sister in danger and watching her business burn. At least the flames hadn't spread next door to Starr's home.

"Thank you for going in there." Starr blinked back tears and shoved a hank of wild curls from her face. "We'll never be able to repay you."

Matthew tugged at his tie, too aware of Ashley a few inches away, close enough she could overhear. He doubted Starr would keep thanking him if she knew the full story about what had happened last night and how it had ended.

He settled for a neutral, "I'm just glad to have been in the right place at the right time."

"What amazing good luck you were around." Starr smoothed a hand over her sister's head. "Why were you here? Beachcombers doesn't open for another hour."

His eyes snapped to Ashley's. He didn't expect she would say anything here, now. But would she be sharing sister girl talk later? He sure as hell didn't intend to exchange locker-room confidences with anyone about this. Keeping his life private was tough enough with the press hounding him and everyone around him for a top-dollar tidbit of gossip.

Starr frowned. "Matthew?"

"I came by for—"

"He came to—" Ashley brushed aside Starr's hand and lifted the oxygen mask. "He needed to pick up contracts for the fund-raiser. Please, don't worry about me. What's going on with Beachcombers? Is that another police siren?"

She tugged the blanket tighter and tried to stand. No surprise. While he hadn't known Ashley for more than a few months, she clearly preferred people didn't make a fuss over her. A problem for her at this particular moment, because he wasn't budging until he heard the all clear from her EMS tech.

Matthew turned to the burly guy, who tucked a length of gauze back into a first-aid kit. "Shouldn't she be in a hospital?"

"Congressman Landis?" a voice called from behind him, drawing closer, louder. "Just one statement for the record before you go."

Holy hell. He glanced over his shoulder and took in

the well-dressed reporter holding a microphone, her cameraman scurrying behind her with a boom mike and video recorder. He recognized this woman as an up-and-coming scrapper of a journalist who was convinced he would be her ticket to a big story this election season.

How could he have forgotten to look out for the press, even here, at a restaurant buried in an exclusive stretch of beachside historic homes? He'd been a politician's son for most of his life. A South Carolina congressman in his own right. Now a candidate for the U.S. Senate.

He might not always be able to keep his private life quiet, but he would make sure Ashley's stayed protected. He'd hurt her enough already.

Matthew pivoted and before he could finish saying, "No comment," he heard a camera click. So much for his resolve to close the book on his time with Ashley.

Showering in the hospital bathroom, Ashley finished lathering her soot-reeking hair and ducked her head under the spray. The *tap, tap, tap* of the water on green tile reminded her of the sound of cameras snapping photographs earlier. At least the EMS technicians had hustled her into the ambulance and slammed the doors before any members of the media could push past Matthew's barricading body.

Still, no matter how long she stood under the soothing spray, she couldn't wash away the frustration burning along her nerves. Matthew Landis had only blown through Charleston a few times and already he'd turned her life inside out, like a garment tugged off too quickly.

Had he really stared at her for a second too long when

the blanket slipped? Part of her gloried in his wide-eyed expression, especially after his hasty retreat earlier that morning. Then tormenting images came to mind of him risking his life to save her when she'd been trapped in the powder room. Ashley grabbed the washcloth and scrubbed away the lingering sensation of smoke and Matthew's touch.

Once she'd dried off and wrapped her hair in a towel, she felt somewhat steadier. She slipped into the nightgown and robe her sister had brought by her hospital room, giving only a passing thought to the ruined pink peignoir. Yes, she was well on her way to putting the whole debacle behind her. She had more important things to concentrate on anyway—like the fiery mess. Ashley yanked open the bathroom door.

And stopped short.

Matthew Landis sat on the hospital room's one chair, stretching his legs in front of him. He wore a fresh gray suit with a silver tie tack that she could swear bore the South Carolina state tree—a palmetto. How he managed such relaxed composure—especially given today's circumstances—she would never know.

He appeared completely confident and unfazed by their near-death experience. The small square bandage on his temple offered the only sign he'd blasted into a burning building and saved her life.

Her throat closed up again as she thought of all that could have happened to him in that fire. She needed to establish distance from him. Fast.

He held a long-stemmed red rose in one hand. She refused to consider he'd brought it for her. He'd undoubtedly plucked it from one of the arrangements already filling the rolling tray and windowsill. He twirled the stem between his thumb and forefinger. Why had he stuck around Charleston rather than returning to his family's Hilton Head compound?

Ashley cinched the belt on her hospital robe tighter. Her other hand clutched the travel pack of shampoo, mouthwash and toothpaste. "I didn't, uh, expect..."

He didn't move other than a slow blink and two twirls of the flower. "I knocked."

She unwrapped the towel, her hair unfurling down her back. "Obviously I didn't hear you."

Silence mingled with the scent of all those floral arrangements. Matthew stood. Ashley backed up a step. She hooked the towel over the doorknob and looked everywhere but at his piercing green eyes that had so captivated constituents for years.

Everyone in this part of the country had watched the four strapping Landis brothers grow up in the news, first while their father occupied the senate. Then after their dad's tragic death, their mother had taken over his senatorial seat.

Matthew had followed in his family's footsteps by running for the U.S. House of Representatives after completing his MBA, and now that his mom was moving on to become the secretary of state, Matthew was campaigning for her vacated senate seat.

The name Landis equaled old money, privilege, power and all the confidence that came with the influential package. She wanted to resent him for being born into all of those things so far outside her reach. Except his family had always lived lives beyond reproach. They were known to be genuinely good people. Even their political adversaries had been hard-pressed to find a reason to criticize the Landises for much of anything other than their stubborn streak.

He cleared his throat. "Are you okay?"

She spun to face him. "I'm fine."

"Ashley." He shook his head.

"What?"

He stuffed his hands in his pockets. "I'm a politician. Word nuances don't escape me. *Fine* means you're only telling me what I want to hear."

Why did he have to look so crisp and appealing while she felt disheveled and unsettled? The scene felt too parallel to the one they'd played out just this morning. "Well, I am fine all the same."

"It's good to hear that. What's the doctor's verdict?"

"Dr. Kwan says I can leave in the morning." She skirted around Matthew toward the bedside table to put away her toiletries. "He diagnosed a mild to moderate case of smoke inhalation. My throat's still a little raw but my lungs are fine. I have a lot to be grateful for."

"I'm glad you're going to be all right." Still he watched her with that steady gaze of his that read too much while revealing only what he chose.

"I've sucked down more cups of ice chips than I care to count. I'm lucky, though, and I know it. Thank you for risking your life to save me." She tightened the cap on her toothpaste, then rolled the end to inflate the thumbprint in the middle. The question she'd been aching to ask pushed up her throat just as surely as the toothpaste made its way toward the top of the tube. "Why did you come back this morning?"

"I forgot my briefcase." He set the flower aside on the rolling tray.

Her thumb pushed deeper into the tube of Crest. She looked down quickly so he wouldn't be able to catch her disappointment. "I hope you didn't have anything irreplaceable in there because I'm pretty sure that even if it didn't burn up, the papers are suffering from a serious case of waterlog."

She tried to laugh but it got stuck somewhere between her heart and her throat. For once, she was grateful for the cough that followed. Except she couldn't stop.

Matthew edged into sight, a cup of water in his hand. She took it from him, careful not to brush fingers, gripped the straw and gulped until her throat cleared.

Ashley sunk to the edge of the bed, gasping. "Thank you."

"I should have gotten you out faster." His brow furrowed, puckering the bandage.

"Don't be ridiculous. I'm alive because of you." Her bare feet swinging an inch from the floor, she crumpled the crisp sheets between her fingers to keep from checking the bandage on his temple. "Uh, how bad was the damage to Beachcombers? Starr gave me some information, but I'm afraid she might have soft-soaped things for fear of upsetting me."

He pulled the chair in front of her and sat. "The structure is intact, the fire damage appears contained to downstairs, but everything is going to be waterlogged from the fire hoses. That's all I could tell from the outside."

"Inspectors will probably have more information for us soon."

"If they show any signs of giving you trouble, just let me know and I'll get the family lawyers on it right away."

"Starr said pretty much the same when she came by earlier. She just kept repeating how glad she is that I'm alive."

Their other foster sister, Claire, had echoed the sentiment when she'd called from her cruise with her husband and daughter. Insurance would take care of the cost. But Ashley still couldn't help feeling responsible. The fire had happened on her watch and she'd been so preoccupied with Matthew she may well have screwed up in some way. How could she help but blame herself?

Matthew shifted from the chair to sit beside her on the bed and pulled her close before she could think to protest. His fingers tunneling under her damp hair, he patted between her shoulder blades. Slowly, she relaxed against his chest, drawn by the now-familiar scent of his aftershave, the steady thud of his heart beneath his starched shirt. After a hellish day like the one she'd been through, who could fault her for stealing a moment's comfort?

"It'll be okay," he chanted, his husky Southern drawl stroking her tattered nerves as surely as his hands skimmed over her back. "You've got plenty of people to help."

His jacket rasped against her cheek and she couldn't resist tracing the palmetto-tree tie tack. Being in his arms felt every bit as wonderful as she remembered. And here they were again.

Could she have misread his early departure this morning? "Thank you for stopping by to check on me."

"Of course. And I was careful not to be seen."

Her heart stuttered and it had nothing to do with the whiff of his aftershave. "What?"

He smoothed her hair from her face, his strong hands gentle along her cheeks. "I was able to dodge the media on my way inside the hospital."

She thought back to the barrage of questions shouted their way as she'd been loaded into the ambulance. Uneasily, she inched out of his arms. "I imagine there will be plenty of coverage of your heroic save."

Matthew scrubbed a hand along his jaw. "That's not exactly the angle the media's working."

Apprehension prickled along her spine nearly managing to nudge aside the awareness of his touch still humming through her veins. "Is there a problem?"

"Don't worry." His smile almost reassured her. Almost. "I'll take care of everything with the press and the photos that are popping up on the internet. Once my campaign manager works his magic with a new spin, nobody will think for even a second that we're a couple."

Chapter 3

Not a couple? Wow, he sure could use some lessons on how to let a girl down easy.

Ashley shoved her palms against his chest. His big arrogant chest. So much for assuming he'd been attracted to her after all. It would be a cold day in hell before she fell into those mesmerizing eyes again. "Glad to hear you've got everything under control."

Matthew eased to his feet, confidence and that damned air of sincerity mucking up the air around him. "My campaign manager, Brent Davis, is top—"

Ashley raised a hand to stop him. "Great. I'm not surprised. You can handle anything."

He searched her with his gaze. "Is there something wrong? I thought you would be pleased to know about the damage control."

Damage control? Her experience with him fell under the header of freaking *damage* control? Her anger burned hotter than any fire.

But the last thing she needed was for him to get a perceptive peek into her emotions. She scrambled for a plausible excuse in case he picked up on her feelings. "I'm dreading going over to the store tomorrow, but at the same time can't wait to set things in order. It's a relief to know I don't have anything to worry about with the press." Damn it all, she was babbling now, but anything was better than an awkward silence during which she might do something rash—like punch him. "So that's that, then."

He didn't leave, just stood, his brows knitting together. Her heart tapped an unsteady beat in spite of herself.

Okay, so he was *hot* and confident and sincere looking. And he didn't want her. She shouldn't be this pissed off. It was just an impulsive one-night stand. People did that sort of thing.

She just never had. But she wasn't totally inexperienced. Why, then, did a single lapse against his chest plummet her into a world of sensation that a bolt of silk couldn't hope to rival?

She wanted, needed, him gone now. "Thanks again for visiting, but I have to dry my hair."

Oh, great. Really original brush-off line.

He massaged his temple beside the bandage. "Promise me you'll be careful. Don't rush into Beachcombers until you get official notice that it's safe."

"I pinky swear. Now you really can go." Why wouldn't he leave the hospital? Better yet, return to Hilton Head altogether.

"About this morning... Ah, hell." He stuffed his hands in his pockets. "You're still okay with everything. Right?"

Full-scale alert. The man was rolling out the pity party. How mortifying.

If he said anything more, she might well slug him after all, which would rumple his perfectly tailored suit and show far more than she wanted him to see concerning his effect over her. "I have bigger concerns in my life right now than thinking about bed partners."

"Fair enough."

"I have to deal with the shop, my sisters, insurance claims." She was a competent businesswoman and he should respect her for that. No pity.

"I've got it." He held up his hands, a one-sided smile crooking up. "You're ready for me to leave."

Sheesh. How had he managed to turn the tables so fast until she felt guilty? Blast his politician skills that made her feel suddenly witchy.

She softened her stance and allowed herself to smile benignly back. "Last night was…nice. But it's back to real life now."

He arched one aristocratic brow. "Nice? You think the time we spent naked together was *nice?*"

Uh-oh. She'd thrown down a proverbial gauntlet to a man who made a profession out of competition. A chill tightened her scalp.

She shuffled to the window, offering him her back until she could stare away the need to explore the heat in his eyes again. Her poise threatened to snap. Matthew's return had already left her raw, and today she had little control to spare.

"Matthew, I need for you to go *now.*" She toyed with the satin bow in a potted fern, the ribbon's texture reminding her of the gown she'd foolishly donned earlier.

"Of course." His voice rumbled, smoother than the ribbon in her hand or the fabric along her body.

Two echoing footsteps brought him closer. His breath heated through her hair. "I'm sorry about the media mess and for not keeping my distance when I should have. But there's not a chance in hell I would call last night something so bland as *nice*."

If he touched her again, she'd snap, or worse yet, kiss him.

Ashley spun to face him, the window ledge biting into her back. His gaze intense, glowing, he stared down at her. The bow crumbled in her clenched hand.

Forget courtesy. "My sister is on her way with a blow-dryer. She forgot to bring one when she brought by my other things."

He nodded simply. "Call me if you have any unexpected troubles with the press or the insurance company."

The door hissed closed behind him. Snatching up the rose he'd held, Ashley congratulated herself on not sprinting after him. Especially since her lips felt swollen and hungry. She'd always been attracted to him. What woman wouldn't be?

Her body wanted him. Her mind knew better—when she bothered to listen. She'd vowed she wouldn't be one of those females who lost twenty IQ points when a charming guy smiled.

She sketched the flower against her cheek, twirling the stem between two fingers. How would she manage to resist him now that she'd experienced just how amazing his touch felt on her naked skin?

Straightening her spine, she stabbed the long-stemmed bud back into a vase. The same way she'd done everything else since her parents tossed her out before kindergarten.

With a steely backbone honed by years of restraint.

It took all his restraint not to blow a gasket when he saw the morning paper.

Matthew gripped the worst of the batch in his fist as he rode the service elevator up to Ashley's hospital room. He'd known the press would dig around. Hell, they had been doing so for most of his life. Overall, he took those times as opportunities to voice his opinions. Calmly and articulately.

Right now, he felt anything but calm.

He unrolled the tabloid rag and looked again at the damning photos splashed across the front page. Somehow, a reporter had managed to get shots of his night with Ashley. Intimate photos that left nothing to the imagination. The most benign of the batch? A picture of him with Ashley at her front door, when she'd been wearing her robe. When he'd leaned to kiss her goodbye.

The photographer had gerrymandered his way to just the right angle to make that peck on the cheek look like a serious lip-lock.

Then there was the worst of the crop. A telephoto-lens shot through one of the downstairs bay windows when he and Ashley had been in the hall, on their way to her room, ditching clothes faster than you could say "government cheese."

Had she seen or heard about the pictures yet? He would find out soon enough.

The elevator jolted to a stop. Door swished apart to

reveal a nurse waiting for him with a speculative gleam in her matronly eyes. He managed not to wince, and gestured for her to lead the way.

The nurse's shoes squeaked on the tile floors as he strode behind her, the sounds of televisions and a rattling food cart filling the silence as people stopped talking to stare when he walked past.

He understood well enough the ebb and flow of gossip in this business. For the most part, he could shrug it off. But he wasn't so sure someone as private and reserved as Ashley could do the same.

Matthew nodded his thanks to the nurse and knocked on Ashley's door. "It's me."

The already cracked-open door swooshed wider. Ashley sat in the chair by the window, wearing jeans and two layered shirts, all of which cupped her curves the way his hands itched to do.

He shoved the door closed behind him.

Ashley nodded to the paper in his fist. "The political scoop of the year."

Well, that answered one question. She'd already seen the paper. Or watched TV. Or listened to the radio.

Hell. "I am so damn sorry."

"I assume your campaign manager hasn't rolled out of bed yet," she said quietly, as stiff as the industrial chair.

"He's been awake since the phone rang at 4:00 a.m. warning him this was coming."

"And you didn't think it would be prudent to give me a heads-up?" While her voice stayed controlled, her red hair—gathered in a long ponytail—all but crackled with pent-up energy as it swept over her shoulder, along her pink and green layered shirts.

"I would have called, but the hospital's switchboard is on overload."

She squeezed her eyes shut, a long sigh gusting past her lips. Finally, she unclenched her death grip on the chair's arms and looked at him again. "Why does the press care who you're sleeping with?"

She couldn't be that naive. He raised an eyebrow.

"Okay, okay." She shoved to her feet and started pacing restlessly around the small room. "Of course they care. They are interested in anything a politician does, especially a wealthy one. Still why should it matter in regards to the polls? You're young, unattached. I'm single and of legal age. We had sex. Big deal."

As she passed, a drying strand of hair fluttered, snagging on his cuff link and draping over his hand. Each movement of her head as she continued talking shifted the lock of hair without sliding it away.

Why couldn't he twitch the strand free? "You may or may not have read about how my last breakup ended badly. My ex-girlfriend didn't take it well when I ended things, and she let that be known in the press. Of course the media never bothered to mention she was cheating while I was in D.C."

Her answer dimly registered in his mind as he stared while the overhead light played with the hints of gold twining through the red lock. He kept his arm motionless. The strand slashed across his hand the way her hair had played along his chest when she'd leaned over him, her beautiful body on display for him.

Naked.

He cleared his throat and his thoughts. He needed to prepare her for what she would face once she left this room. "The media are going to hound you for details. You can't comprehend how intense the scrutiny will be until you've lived with it. Do you have any idea how many reporters are out there waiting for a chance to talk to you right now?"

"When my sister gets here, we'll slip out the back entrance." She eyed the door with a grimace. "I'm sure the hospital staff will be happy to help."

He scratched behind his ear. "It's not that simple. And your sister's not coming."

She pointed to his hand. "Stop scratching."

What the hell? "Pardon?"

"Scratching. It's your poker tell. You only do that when you're trying to think of a way around a question. What are you hiding—" She paused, scowled. "Wait. You told my sister not to come, didn't you?"

Matthew dropped his arm to his side. Damn it, he'd never realized he had a "tell!" sign. Why hadn't he or his campaign manager picked up on that before? At least Ashley had alerted him so he could make a conscious effort to avoid it in the future.

Meanwhile, he had to deal with a fired-up female. "Her husband and I thought it would be safer for her to stay out of the mob outside."

"You and David decided? You two have been as busy as your campaign manager." She scooped up her overnight tote bag. "I'll take a cab."

Matthew eased the canvas sack from her hand before she could hitch the thing over her shoulder. "Don't be ridiculous. My car is parked right by the back exit."

Her eyes battled with him for at least a three count before she finally sighed. "Fine. The sooner we go the sooner this will be past us."

A short ride down the elevator later, he opened the service entrance—and found four photographers poised and ready. He shielded Ashley as best he could and hustled her into his car. More pictures of the two of them wouldn't help matters, but better he was there to move this along than having her face them alone.

He plowed past a particularly snap-happy press hound and slid into the driver's side of his Lexus, closing the door carefully but firmly after him.

Ashley sagged in her seat. "God, you're right. I didn't realize it would be this bad."

"Bad?" He gunned the gas pedal. "I hate to tell you, but we got off easy, and they're not going to give up anytime soon. They will pry into every aspect of your private life."

Her face paled, but she sat up straighter. "I guess I'll just have to invest in some dark glasses and really cool hats."

He admired her spunk, even more so because he knew how much harder this was for her than it would be for others. "The press isn't going to leave you alone. They've been trying to marry me off for years."

"I'm tough," she said with only a small quiver in her voice. "I can wait it out."

Except she shouldn't have to. This was his fault and he should be the one bearing the fallout. Not her.

Then the answer came to him in a sweep of inspiration as smooth as the luxury car's glide along the four-lane road. Hadn't he already noted how much easier managing the media would be for her with him by her side? He knew the perfect way to keep her close *and* tamp down the negative gossip.

Decision made, he didn't question further, merely forged ahead. "There's a simpler way to make this die down faster."

"And that would be?" She swiped her palms over her jeans again and again, her frayed nerves all the more obvious with each passing palmetto and pine tree.

Stopping for a traffic light, he hitched his arm along the seat behind her head and pinned her with his most persuasive gaze. "We'll get engaged."

"Engaged?" Her eyes went wide and she jerked away from the brush of his arm as if scorched. "You've got to be kidding. Don't you think getting married to pacify the press is a little extreme?"

Marriage. The word stabbed through him like a well-sharpened blade. He absolutely agreed with her point about staying clear of the altar.

The light turned green and he welcomed the chance to shift his eyes back to the road. "It won't go that far. Once the buzz dies down and they focus on the issues again, you and I will quietly break up. We can simply turn the tables and state that the pressure from so much media attention put a strain on our relationship."

Yeah, the idea of lying chafed more than a little since he considered his ethics to be of the utmost importance. But right now, only one thing dominated his thoughts.

Keeping Ashley's reputation from suffering for his mistake.

He would have to live with the fallout from that, not her. This was the best way to protect her. "We'll set up a press conference of our own to make the official announcement."

She crossed her arms over her chest, her brown eyes glinting nearly black with a determination that warned him he may have underestimated the strength of the woman beside him.

"Congressman Landis, you are absolutely out of your flipping mind. There's not a chance in hell you're putting an engagement ring on my finger."

Chapter 4

Uh-oh. She'd thrown down the proverbial gauntlet again.

Ashley gripped the sides of the butter-soft leather seat. She couldn't miss the competitive gleam in Matthew's eyes as he drove the luxurious sedan.

"Matthew," she rushed to backtrack. "I appreciate that you're concerned for my reputation, but one night of sex does not make me your responsibility. And it doesn't make *you* my responsibility, either."

He reached across to loosen her grip and link hands as they sped down the road. She looked away and tried to focus on the towering three-story homes, their deep porches sheltering rocking chairs and ferns. Anything to keep from registering how Matthew's thumb brushed back and forth across the sensitive inside of her wrist.

His callused thumb rasped against her tender skin, bringing to mind thoughts of all those photos of him in the paper featuring the numerous times he'd worked on Habitat homes. He came by the roughened skin and muscles the honest way. Her traitorous heart picked up pace from just his touch, a pulse he could no doubt feel.

Yep, there he went smiling again.

She snatched her hand away and tucked it under her leg. "Stop that. The last thing we need is to provide more photo ops for gossip fodder."

"Be my fiancée," he stated, rather than asking.

"No."

"I'll make it worth your while." He winked.

She covered her ears. "I am Ashley Carson and I do *not* approve this message."

Laughing, he gripped one of her wrists and lowered her arm. "Cute."

"And hopefully understood."

"Ashley, you're a practical woman, an accountant, for God's sake. Surely you can see how this is the wisest course of action."

Practical? He wanted her for "practical" reasons? How romantic.

"Thanks, but I'll take my chances with the press." She tried to tug free her recaptured hand.

No such luck.

He held on and teased her with more of those understated but potent touches all the way to her sister's house—which just happened to have a red-and-blue Landis For Senate sign on the front lawn. Ashley shifted her attention to Beachcombers instead. And gasped from the shock and pain.

The sight in front of her doused passion and anger faster than if she'd jumped into the crashing surf in front of them. Beachcombers waited for her like a sad, bedraggled friend. Soot streaked the white clapboard beside broken windows, now boarded over. The grassy lawn was striped with huge muddy ruts from fire trucks and the deluge of water.

If she kept staring, she would cry. Yet looking away felt like abandoning a loved one. She had bigger problems than her reputation—or some crazy mixed-up need to jump back into bed with a man certain to complicate her life.

She needed to regroup after the devastation, to meet with her sisters and revise her whole future. And no matter what plan they came up with, Matthew Landis would not be figuring into the strategy.

This time, when she pulled her hand back, she would make sure he understood that no meant no.

Waiting for Starr to come downstairs, Ashley peered through the living room window, watching as Matthew drove away.

A marriage proposal. Her first, and what a sham.

Now that she'd gotten over the shock of his *faux* fiancée proposition, she had to appreciate that he wanted to preserve her reputation. An old-fashioned notion, certainly, but then his monied family was known for their by-the-rules manners. How ironic that Starr belonged in this kind of world for real now that she'd married into an established Charleston family.

The Landis's Hilton Head compound might be more modern than this place—she'd pored over a photo spread in *Southern Living*—but his home proclaimed all the wealth and privilege of this Southern antebellum house that had been in Starr's husband's family for generations.

Her artsy sister had put her own eclectic stamp on the historic landmark, mixing dark wood antiques with fresh new and bright prints. All the dour drapes had been stripped away and replaced with pristine white shutters that let in light while still affording privacy when needed.

Like now.

Ashley wandered across the room, past the Steinway grand piano to the music cabinet beside it. Photos in sterling-silver frames packed the top. One of Starr and David on their wedding day. Another of David's mother perched royally in a wing-back chair holding her cat.

And yet another of Starr, Claire and Ashley standing in front of the Beachcombers sign when they'd officially opened the business three years ago. Most restaurants failed in the first year, but they had defied the odds despite having no restaurant experience. Their clientele swelled as Charleston's blue-blooded brought their well-attended bridal breakfasts and showers to Beachcombers, drawn by hosting their events in such a scenically placed historic home.

Once Starr lured them in with her decorative eye for creating the perfect ambiance, their sister Claire's catering skills sealed the deal and Ashley tallied the totals. Their foster mother may have used up her entire family fortune taking in children, but she'd left a lasting legacy of love.

Ashley cradled a picture of Aunt Libby.

Their foster mother had lost her fiancé in the Korean War and pledged never to marry another man. Instead, she'd stayed in her childhood house and used all her inheritance to bring in girls who needed a home. Many had come and gone, adopted or returned to their parents. Just Claire, Starr and Ashley had stayed.

God, how she missed Aunt Libby. She could sure use some of her cut-to-the-chase wisdom right about now. Aunt Libby had never cared what other people thought about her, and heaven knew there had been some hateful things said when Libby had brought some of her more troubled teens to this high-end neighborhood

The light tread of footsteps on the stairs pulled her from her thoughts. Ashley turned to find her fireball of a sister sprinting toward her.

"Welcome! I'm so sorry I wasn't here to greet you."

"Not a problem." Ashley stepped into the familiar hug. This woman was as dear to her as any biological sibling ever could be. "Your housekeeper said you've been battling the stomach flu. Are you okay?"

"Nothing to worry about. I'm fine." Starr stepped back and hooked an arm through Ashley's. "Let's go up to my room. I've been sorting through my clothes to find some you can borrow until you get your closet restocked. I'm shorter than you are, but there are a few things that should work."

Starr pulled her sister up the stairs and into her bedroom…and holy cow, she'd meant it when she said she'd gone through all her clothes. The different piles barely left any room to walk, turning the space into a veritable floordrobe.

"Really, you're being too generous. I don't want to put you out."

Starr smiled and slid her hand over her stomach. "Don't worry. I won't be able to fit in my clothes soon anyway. I don't have the stomach flu."

The hint flowered in her mind, stirring happiness and, please forgive her, a little jealousy. "You're pregnant?"

Starr nodded. "Two and a half months. David and I haven't told anyone yet. I would have said something sooner, but it was totally a shock. We weren't planning to start a family yet, but I'm so happy."

"Of course you are. Congratulations." Ashley folded her in a hug. "I'm thrilled for you."

And she was. Truly. Both of her sisters were moving on with their lives, building families. She just wanted the same for herself. Someday. With a man who wasn't proposing a "practical" engagement.

Her sister held tight for a second before pulling back. "Okay, so?"

"So what?"

Starr picked up a newspaper on her bed stand and flopped it open. "Holy crap, kiddo, I can hardly believe my eyes. *You* slept with Matthew Landis?"

"Thanks for the vote of confidence." She knew she wasn't Matthew's type, but it hurt hearing her sister's incredulity. For that matter, why in the world would Matthew think the press would even believe an engagement announcement?

"I'm simply surprised because it's so sudden. I didn't realize you two had known each other that long." She folded the paper to cover the incriminating pictures. "Although given these, I guess you've been keeping a lot from me lately. I can't believe you didn't say anything when I brought the clothes to the hospital." There was no missing the hurt in her tone.

"I'm sorry and you're right—about the not-knowing-each-other part. You already heard or read most of what there is to tell. We've seen each other during the course of planning functions and smaller gatherings for his campaign. That night, was just…well…"

"Spontaneously human?"

"Neither one of us was doing much thinking."

"Well, I'm glad you're all right."

"But?"

"It's such a tight race." Her sister picked at a pile of sparkly painted T-shirts that looked designer made yet had been created by artsy Starr. "I'd hate for his opponent to get any kind of leg up at a time when even a few votes can make a difference. There are some important issues at stake—like Martin Stewart's history in the state legislature and how he has hacked away funds that feed into the foster-care system."

Certainly discussion of the race had been bandied about among Beachcombers clientele with everyone weighing in. Ashley and her sisters had gotten behind Matthew early on given their strong stance on foster care. "That issue hits close to home, no question. But I'm sure the voters will see Martin Stewart for the phony snake he is by the time the campaign runs its course. The guy does the Potomac Two-Step changing his stance on issues so often he's a prime candidate for *Dancing With the Stars.*"

Starr's packing slowed to a near halt. "I wish I could be so certain."

"I truly believe that. Remember when you worked after school in his office? It only took you a couple of months to quit that job. You said he was hell to work for. If you sensed that at seventeen, surely older more mature voters will figure it out, too."

Starr resumed stacking piles in the box quietly. Too quietly. Her sister never ran out of things to say.

Ashley tried to catch her sister's eye. "What's wrong?"

Starr pivoted on her heel, her eyes awash with pain—and anger. "I didn't quit that job. I was fired."

"Oh, my God, why?"

"Because I wouldn't sleep with him."

Whoa. The impact of Starr's revelation set Ashley back a step. Then another until she sagged into a chair. "You were only seventeen. He must have been in his thirties then."

"Yeah, exactly." Starr stalked around the room, dodging piles of clothes. "He fired me, and to top it off, just before that I had asked him to write a recommendation for me to get into that art school in Atlanta. Well, afterward, he made a call that ruined any chance I had at the scholarship."

"Starr, that's horrible." Ashley tried to hide her hurt that her sister hadn't shared something so life critical with her before now, but her firebrand of a sister seemed suddenly fragile. Plus, she didn't want to upset a pregnant woman, so Ashley settled for, "I'm surprised Aunt Libby didn't string him up by his toenails."

She smoothed her hand along a bright red angora sweater with jet beads along the neckline, wondering how her vibrant sister had put up with that kind of treatment.

"I didn't tell her. I was embarrassed and—" Starr shrugged a shoulder "—afraid no one would believe me since my parents had been such scam artists. Then as time passed, it seemed best to just put it all behind me. I may seem more outgoing than you, but in those days it was mostly bravado."

Ashley hugged her again, holding on until her sister stopped shaking. "I'm so, so sorry you had to go through that."

Starr inched away and swiped her wrist across her eyes, bracelets jangling a discordant tune. "I could go to the press now, but since I'm your sister…"

"They would assume you're lying to help me out." Which would only make things worse.

"I'm afraid so. Maybe now you understand better why I've been so active in campaigning for Matthew Landis."

What a mess. If Matthew lost the election because of one night of consensual sex between two adults, that would be horribly unjust, but she knew well enough that life wasn't always fair. She had to do something to clean up the mess she'd made. She had to do something for Starr.

The obvious answer sat there in front of her in the way her sister had supported her and been the family she never had. She would do anything for the sisters who'd been so self-sufficient they didn't need much of anything from the youngest of their clan. "Don't worry about it. The press will have plenty to talk about before long."

"What do you mean?"

Ashley sucked in a bracing breath. "You aren't the only one with big news today. Matthew and I are engaged."

* * *

She would tell Matthew her decision to go forward with the engagement. Soon, since she'd called and asked him to stop by and pick her up for a late supper after she looked through the charred mess.

Her life would be changing at the speed of light once she accepted his proposal. Even though she would be staying at Starr's during the Beachcomber renovations, Ashley knew the announcement would bring down a hailstorm of media attention. She only needed a few minutes alone inside her old world first—however wrecked it might be.

The air was heavy with humid dew. While crickets chirped, Ashley climbed the rear entrance steps toward the only real home she'd ever known. At least the press couldn't get too close to her in the gated backyard. She panned her flashlight around the lawn and didn't see anyone lurking in the bushes.

Rubbing a hand over the cream-colored clapboard, she thought of the hours she'd spent developing the business with her sisters. A deep breath later, she pushed on the door. It stuck until an extra jolt of her shoulder nudged it loose.

The acrid pall nearly choked her. Who would have thought the smell could linger so long? Soot mingled in the air, hanging on the humidity like whispery spiderwebs.

No doubt even walking through her shop would be messy, so Ashley tied her hair through itself into a loose slipknot. A quiver of dread fluttered to life. She squashed it before it could rob her of the drive she needed to face the damage.

A soaked rug squished beneath her shoes as she padded down the hallway. Pausing at her office, she tapped the door open, sighing to find all intact. A film of black residue smudged the surfaces of desks and shelves, but just as Matthew had promised, no fire damage.

She would come back to it later. First, she needed to confront the worst. Each step bubbled gray water from beneath her shoes, the squelching sound weakly echoing memories of Matthew's leather loafers pounding down the hall as he'd carried her.

Around the corner waited the main showroom. The horrid sense of helplessness returned, crawling between her shoulder blades like a persistent bug she couldn't swat away. Above all, Ashley hated feeling powerless.

She shook off the wasted emotion. Time to take control and face the nightmare so she could wake up and get her life back. Ashley plowed around the corner and into a broad male chest. She jumped back with a scream, slipping on the squishy rug.

But it wasn't the paparazzi.

Matthew filled the doorway. Apparently she would be talking to him sooner than she'd expected.

"Hold on a minute, darlin'." Matthew gripped her shoulders, his voice rumbling into the silence. "It's just me."

"Matthew, of course it's you." Shuddering with relief, she instinctively sagged against him—then stiffened defensively.

He pulled her firmly against him anyway until she could only hear the steady thrum of his heart pulsing beneath her ear. His musky scent encircled her, insulating her from the fiery aftermath.

Her skin burned with a prickly sensation, almost painful. A rush of heat deep in the pit of her stomach made her long to melt against him, press her breasts to his chest until the ache subsided or exploded into something magnificent.

Ashley flatted her palms on his chest and shoved. "You scared the hell out of me."

"Sorry." Matthew squished back a step, hands raised in surrender, his flashlight casting a dome of light. "I saw you crossing the yard and I came in through the front."

"It's okay. Now that I can breathe." It wasn't fair that she felt like death warmed over and he looked so damned good. Even in khakis and a polo shirt, he rippled with power.

Still, she felt tired and cranky, and his appeal left her edgy and vulnerable. She didn't like it—and she still had to tell him they were engaged after all. "What are you doing here so early?"

"You said you were coming to check out the damage." He absently scratched behind his ear, then stopped. "I thought you could use some help."

Miffed with herself for losing her temper, Ashley reined in her wayward emotions. She'd never used anger to get her way before. She couldn't see any reason to start now. Must be nerves from what she had to tell him.

She'd wanted a good night's sleep to brace herself, but so much for wishes. "I apologize and you're right, I did need to speak with you. We can talk while I do my walk-through of the place."

For the first time since she'd slammed into Matthew, his poster-boy-perfect mask slid. Concern wrinkled his brow. "Are you sure you're ready for this? Hire a cleanup crew and spare yourself some heartache."

"I'm not going to clean the place yet. Actually, I can't until the insurance company completes its assessment. I just wanted to look. It shouldn't take long."

He stepped aside. She gasped.

The whole room loomed like a black hole, void of color. Boards over the window even kept out much of the streetlights from lending any relief to the drab grays. Maybe she should have waited until morning after all and seen the place in the light of day. Surely the dark made everything seem worse than it was.

But probably not.

She'd hosted so many beautiful prewedding events here in the past, imagining celebrating her own engagement someday. What a crummy, crummy way to get her wish.

Matthew wondered how Ashley could stand so stoically still in the face of such a damn mess.

The second she'd told him she planned to come here, he'd known he would have to be there with her. For safety's sake and for support.

Her chin quivered. Totally understandable. He'd expected just such a reaction. He hadn't anticipated how her sadness would sucker punch him.

Matthew crossed his arms, trapping his hands so he wouldn't reach for her. She eased past him, the sweep of her peasant top brushing against his arm. What did she have on underneath? His throbbing body begged him to discover the answer.

Odd how he'd never considered that practical Ashley might wear her merchandise. Her merchandise. How could he have been so focused on thoughts of getting Ashley naked that he momentarily forgot about the mess around them?

Clothing racks lay on their sides, having been tipped by the force of spraying water. Curled wisps of melted fabrics stuck to the floor and hangers. That same material could have melted to her skin.

Matthew heard a bell chime behind him, followed by Ashley's chuckle. Her laugh rippled over his taut nerves, just as enticing as any slip. Damn. He was in trouble. "What did you find?"

Ashley reached inside the antique gilded cash register and pulled out a soggy stack of bills. "A few blasts with the blow-dryer and I'll be solvent."

Only Ashley could stand in the middle of a charred-out room, holding what probably amounted to a couple hundred bucks and still manage a laugh.

He stepped deeper into the room. "So supper's on you tonight."

"Sure. I could probably afford to spring for burgers, if you don't mind splitting the cola?"

"How about I give you some money just to tide you over?"

Her pride blazed brighter than their two flashlights combined. "I'll be fine once the insurance check arrives. I don't mind working off my deductible with sweat equity."

"It's a standing offer."

"Thanks, but no."

Matthew bit short a rebuttal. He could see she wouldn't be budged. He would just find other ways around her counterproductive need for independence. "All right, then."

He followed her back down the hall, her gathered long hair swaying with each step, baring a patch of her neck, and just that fast he started forgetting about the charred mess around them.

Until they reached her open bedroom door.

What if she'd been asleep in her bed when the fire started and he hadn't returned? Being inside the powder room could very well have saved her life.

His chest tightened, his breathing ragged. He braced a forearm against the fire-split molding. His arms trembled with the tension of bunched muscles as he fought the image of Ashley dead.

She made a slow spin around to face him again. "Well, you were right, Matthew. There's not much I can do here for now. I feel better, though. Knowing the worst somehow makes it easier to go forward."

"Right." He only half registered her words, still caught in the hellish scenario of her stuck in this place while it burned. Thank God she wasn't his fiancée, someone like Dana who could wreck his world in a stopped heartbeat.

"I accept."

Ashley's words snapped him back to the present.

"Accept the money?" He was surprised, but damn glad. "Of course. How much do you need?" His eyes swept over her, unable to read her body language but sensing the tension coiling through her.

"Not that. I accept your, uh—" she chewed her lip "—your proposal. If you still think it will help your campaign, I'll be your fiancée."

Chapter 5

He was engaged. Hell.

Matthew creaked back in the chair at his bustling campaign headquarters in Hilton Head. Even four hours after Ashley's official acceptance, he still couldn't believe she had actually agreed. He'd gotten his way, but still, the whole notion had him itching with the same sensation that had urged him to get out of her place as quickly as he could after their night together.

He stared at the computer screen full of briefing notes in front of him, but it registered as vaguely as the ringing of telephones and hum of the copy machine outside his office.

Thumbing the edge of a shiny red-and-blue stack of "Landis for Senate" bumper stickers, Matthew wondered why the thought of even a fake engagement floored him so much. After all, he'd gotten exactly what he wanted from her. It wasn't real, like with Dana.

He just hadn't expected Ashley to be so damn reluctant in her agreement. Okay, so yeah, maybe his ego smarted a little. *He* was the one who wanted to keep his bachelor life.

Wouldn't his brothers enjoy yukking it up over this mess?

A light tap sounded on his open door. He glanced up to find his campaign manager—Brent Davis—filling the opening. "Are you getting enough sleep?"

"You're kidding, right?" Matthew waved Brent to take the chair in front of the mahogany desk.

Older than Matthew by twenty years, the wiry manager had been an energetic force behind Matthew's mother's campaign and had acted as a consultant when Matthew ran for the House of Representatives. Brent had been the natural choice to head the campaign when Matthew had made his decision to seek his mother's vacated senatorial seat.

For the first time, Matthew wondered if he'd decided to push too hard, too fast, politically. He could have hung out in the House for another ten years or so and still been on track to run for the senate by the time he was forty. But he'd been so hell-bent on not letting go of the seat that started with his father before shifting to his mom. He'd worried that someone else might get a lock on the spot that couldn't be broken.

Had his ambition pushed him to sacrifice anything—including an innocent person like Ashley?

Damn it all, he was doing this to help preserve her reputation. He'd made his decision and he wouldn't hurt her more by changing his mind and offering her a trip to the Bahamas to hide out until the frenzy died out. While yes, he could have handled the scandal, it would have been a hell of a lot more taxing on everyone in his campaign who had worked so hard to get him here.

Time to step up to the plate and be a man. He leaned forward on his arms, shirtsleeves rolled up, and looked Brent Davis square in the eye. "Ashley Carson and I are engaged."

His campaign manager froze—no expression, no movement, not so much as a blink to betray his thoughts. Matthew knew from experience the guy only did that when he'd been tossed a curve ball that whacked him upside the skull. The last time Matthew had seen that look on Brent's face, he'd gotten the news flash that Ginger Landis had decided to elope with her longtime friend General Hank Renshaw during a goodwill tour across Europe.

Finally, Brent templed his pointer fingers and tapped them against his nose. "You're joking."

"I'm serious." Matthew straightened, unflinching.

One blink from Brent. Just one, but a fast flick of irritation. "You're engaged to the mouse of a girl in the compromising photos."

Anger blazed hot and fast. "Watch how you talk about Ashley."

Brent's eyes went wide. "Whoa, okay, take it down a notch there, big fella. I hear you loud and clear. You're totally in lust with this female."

"Davis…" Matthew growled his final warning.

Besides, the last thing he needed right now was to dwell on that night with Ashley, a train of thoughts guaranteed to steal what cool he had left at the moment. "She's my fiancée, my choice—deal with it. That's your job."

"Why didn't you tell me you were dating her when those damning photos hit the news?" Brent flattened his palms on the desk. "You left me to spin one helluva nightmare with incomplete informati— Wait." He leaned back with narrowed laser eyes. "This is one of those fake deals, isn't it? The two of you are making this up to get the heat off."

"I never said that," he hedged, unwilling to expose Ashley to any more embarrassment.

"You need to be honest with me if I'm going to help you make it through the November elections on top." Brent tapped the stack of bumper stickers with his pointer finger repeatedly for emphasis. "In fact, you should have told me before you proposed to her in the first place."

On the one hand, Matthew could see his point. On the other, it seemed damned ridiculous—not to mention unromantic—to clear his bridal choice with his campaign manager first.

If he really was getting married. Which he wasn't. But that was beside the point.

He wouldn't sacrifice Ashley to the media hyenas just to win an election. In spite of all his competitive urges that totally agreed with Brent, Matthew couldn't bring himself to say anything that might bring Ashley further embarrassment.

Something deep inside him insisted if he was the kind of man to abandon her, then he didn't deserve to win. "Ashley and I were work acquaintances who were surprised to find there was something more. Call it a whirlwind romance in your press release."

Brent nodded his head slowly, a smile spreading

across his angular face for the first time since he'd entered the office. "If we put that out there to the media, then everyone will understand when the two of you decide to break off the impetuous engagement."

"I never said that, either."

"Damn it, Matthew—" his smile went wry "—I taught you how to use those avoidant answer techniques with the press back when your mother was running for office. Don't think you can get away with using those same techniques on me."

Why couldn't he bring himself to close the office door and tell Brent the truth? It all came back to protecting Ashley, her reputation and her pride as best he could until he set things right again in her life.

Matthew angled forward with a long creak of the wheels on the antique leather chair he'd inherited from his father. "I said Ashley and I are engaged, and that's exactly what I mean. We're going to pick out a ring tomorrow."

A ring?

Hell, yeah.

Of course they would need a ring. If Ashley balked, he would suggest they could sell it afterward and donate the proceeds to her favorite charity. Ashley, with all her generous ways, would get into a notion like that. He wasn't actually purchasing any token of commitment, rather protecting Ashley while contributing to a worthy cause.

Brent eyed him narrowly. "Why not give this Ashley Carson woman your mother's ring from her marriage to your father?"

Good question.

"Ashley wants her own," he neatly dodged. "As a foster child, she lived her life receiving hand-me-downs from others, rarely getting the chance to choose what suited *her* best. She deserves to have a ring of her choice and start traditions of her own."

Yeah, that sounded plausible enough, especially given he'd only had half a second to come up with an answer. As a matter of fact, it actually resonated as true inside him, the decision he would reach if he and Ashley were doing this couple thing for real.

Matthew aligned the stack of bumper stickers. "I imagine the news will leak from someone in the jewelry store, but we'll still want to make our own official announcement. When do you think is best to call a press conference? Tomorrow night or the next morning?"

"You actually love this woman?" His manager didn't even bother hiding the jaded tone in his voice.

Love? The word brought to mind the endless times he'd heard his mother crying on the other side of the door after Benjamin Landis's death. Ginger had been damn near incapacitated. If it hadn't been for her kids and the surprise offer to take over her husband's senate seat, Matthew still wasn't sure how long it would have taken his mother to enter the world of the living again.

He would have chalked it up to emotions growing over a long-term relationship, but he'd felt much the same crippling pain when his fiancée died in college. No way was he going back for round two of that pathway to hell. The possibility of letting anyone have that kind of control over him again scared the crap out of him.

He'd been right to try to end things after their ac-

cidental night together. Circumstances, however, had
forced them to bide their time before going their separate and diverse ways.

He thought about Ashley, and yeah, she stirred a
protectiveness inside him along with that hefty dose
of arousal. Just thinking about her naked body tangled
in the sheets with her auburn hair splayed over the pil-
low...

Damn. He wouldn't be standing up from behind the
protective cover of his mahogany desk anytime soon.
"I am captivated by her."

Brent stared him down and Matthew held his gaze
without wavering. Finally, his old family friend nodded. "Either you're a brilliant liar or in more trouble
than you realize, my friend."

The camera flash blinded her.

Ashley blinked to clear the sparks of light as the intense reflection bounced off the marquise-cut diamond
on her finger as she stood in front of the podium outside Matthew's campaign headquarters in Hilton Head.

She hadn't wanted him to spend so much on the ring,
but he'd swayed her by telling her the proceeds from
hocking the rock afterward would go to the charity of
her choice. That he knew her and her wishes so well
after such a short time swayed her more than anything.

His campaign manager, Mr. Davis, stepped between
them and the microphone. "Thank you, ladies and gentlemen of the press. That officially concludes our conference for this afternoon."

Ashley forced a smile on her face as cameras continued to click while Matthew escorted her toward a

chauffeur-driven Suburban. The weight of the stone on her hand provided a constant reminder that while she might not be committed to this man, she was committed to her decision to help him with his campaign to beat his scumbag opponent.

She extended her fingers and stared at the brilliant diamond in the shiny gold setting, thought of their night together, followed by his cageyness the next morning.

She feared she'd made a mistake.

Not in deciding on the engagement. She still believed in making sure that rat bastard running against him didn't get to exploit anyone else.

But this ring? She turned her hand to catch fragments of sunlight in the facets of the stone. The ring was perfect, exactly what she would want in a real engagement, and now she could never have it because the marquise cut would always remind her of Matthew Landis and the way he'd hurt her.

She couldn't help but think of how he'd hotfooted toward her door. When this relationship didn't benefit him anymore, he would likely hotfoot his way out of her life just that fast. She didn't want to view him in such an unfavorable light, but what else could she think? That was what he'd shown her, and he *was* a politician after all.

Although she'd seen signs he wasn't the typical politician, she reminded herself he was used to spinning things to his own advantage. She needed to remember that in order to survive this debacle.

Ashley slid into the backseat of the Suburban, the driver closing the door after her while she settled into the decadently soft leather. A built-in television played a twenty-four-hour news channel.

Matthew tossed his briefcase to the floor before buckling his seat belt. "Thank God, that's past. We should have some time to talk before we reach my place."

Her ears perked up and she lost focus on the ring. "Your place?"

"Yes, you should familiarize yourself with the property." He angled to face her, his knee brushing against hers and stirring more than nerves in her stomach. "It would seem strange if you're unfamiliar with where I live."

"Of course. That makes sense." She forced her face to stay blasé even though inside she couldn't ignore the frustrated twinge that his reasons for taking her home were merely practical. "Why didn't your campaign manager come along, then? Where is he now?"

"Don't know." Matthew shrugged as a golf course with a lush lawn and palm trees whizzed past.

"I thought he wanted to tell me more about the upcoming agenda." She tugged her lightweight sweater closed over her floral sundress she'd borrowed from Starr. The outfit was pretty, but Starr wasn't as busty so the darn thing didn't fit quite right and the press of Matthew's knee against hers was starting to make the dress even more uncomfortably tight as her breasts ached for his touch.

She should have been shopping for clothes rather than a ring in order to pull off this charade.

"Brent and I decided I could give you the information just as easily. He has enough to keep him busy." Matthew clicked open his briefcase and pulled out a printed agenda roster. "I'm slated to speak at a Rotary breakfast in the morning and a stump gathering in the afternoon. On Saturday evening, there's a harbor cruise fund-raising dinner."

He paused reading to glance over at her, seemingly unaware of the havoc he wreaked on her senses with just the touch of his kneecap, for Pete's sake. If only the photographers hadn't caught those compromising photos, she could have gone on with her life, pissed off at him, certainly, but free of this painful attraction.

"Ashley?" He ducked his head into her line of sight. "Are you with me? Do you have a problem with any of this? You don't have to attend everything. It's not like you're a politician's wife."

"Of course I want to come. It's fascinating to hear all of the political ins and outs up close. And it's not as if I have a job at the moment. Everything's at a standstill with Beachcombers until the insurance company finishes its report and cuts us a check."

She forced her eyes to stay dry when more than anything she wanted to shout her frustration over her out-of-control life. She liked simple and uncomplicated.

Matthew Landis was anything and everything except simple and uncomplicated.

His handsome face went somber with concern. "I could always float you a loan—"

"Shut up about the money already." God, he really didn't have a clue about her values and pride, in spite of the ring. Still, she eased her words with a smile even as constant reminders of his affluent world whipped by outside in the shape of waterside mansions and high-end cars. "But thank you for the offer. It's very generous of you."

"Don't overrate me. The amount you need wouldn't even put a dent in my portfolio."

She wrinkled her nose and planted her legs firmly on her side of the car—away from his. The leather seats teased at the back of her calves with a reminder of lush accessories she could never afford. "Why did you have to take such a nice offer and downplay it that way?"

"I'm not bragging, only speaking the truth."

That might be so, but it still didn't mean she planned to let him open his wallet to her. Taking money from a man she was sleeping with seemed…icky.

She'd already come too close to crossing a moral conscience line with this fake engagement. She couldn't take one step further. "I see plenty of wealthy people traipsing through Beachcombers who will stiff the waitress on a tip without thinking twice. I know affluence and generosity do not always go hand in hand."

"Since I already have enough debates on my schedule, I won't bother disputing your kind assessment of my character."

She chewed her lip to keep from arguing further and simply listened to the roar and honks of street traffic. The last thing she wanted was to wax on about the wonderful attributes of Matthew Landis. That would do little to bolster her self-control.

He tapped her brow with a warm, callused finger. "Penny for them."

She forced a lighthearted smile on her face. "Come on, surely with your portfolio you can do better than that."

"Touché." He chuckled low, the rumble of his laugh

sliding as smoothly over her senses as his arm along the back of the seat to cup her shoulders.

His touch burned along her already heightened nerves, tightening an unwelcome need deep in her belly. She'd always been attracted to him, but the sensual draw was so much more intense now that she knew exactly how high he could nudge her pleasure with even one stroke of his body inside hers.

She inched forward on the seat, her light linen sundress suddenly itchy against her knees. "You don't need to keep up the shows of affection. No one is around to snap a promo shot."

Slowly, torturously so, he slid his arm away, his green eyes glinting with a hint of bad-boy charm that showed he knew exactly how much his touch affected her. "I didn't mean to overstep."

"Apology accepted."

Sheesh, she hated sounding so uptight, but she could barely hold her own with this guy when he *wasn't* touching her. She'd enjoyed having his hands all over her, but she'd hated the way he made her feel the next morning.

"So what's the going rate for your thoughts?"

"Actually, they're free at the moment." She struggled for some new direction to take their discussion that had nothing to do with touching, needing, wanting. "I'm just not sure if my question is polite."

"I've developed a thick skin over the years."

She wished she could say the same. "All right, then." She tipped her face confidently—and so the vents could shoosh some cooling air against her warming skin. "I can't hush up the accountant in me that's wondering how your family accumulated such a hefty portfolio."

"Dumb luck, as a matter of fact." He scratched his hand along his jaw, which just happened to draw his pointer finger over his top lip in a temptingly seductive manner. "My great-grandfather bought into a big local land deal that paid off well when it just as easily could have tanked."

She remembered clearly how that mouth of his felt exploring every inch of her body, lingering once he'd discovered a particularly sensitive region. She cleared her throat, if not her passion-fogged thoughts. Too easily she could be lured under his sensual spell again and she needed to hold strong. "Uh, where were these land plots?"

"Myrtle Beach." He dropped his hand back to his knee, giving her overloaded senses a momentary reprieve.

"Ah, that explains a lot." Interesting how he downplayed his family's fortune. Wealth that large didn't accumulate on its own or grow by taking care of itself. "But it doesn't explain everything. Plenty of people blow a fortune before it ever reaches their kids."

"We've invested wisely over the years," he conceded, fingering his cuff links, an antique-looking set that she suspected must have family sentimentality. As she looked closer, she recognized his father's initials. "We've lived well, without question, but always kept an eye on growing the principal."

"Very smart move." Her accounting brain envisioned numerous creative ways to diversify a large holding. Some lucky number cruncher must be having a field day playing with all that capital. "Families expand, so if you don't increase the size of the pie, the pieces will get smaller with each generation."

"Exactly." His thumb polished a rounded cuff link. "We're lucky that we've been able to pursue whatever career dream we wanted without worrying about putting a roof over our heads."

His grassroots practicality touched her as firmly and stirringly as those callused fingers ever had, and that scared her. This man could hurt her, badly, if she wasn't careful.

"It's admirable that you all think that way rather than simply living a life of leisure." The Suburban slowed to a crawl behind cars backed up from a wreck ahead. She forced her drying-up mouth to keep the conversation flowing. "You could simply see the world or something, and nobody would think less of you."

"I could go stark raving nuts, you mean. I like playing golf as much as the next guy—" he gestured at the rolling course packed with players "—but I'm not good enough to make a living at it, therefore it can't be my life's pursuit. For me, politics keeps me in touch with the rest of the world and how they're living. That's a real grounding kind of thing. My brother Kyle says the same about serving in the air force."

So this conversation thing wasn't working out as well as she'd expected since he actually got nicer with each sentence. If the traffic jam didn't clear soon she would be in serious trouble. "What about your other brother Sebastian?"

"He's the business lawyer who keeps us all bankrolled for the next generation."

"And Jonah?"

His smile tightened. "The jury's still out on him."

"He's the youngest, right?" She seemed to recall from the publicity photos of Ginger Landis Renshaw with her boys. "I seem to remember reading he only just graduated from college."

"So did you, but you're not jaunting around the world." He thumbed the crease between his eyebrows. "I'm just not sure how my parents brought up a playboy son."

She followed his words and the mounting proof that there might be something more to him than a fat wallet, a handsome face and slick politician's persona. Definitely dangerous, with a warm magnetism that radiated from him and reached to her even when they didn't touch.

"You're a good listener, Ashley."

"You're an interesting speaker." And that was the truth, damn it. Why couldn't he have been a pedantic slug? "I look forward to hearing what you have to say at all those functions. I honestly believe you're the better man for this job and I want to do whatever I can to help make that happen."

"Thank you. You sound like you actually mean that."

She shared a quiet smile with him, unable to miss the enclosed intimacy of just the two of them in the back of the Suburban with a privacy window closed. She started to sway toward him, then jerked her body rigid.

"What's the matter, then?" He smoothed a finger along her furrowed forehead much the way he'd smoothed the crease between his own eyebrows.

"I don't have a problem with attending the events with you." She forced her best prim tone in place to put things back on a more practical keel. "My concern is actually more logistical. I don't know how I'm going to get to Charleston and back in time to make everything."

"Who says you have to go back and forth to Charleston?"

Her jaw dropped as her pulse skyrocketed. A fake engagement was one thing. But moving in together? Matthew must have been dipping into the vehicle's liquor cabinet.

Chapter 6

Ashley considered availing herself of the Suburban's drink selection after all, time of the afternoon be damned. She could be stuck in here with Matthew for hours if the cops didn't clear the wreck soon.

She tugged at the hem of her dress, because yes, she'd felt his heated gaze stray to her calves more than once during the ride to his house. "You can't be suggesting I should move in with you. The press will chew us up."

"We're engaged." He cupped her elbow.

She shrugged her arm free. She'd been lured by his sexual draw once before and look where that had landed her. Half-dressed on the front page of countless newspapers. "Don't be obtuse and stop touching me."

His eyes narrowed and Ashley mentally kicked herself. Another gauntlet moment.

He slowly removed his hand. "So you're still every bit as attracted to me as I am to you."

Ouch. He played tough.

Well, she would have to meet the challenge. "That

line of discussion will not go far in persuading me to stay with you."

One side of his mouth kicked up in a smile. "Point well made." He stretched his arm along the back of the seat, this time without so much as brushing any part of her. "I live in a family compound, as do two of my brothers. We all have our own quarters. Mom and the general live in both D.C. and South Carolina. The general's at the Pentagon right now, but Mom's around, so you even have a chaperone."

"By living quarters, what do you mean?" She eyed him warily. He'd made it clear he was still attracted to her and that it wasn't an act. Yet having an affair with a ring on her finger and the intent to break things off felt wrong. How ironic that she'd been willing to consider sleeping with him when there'd been no jewelry or fake commitments involved. "Is everybody in the same house with a suite, but all still bump into each other walking around in the hall?"

"I thought you objected to me not being around in the morning."

She narrowed her gaze and considered elbowing him in the kidney, but that would show he had too much sway over her emotions. "Old issue. No longer relevant."

"Fair enough. Jonah and Sebastian both have suites of rooms in the main house since Jonah graduated and Sebastian's separated from his wife. Kyle has a condo near the air force base in Charleston. And I live in the renovated groundskeeper's carriage house behind the main place. Does that work for you?"

His plan sounded solid and her sister's husband had just arrived home from assignment. While Starr and

David would say they didn't mind having her around and they had plenty of space, she had to imagine they would want some privacy. They hadn't been married long and they had the pregnancy news to celebrate. She would be most decidedly a third wheel and it was downright silly to drive back and forth from Charleston to Hilton Head multiple times a day.

Matthew's idea was sensible, and bottom line, she was painfully practical.

"Okay and thank you. As long as your brothers don't run around in their boxer shorts, I guess this should work out all right."

"No worries." Matthew's grin stretched from appealing to downright wicked, sending a shiver of premonition up her spine as the Suburban finally jolted forward. "If I find any of them wearing nothing but their skivvies around you, I'll kick their asses."

Wow, Matthew sure knew how to deliver a zinger line to close up shop on conversation. His silence left her with nothing to do but stare out the window.

She'd grown up in Charleston, but this exclusive area of coastal beauty had been meticulously manicured in a way that seemed to preserve yet tame the natural magnificence.

Of course, given the size of the mansions and golf courses they'd passed, the people who lived here could obviously afford to sculpt this place into anything they wished.

The driver steered the SUV along a winding paved drive through palm trees and sea grass until the view parted to reveal a sprawling white three-story house with Victorian peaks overlooking the ocean. A lengthy set of stairs stretched upward to the second story wrap-around porch that housed the main entrance. Lattice-work shielded most of the first floor, which appeared to be a large entertainment area. Just as in Charleston, many homes so close to the water were built up as a safeguard against tidal floods from hurricanes.

The attached garage had so many doors she stopped counting. His SUV rolled to a stop beside the house, providing a view of the brilliant azaleas behind them and the ocean in front of them. An organic-shaped pool was situated between the house and shore, the waters of the hot tub at the base churning a glistening swirl in the afternoon sun.

"My place is over there." He pointed to the cluster of live oaks and palmettos, a two-story carriage house just visible through the branches.

White with slate-blue shutters, this carriage house was larger than most family homes. She understood he came from money. She had even grown up among wealthy types in Aunt Libby's old Charleston neighborhood. But seeing Matthew's lifestyle laid out so grandly only emphasized their different roots.

She walked up the lengthy stretch of white steps toward the large double doors on the second floor. She gripped the railing and looked out over the water. "This view. It totally rocks."

He slid an arm around her again. This time she couldn't bring herself to pull away and ruin the moment. She let herself believe she leaned into his embrace simply because they might be seen by someone, the staff, his family.

Had he even told his family the truth? She assumed
so but hadn't thought to ask. It was one thing to keep
his silence with his campaign manager because as much
as you thought you could trust someone, she'd learned
it never hurt to be extracareful.

The sound of an opening door plucked her from her
reverie. She jerked in Matthew's spicy-scented embrace
and turned to find an older woman coming through the
main entrance. Even if she hadn't recognized the senator from her press coverage, Ashley would have figured out her identity all the same. Her deep green eyes
declared her to be Matthew's mother, even if her fair
head contrasted with his dark brown hair.

Ginger Landis Renshaw strode toward them, her
shoulder-length gray-blond hair perfectly styled. Ashley recalled from news reports the woman was around
fifty, but she carried the years well. Wearing a pale pink
lightweight sweater set with pearls—and blue jeans—
Ginger Landis wasn't at all what Ashley had expected.
Thank goodness, because the woman in front of her
appeared a little less intimidating.

She had seen the woman often enough on the news—
always poised and intelligent, sometimes steely, determined. Today, a softer side showed as she looked at her
son, then over to Ashley.

"Mother, this is Ashley. Ashley, my mother."

Ginger extended her hands and clasped Ashley's.
"Welcome to our home. I'm sorry to hear about what
happened to your business, but I'm so glad you're all
right and that Matthew brought you here to stay with us."

"Thank you for having me on such short notice, Senator."

"Ginger, please, do call me Ginger."

"Of course," she replied, not yet able to envision herself using the first name of this woman who dined with heads of state.

Matthew's mother studied her, inventory-style, and suddenly Ashley realized the reason for the woman's presence here instead of in D.C. with her husband. Matthew's mother must have been called to give her a Cinderella makeover.

Ashley released Ginger's clasp and crossed her arms over her ill-fitting dress. "It's a pleasure and honor to meet you."

Ginger tipped her head to the side. "Is something wrong, dear?"

Visions blossomed to mind of being stuffed into some stiff sequined gown with her hair plastered in an overdone crafted creation that would make her head ache. She might even be able to pull the look off without appearing to be a joke. She might even look presentable enough to turn a head or two.

But she would feel wretchedly fake and uncomfortable the whole time. "No, of course not. I'm grateful for your generosity in letting me stay here."

"But...?" Ginger prodded.

Ashley let the words tumble free before she could restrain them and end up stuffed in a fashion runway mess. "I just can't help but wonder if Matthew's campaign manager expects you to give me some kind of makeover."

"Why would I want to change you? My son obviously finds you perfect as you are."

"That's very kind of you to say. Thank you." Ash-

ley expected relief only to find something different altogether. She resented the twinge of disappointment
sticking inside her chest like an annoying thorn. She
truly didn't want some fake redo. She liked herself just
fine, but still...

Then another implication of his mother's words
soaked in. She didn't appear to know the engagement
was fake. That Matthew would keep himself so closed
off from even his family gave her pause. Except wasn't
she doing the same with her own sisters?

Matthew kissed his mother's cheek. "Always the diplomat." He backed a step. "I'll just go help the driver
with our luggage."

Ashley couldn't miss how it didn't seem to dawn on
him to allow the chauffeur to haul their suitcases by
himself. Yet another touch that made Matthew all the
more appealing.

Forcing herself to stop watching him lope down the
steps with a muscled grace, she turned her attention to
following Ginger back into the house. No mere maga-
zine layout could have done the place justice.

A wall of windows let sunshine stream through and
bathe the room in light all the way up to the cathe-
dral ceilings. Hardwood floors were scattered with
light Persian rugs around two Queen Anne sofas up-
holstered in a pale blue fabric with white piping. Wing-
back chairs in a creamy yellow angled off the side. The
whole decor was undoubtedly formal, but in an airy,
comfortable way.

Ginger spun on her low heel. "I'll show you to your
room shortly. The view of the ocean is breathtaking."

Having grown up at Aunt Libby's on the water, she

appreciated the sense of home she would get from the sound of the waves lulling her to sleep. Come to think of it, this woman had an Aunt Libby–like air of kindness to her.

"Your home is gorgeous." Ashley turned to the picturesque windows overlooking the pool and ocean. "Thank you again for letting me stay. I can't wait to unpack my suitcase."

"Oh, my dear, don't worry about doing that. You won't need to use your sister's clothes."

Ashley pivoted away from the windows to the room filled with the beauty and scent of fresh-cut flowers in crystal vases. "Excuse me, but I thought you said we weren't going to do the makeover deal."

"I never said we weren't going shopping."

"You didn't?" This woman was as good at wordplays and nuances as Matthew. Ashley would have to watch her step around both of them. "What do you mean, then?"

"Your entire wardrobe was ruined. It's obvious you need new clothes, even more so because of the predicament with my son and all the appearances you'll need to make together."

"I can't let him pay for my clothes."

Matthew's mother planted her fists on her hips in a stance that brooked no argument. "Since he's the reason you have to attend the functions, it's only fair he pay."

Ashley stayed silent because she knew she wouldn't win a war of words with this master stateswoman.

Ginger smiled. "Prideful. I like you more and more by the minute." She waved a manicured hand. "I wasn't born into all of this. I didn't even know about it when

I met my first husband, an air force jet jock who swept me off my feet so much we eloped in two weeks."

A bittersweet smile flickered across her face as the soft sounds of someone turning on a vacuum in the next room filled the silence.

Ashley touched her arm. "How long has he been gone?"

"Nearly eleven years. I never thought I would fall in love that way again. And in a sense, I was right. Love built slower for me the second time around, but no less strong."

Ginger's eyes took on a faraway look and Ashley realized the woman was staring at an old family photo across the room for at least half a minute before she returned her attention back to the present. "So, Ashley, about the shopping spree. I adore the general and my boys, but there are times I need a girls' day out."

Wow, this lady had a way of working a person around to her side of the argument. "How about this? He can pay for the clothes I use at official functions, but I pay for anything else I wear."

"That sounds entirely fair and wonderfully honorable."

"Matthew's campaign manager says the media will eat me alive."

Ginger cupped her cheek, her charm bracelet jingling. "No one expects you to change who you are. We're only here to help you be comfortable as *yourself.* We'll be doing that with new clothes of your choosing and some helpful tips for dealing with the press."

Oh, man, she really didn't want to like this woman so much. Forming any kind of bond with Matthew's family would only make things all the tougher when she walked away.

At least she could take some comfort in the sincerity lacing Ginger's words. Matthew's mother would help her choose appropriate clothes that stayed true to her own tastes.

There wouldn't be a Cinderella makeover after all. Which was a relief. Except that as much as she knew she and Matthew weren't right for each other long-term, part of her wouldn't have minded knocking him flat on his awesome butt.

He was only just finishing up his first speech of the day and already he was sweating—big-time.

Except he couldn't blame the crowd or the press or even the cranking summer heat. His pumping blood pressure had more to do with the demure woman sitting serenely to his right in his peripheral vision, her attention unwaveringly focused on him.

The way Ashley's sheath dress kept hitching up over her knees was about to send him into cardiac arrest at thirty years old. His mother had absconded with Ashley yesterday afternoon, not returning until well after supper. Call him crazy, but he'd been expecting pastel suits and pearls like his mother wore.

Instead, his mother had picked an emerald-green form-fitting dress with a scooped neck and a pendant that drew his gaze south. A daring choice given all he'd heard about everyone appearing subdued during a campaign. Yet Ashley, with her long auburn hair pulled back with a simple gold clasp, looked classically elegant. The no-heel strappy sandals accented with gold stones matching the necklace flashed a tribute to her glowing youthfulness. She would easily appeal to a cross section of voters.

She'd easily appealed to *him* at a time when he'd sworn he would keep his distance.

He resisted the urge to swipe his wrist over his brow, a dead giveaway to anyone with a camera that he was rattled. He glanced quickly at his notes to scoop up his ender. Thank God, he must have said something coherent because everyone clapped and smiled.

The rotary president stepped up to the microphone to invite questions from the media.

An older woman stood, her press pass around her neck tangled in the buttons of her tan sweater. "Miss Carson, tell us how Congressman Landis proposed? Was it before or after the revealing photos of the two of you hit the papers?"

Yeah, that had lots to do with the issues.

His campaign manager on his left shot to his feet. "Come on, Mary." Brent smiled at the seasoned reporter. "You know Ashley's still new to all of this. How about you don't put the screws to her just yet?"

Ashley placed a soft hand on Matthew's arm, gently nudging him from the podium. "It's all right. I would like to answer."

Matthew heard his campaign manager suck in air faster than a dehydrated person gulped down water. Matthew worried more than a little himself, but he wouldn't embarrass Ashley by silencing her. He would simply stand by in case she threw him a panicked "save me" look.

"As you can tell, Matthew has concerns for me and

the stresses of campaign scrutiny. That's why he tried to keep me out of the limelight. So I solved the problem by proposing to him."

Chuckles rumbled through the crowd while reporters went wild taking notes. He had to admit, she'd handled the question well while sticking to the truth.

She cast a shy glance through her eyelashes. "You'll have to pardon me if I insist the rest of the details are *very* personal and private." The laughter swelled again. Ashley waited patiently for the hubbub to subside. "And I know when to end on a positive note. Thank you for having us here today."

Matthew palmed the small of her back and ushered her toward the exit behind the podium. The door swooshed behind them, muffling clicking cameras. He leaned and captured her lips with his—hey, wait, where had that idea come from?—but too late, he'd already done it. He was totally entranced with the way she'd glowed behind that podium. So much so, all his good intentions for protecting her with distance had flown right the hell out the window.

Now that he had her against him again, the taste of her fresh on his tongue, he had to savor the moment for an extra stroke longer before easing the kiss to an end. He settled her against his chest instead while he regained control.

"You did a fantastic job handling that reporter, Ashley."

"I answered truthfully." Her fingers gripped his lapels, her words breathy in the narrow corridor leading to a brightly lit exit sign out of the small community college auditorium.

"You answered artfully." He forced himself to step back, but couldn't bring himself to release her arms, convenient since she still held his jacket. "There's a skill to that."

"It was worth it to hear your campaign manager go on life support."

"I was hoping you wouldn't notice."

"He has no reason to trust me. I don't have a track record." Her eyebrows pinched together. "Matthew, I've been waiting for the right time to ask you something, but there are always people around, so I may as well spill it now. Why haven't you told your family the truth?"

"Why haven't you?"

"Answering a question with a question isn't going to work this time."

He gave her the truth as best he understood it. "So much of my life is an open book. I prefer to keep things private when I can." As he'd done about his relationship with Dana. Ashley had a way of pushing his buttons and making him open up before he realized it, a decidedly uncomfortable feeling. "Besides, my family would only worry if they knew, which I suspect is the same reason you haven't told your sisters."

"You're very perceptive." She relaxed against his chest, soft, sweet smelling and too sexy given the way she'd been turning him inside out all morning long.

"I'm sorry you're in this position at all." And damn but he knew to be more careful in his word choices. Now the word *positions* had him thinking of all the different ways he would like to have Ashley under him, over him, around him. "If I could go back and do things different, I—"

He stopped. He couldn't complete the sentence because he realized without question that he wouldn't give up that night with Ashley, even realizing how things would turn out. God, but that made him a selfish bastard.

Her eyes locked with his, her lips parting slightly. She arched up on her toes just as he felt his head magnetically drawn back down toward her. His mouth grazed hers, once, twice, only long enough for a gentle nip that sent his insides aching for more. What harm could there be in exploring the sexual side of things? A brief affair... More of the taste of Ashley...

The door swung open, cutting short the moment, if not his desire. His campaign manager barged toward them, not bothering to slam the door, damn him, undoubtedly more than happy for the reporters to snap a shot now.

Brent clapped his hands together. "Okay, lovebirds, time to get this show on the road."

Matthew watched Ashley as she followed Brent out the door. He didn't want a committed relationship and he most definitely was not giving his heart away again. However, something told him as he watched Ashley, new confidence swinging in her step, he might not be able to walk away as easily as he'd imagined.

Chapter 7

Enjoying the play of moonlight across the ocean, Ashley gripped the railing of the harbor-cruise paddleboat as it docked and thought of the thousand questions she'd answered since yesterday morning. Hands she'd shaken. Babies she'd cradled.

The last part had been the easiest because those little constituents didn't vote. She hadn't realized until the morning paper that she'd been lured into the most cliché campaign moment possible. Thinking about her every move and word was downright exhausting, especially when she and Matthew actually knew so little about each other. She really should make out a questionnaire asking about funky facts from his past.

Tonight had been pleasant with the romantic setting and fairly tasty meal—Beachcombers could have provided better, of course—but the evening had been nice. Except for the fact she'd barely seen Matthew. She rubbed her arms, trying to will away the irritation she had no right to experience. She focused instead on the beauty around her.

Lights were strung along the paddleboat cruiser. Dinner tables were littered along one deck. The upper deck rang with swing-band dance music. A waiter strolled by with a silver platter resting on one palm, perfectly balancing the tray of champagne flutes.

Matthew stepped from the shadows, sipping his seltzer water. His eyes scanned down with obvious approval glinting and she winged a prayer of thanks to Ginger Landis Renshaw, her fairy godmother who'd been wise enough not to try to transform her into Cinderella. Instead, she'd simply helped Ashley fine-tune her own tastes in ways she never could have envisioned on her own.

She certainly wouldn't have thought to select a dress that left her shoulders bare. She'd always tried to cover the uneven tilt with layers—the more the better. But then Ginger had pulled out the simple cream dress stitched in gold with a plunging V-neck in the front and back. She'd dreamed of this sort of satiny fabric sliding over her skin. Ginger had added a lightweight gold shawl.

Matthew tipped back his water glass and drained the whole thing as if his throat was parched.

Ashley savored the moment and searched for small talk to keep him standing with her. "You're not drinking any of that top-notch champagne?"

"Seems like a recipe for disaster, mixing alcohol and reporters." He glanced at Ashley's drink.

She rattled her ice, saddened again that they knew so little about each other. "Seltzer water for me, too, but with a lime."

"My apologies for jumping to conclusions. Let me get you a refill to make up for ignoring you all evening."

"Thank you." Most of all for noticing that she'd been left to her own devices. That eased the sting.

She leaned back against the rail, studying the couples dancing up on the deck. The ocean wind carried snippets of conversations her way from partiers as well as people milling about and disembarking down the gangplank. She paid little attention until her ear snagged on a familiar voice, the campaign manager's brisk baritone.

"She did better than I expected."

"That's not saying much," another man responded, a voice she vaguely recognized from a telephone briefing she'd received earlier. "Your expectations weren't very high."

"Well, what can I say?" Brent answered. "She wasn't what I would have chosen for him on the campaign trail or as a senator's wife. She brings nothing to the table politically except that shy little smile. However, what's done is done. He will have to make the best of things. At least she won't outshine him."

Ouch. That one hurt more than a little. But then, eavesdroppers rarely heard good about themselves.

"I thought Ginger did a decent job with the makeover," the other man continued. "Not too flashy, not too schoolmarmish. The outfit is classy but Ashley doesn't look like someone playing dress up with her mother's clothes."

"Yeah, about that age thing. What the hell was Matthew thinking? She's only what, twenty-four? The pressure is going to demolish her."

Ashley had heard enough. She refused to stand

around like an insecure wimp, regardless of how much their words hurt, reminding her yet again how she was the wrong kind of woman for Matthew. At least she could make sure they never knew how deeply the barbs dug.

She stepped out of the shadows. "Twenty-*three,* thank you very much. I am twenty-three. You of all people should have your facts in order better than that. But thanks for the extra year of maturity vote of confidence to go along with my honors diploma in accounting from the College of Charleston."

"Ah, hell." Brent had the good grace to wince while music echoed on the sea breeze. "We didn't see you there. I'm sorry for speaking out of turn in a public setting."

"Apology accepted." There was no use in making an enemy of the man. She just didn't want his pity because it played on her already pervasive sense that she couldn't be the kind of woman Matthew needed. "Although I would warn you of a very good piece of advice I received at a briefing recently. Never, *never* speak a sound bite you wouldn't want repeated."

"Point well taken," the campaign manager agreed, hesitating only long enough to check for privacy. "But hear me on this. I've been around this business a long time, and you're not cut out for this. Most important, Martin Stewart is a wily opponent not to be taken lightly, and you're not helping Matthew."

Before Ashley could answer, Matthew rounded the corner with her drink in hand. "Here you are, Ashley. I thought I'd lost you to another reporter." He passed the glass to her. "Your sparkling water, complete with a twist of lime."

"Thank you." The tart taste fit right in with her souring mood.

Matthew's eyes narrowed. "Is everything all right here?"

Ashley stirred her drink with the thin straw, unwilling to risk causing any scene or rift between Matthew and his campaign manager.

She stabbed her straw through the ice. "Everything's fine. Why shouldn't it be? Your manager is just discussing ways I can be more helpful on the campaign trail."

Matthew slid an arm around her waist. "She doesn't have to do anything other than be herself."

Ashley appreciated him saying that, but she knew full well she hadn't offered anything substantive to his campaign beyond stopping rumors he was indiscriminately sleeping around.

Brent leaned back on the rail on both elbows. "I worry about the two of you."

"Just do your job." Matthew's voice took on that renowned Landis icy tone. "If you have anything more to say on this subject, we can take it up at headquarters later."

"You're the boss." Brent shoved away from the rail and walked away with his companion.

Matthew narrowed his eyes at the retreating man, then turned back to Ashley. "Did he say something to upset you?"

"Nothing. Really. Everything's fine."

Matthew brushed a thumb over her cheekbone, glancing around much like Brent when he'd checked to be sure no one could overhear. "You look tired. You've got dark circles under your eyes."

His words, too close to Brent's concerns, pissed her off when her emotions were already raw. She wasn't a weakling, damn it. "What a smooth talker you are."

"Beautiful—but tired. I realize campaigning can be a grind." He stepped away, taking her drink from her and placing it on a deck table alongside his. "We're leaving now."

"You can't go." She looked around at the people still dancing on the upper deck. "This is your party."

"I most certainly can punch out whenever I want. We've docked. Others are disembarking. I learned a while back if I stay till lights out at every function I'm on hand when the party turns wild, and that never goes well for a politician come picture time."

When he put it that way... She tucked her hand in the crook of his elbow. "Well, by all means, then, let's blow this pop stand before Mrs. Hamilton-Reis hangs her bra in place of the flag."

Chuckling, he shuddered. "Thanks for placing that image in my mind."

"Always happy to please."

His eyes narrowed. "You do please me, you know. Very much, Ashley Carson." He dipped his head and brushed his mouth along her ear. "I'm so very sorry I messed things up for the chance to please *you* again."

His words sent a thrill of excitement and power up her spine. Sure, Brent Davis's years of political wisdom attested to reasons she wasn't the wisest choice to stand by Matthew's side, but at least for tonight, she could have one more memory to tuck away.

And she intended to make the most of it.

* * *

Strolling along the private shoreline outside his home with Ashley, Matthew wondered if he'd pushed too hard too fast by saying something suggestive to Ashley on the boat. He wanted an affair with her, but he already sensed they wouldn't have much time. She would cut and run from his lifestyle soon enough, without a doubt.

But all the touching and kissing for the camera was playing hell with his libido. He'd suggested this bare-foot walk alone along the shore to cool them both down before they turned in for the night. A long night. Likely alone, because as much as he wanted her, she would have to set the pace this time.

Ashley kicked her way through the rolling surf, her gold shawl billowing behind her in the breeze. Creamy white fabric with its tantalizing glimmers of gold stitching molded to her chest the way he wanted to fit his palms against her curves.

Gathering the hem of her gown up to her knees, she shot ahead a couple of paces before spinning on her bare feet to face him, her loose hair streaking around her face. "What did you dress up as for Halloween as a kid?"

Her question blindsided him more than anything he'd heard from the most seasoned reporter. Of course that could also have something to do with his lust-fogged brain at the moment. "Excuse me? I'm accustomed to obscure questions from the press, but that one came way out of left field."

"Then I guess it's an excellent question." Her gentle laugh carried on the salty breeze as light as any me-ringue, simple, but damn fine. "It just struck me over the past couple of days that we really don't know that much about each other. Those holes in our knowledge could be a real pitfall in an interview. So? What about your childhood holidays?"

He thought back to all those pictures in his mother's countless family photo albums. "A cop. I trick-or-treated as a cop."

"And?"

Matthew shook his head, his shoes dangling from his fingers. Water slapped at the dock where the family speedboat bucked with each wave. "Always a policeman for Halloween. Drove my mom nuts. She really got into making us new costumes each year and I kept asking for the same one, just in a bigger size."

"If you wanted to be a police officer, what made you want to go into politics?"

"Who said I wanted to be a cop as an adult? Just because I dressed up like one as a kid doesn't mean..." He scratched his head. "Okay, never mind. Fair question. Politics is the family business. It's only natural I would follow this path."

"Your father was in the air force before becoming a senator." She scraped her hair back from her face. "And your brothers chose different paths."

"That they did." He thought back to their childhood years, putting on costumes in preparation for the day they would be able to play out their dreams for real. "We're looking for ways to serve our country."

"You could have done that on the police force."

"My father died."

She slowed to fall in pace alongside him. Not touching, just there. More present in the moment than most people who got right up in somebody's face. "That must have been an awful time for you."

"He didn't get to complete his term." There was something so damn sad about unfinished business—his father's term, his old fiancée's diploma never picked up.

An engagement never fulfilled with vows.

"Your mother served out his term, and very well I might add. Life has a way of working things out, even the bad things, given time."

"You're right." He needed to remember that more often and concentrate on his own reasons for taking on this office rather than doing it for anyone else. Interesting how Ashley focused him with a few words.

And hell, what was he doing selfishly spilling his guts when he was standing under the stars with a beautiful woman? She turned attention to others so artfully he wondered how many missed the chance to uncover fascinating things about her.

He tipped her chin. "What about you?"

"What about me what?"

"Your Halloween costumes." He walked alongside her, smiling down and trying to envision her as a kid, probably skinny with hair that weighed more than she did. And a heart bigger than all of that combined. "What did you pick, and I want a list."

"A pirate, a zebra, a hobo, a ninja, Cleopatra—the fake snake was tons of fun." She ticked off the years on her fingers. "A doctor, oh, and once I was a pack of French fries. Starr was a hot dog and Claire insisted she was a gourmet quiche, but we all knew it was a pecan pie with fake bacon bits sewn on."

"Wow, your foster mom organized that for all her kids?" Did Ashley realize she was walking closer to him?

Her arm skimmed his.

Her leg brushed his with every step.

Was she trying to seduce him, for God's sake?

"Aunt Libby had this huge box full of old costumes and clothes. She was constantly adding items to it throughout the year—picking up additions on clearance or from yard sales." She looked up at him, her brown eyes the perfect backdrop to reflect the stars overhead. "Actually, we didn't only use it for Halloween. We played dress up year round."

"I'd enjoy seeing pictures of that."

Her smile faded. "If they survived the fire."

He slid an arm around her shoulders and tucked her to his side, holding her closer when she didn't object. "Tell me more about the dress-up games."

"We made quite a theatrical troop with our play acting. We could be anything, say anything and leave the world behind once those costumes were in place. Looking back, I can see how she must have been using some play therapy for a group of wounded girls."

"She sounds like an amazing lady."

"She was. I miss her a lot." Ashley stared up at him with far-too-insightful starlit eyes. "The way you must miss your father."

He tried to clear his throat but the lump swelled to fist-size and wouldn't dislodge.

Ashley slipped her arm under his jacket and around his waist. "That's why you're in politics, then, to feel closer to him?"

Her touch seemed to deflate the lump and he found

himself able to push words free again. "That's why I started, yes, and then I found out along the way why it was so important to him. It's not about power. And sure, the chance to make a difference at a grassroots level is…mind-blowing. But there's more to it."

"And that would be?"

"Honestly, this has gotten to be such a dirty business, no sane person would even want to enter a race. Between the sound-bite-hungry press and cutthroat opponents, no one can possibly lead a life clean or perfect enough to undergo that level of scrutiny. There will be blood in the water at some point and sharks will circle."

"Okay, you're really depressing me here, so how about getting to the point soon."

He chuckled low, the crash of waves stealing the sand from under his feet. "Right. Gotta work on paring down my stump-speech skills. My point? I can't let fear keep me out of the race."

"Good people have to step up to the plate, too."

"Thanks." He gave her a one-armed hug.

"For what?"

"For calling me 'good people.'" And damned if that simple hug hadn't pressed her breast against his side, which had him thinking decidedly not-good-guy thoughts about seducing her right here. Right now. Behind the nearest sand dune.

She stopped, dropping her shoes onto the sand, then taking his and tossing them aside, as well. She clasped both of his hands in hers. "You've been worried about our engagement fib."

He stayed silent for three swooshes of the waves.

She squeezed his fingers. "Doing the wrong thing

for all the right reasons is tough to reconcile. I know. I've been wrestling with the same issue."

"What conclusion did you arrive at?"

"Good people are also fallible humans. Sometimes we deserve a break, even if it's only a temporary reprieve."

He skimmed his knuckles over the soft, clear, ivory skin of her face, over her chin, down her neck. She gazed up at him, her eyes so deep and darkening as her pupils expanded.

If he let himself, he could fall…right…in.

He kissed her. He had to. The past couple of days they'd been dancing around this moment and he knew the solid reasons why he should wait to pursue the attraction, give her time, romance her more. But here, tonight, under the stars, he wanted her, and he could feel that she wanted him, too, from the way she wriggled to get closer. He couldn't sense even the least bit of hesitation in her response.

Her breathy sigh into his mouth reminded him of other times she'd gasped out her pleasure. This usually shy woman certainly tossed away her inhibitions when it came to the sensual.

She gripped his lapels, her fists tugging tighter, pulling him closer as she pressed herself to him. Her lips parted, her tongue meeting his every bit as aggressively as he sought hers. She tasted of citrus from her lime water earlier, more potent than any alcohol. Her soft breasts molded temptingly against his chest and his hands itched to stroke her without the barrier of clothes or possible interruption.

As much as he ached to have her here, out in the open

with the sky and waves all around them, he knew that
wasn't practical. "We should take this inside before we
lose control."

"And before someone with a telephoto lens gets an
up close and personal of the total you."

"Not an image I want recorded for posterity."

Laughing, she clasped his hand and dashed toward
his white clapboard carriage house. She kept the hem of
her dress hitched in one fist, a mesmerizing dichotomy
in her formal gown and bare feet.

Matthew tugged at her hand. "Our shoes."

She smiled back at him, her eyes full of total desire.
"To hell with our shoes."

Staring back at her, he knew he wouldn't say no to
Ashley in full-tilt temptress mode. He just wished he
could be sure his conscience would fare better against
the harsh morning light than their shoes would against
the elements.

Chapter 8

Ashley gripped Matthew's hand as he led her past sprawling oak trees to his two-story carriage house. The quaint white home with gray-blue shutters gleamed like a beacon with the security lights strategically placed. Sand clung to her skin, rasping along her hyper-revved nerves as she raced by fragrant azaleas up the stone steps after him.

He swung the gray door wide and hauled her into the pitch-dark hallway. Before she could blink, he'd slammed the door closed and pressed her against the wood panel for a kiss that sent her blood crashing through her veins like out-of-control waves during a hurricane. His hands were planted on either side of her head as he seduced her with nothing more than his mouth on hers. The taste of lingering ocean spray mingled with the lemon from his water earlier. Her shawl shimmied down her arms to pool around her feet.

Her foot stroked along the back of his calf, her sandy feet rasping against the fine fabric of his trousers. She grasped at his back, stroking and gripping and stroking more, lower, urging him closer until his body sealed flush against hers. And oh, yes, she could feel how much he wanted her, too. She rocked against the hard length of him, searching, aching for release.

Matthew tore his mouth from hers and nipped along her jaw until he reached her ear where he buried his face in her hair, his five-o'clock shadow gently abrading her skin. Her eyes adjusting to the dark, she could see the straining tendons in his neck. His breath flamed over her in hot bursts.

"Ashley, we need to slow this down a notch if I'm going to make it to the bedroom, or at least to the sofa."

She didn't want to stop, even for the short stretch of hardwood it would take to reach the leather couch a few feet away in the moonlit living room. "Why move, then? As long as you've got protection in your pocket, I'm more than happy with right here, right now."

His low growl of approval sent a shiver of excitement up her spine.

He tugged his wallet free. "I've been carrying protection since that first night with you. I knew full well the chemistry between us could combust again without warning."

Matthew plucked out a condom and pitched his wallet over his shoulder. The thud of leather against wood snapped what little restraint she had left.

In a flurry of motion she barely registered since he'd started kissing her again, she grappled with his belt while he bunched the hem of her clingy cream dress in his fists, higher, higher still until he reached her waist. With one impatient hand he gripped the thin scrap of her satin panties—and how she delighted in the fact that when she'd shopped for underwear, she hadn't selected so much as a single piece of practical cotton.

She managed to open his fly and encircle him with a languorous glide of her fingers along his hot, hard arousal. His jaw flexed. His grip twisted on her panties until they...snapped.

Cool air swooshed along her overheated flesh in an excruciating contrast. "Now," she gasped against his mouth. "To hell with foreplay."

"If you insist," he groaned between gritted teeth.

She couldn't resist watching every intimate detail as he rolled the sheath into place. Matthew hitched an arm under her bottom and lifted her against the door until the heat of him nudged perfectly between her legs. Inch by delicious inch, he lowered her as he filled her. She hooked her legs around his waist and pressed him the rest of the way home.

Tremors began quaking through her before he even moved and she realized their every touch in the days prior had been foreplay leading to this. He eased away. Then thrust into her with a thick abandon that sent her over the edge without warning.

Her head flung back against the door as she cried out with each wave cresting through her. Her heels dug deeper into his buttocks. Matthew moved faster, taking the waves higher. His shout of completion spurred a final wash of pleasure, and her body went limp.

They stood locked together silently for... Well, she wasn't sure how long. Then he released her and her feet slid to the floor. She started to sag, her muscles too weak with satisfaction to hold her, and he scooped her into his arms.

"I've got you, Ashley. Just relax."

She hummed her approval against his chest. She would figure out how to talk again later.

On his way through the small foyer, he paused for her to flick one of the light switches, bathing the room in a low glow. As he strode into the living room, she lounged sated against his chest and took a moment to learn more about Matthew from his surroundings. Deep burgundy leather chairs and a sofa filled the airy room, angled for a perfect view of both the ocean and the wide-screen television. Striped wool hooked rugs scattered along tile into an open-area dining room and high-tech kitchen.

And dead center across the room—a narrow hallway that undoubtedly led to the bedrooms.

He stopped beside the sofa. "Do you want to stay here or head back there?"

"There, please." She wanted to learn more about him beyond his political standings, affinity for leather furniture and childhood love of cop costumes.

"Lucky for me, that's exactly where I want to be, too. Actually, anywhere you are without your clothes sounds perfect to me."

Even as she told herself to savor the sensations of the here and now, she couldn't help fearing the out-of-control waves of emotion Matthew stirred could drown her in the end. If so, tonight would be all she could afford to risk.

This could all be simpler than he'd predicted.

Matthew carried Ashley back toward his bedroom, wondering if he'd overthought this whole situation. They got along well and the chemistry hadn't been a one-time fluke. Why not ride the wave? Friendship with rocking hot sex could be an awesome, uncomplicated alternative to spending the rest of their lives alone or locked in some relationship where emotions ruled their lives to the exclusion of all else.

He grazed a quick kiss along her passion-swollen lips before easing her onto his bed. Yeah, he liked the look of her there. And he would enjoy it even more once he peeled her clothes from her sweet body.

Apparently Ashley had the same idea, because she arched up from the bed to kiss him with an ardent intent that made it clear she was ready for round two. He draped his jacket over the chair without ever breaking contact with her mouth. She tugged his tie with frantic fingers, loosening until finally the length slid free from his collar. She flicked the silk over her shoulder and set to work on the buttons down the front of his shirt until she glided her cool finger inside along his bare skin.

Matthew kissed aside one shoulder strap of her dress. With the dress's built-in bra and her panties out on the foyer floor, she was perilously close to total exposure.

He smiled in anticipation against her flowery scented skin. "At least we're going to make it to a bed this time."

She shoved his pants down and away. He kicked them to the side. "I liked the hall."

"Me, too." He liked *her* anywhere. "But this time we're going to take it slower."

Matthew brushed away and down both straps of her gown, guiding it over her breasts, teasing along her hips until it slithered to her feet. He couldn't resist stilling for a moment to take her in. It seemed like longer than a handful of days since he'd had the pleasure of seeing her naked.

He remembered her being hot. He'd dreamed of her sexiness. But he'd forgotten or hadn't taken the time to notice some of the more intimate details of her body—such as the enticing mole on her hip that he now traced with his thumb to better imprint it in his memory. Countless other nuances of Ashley burned themselves into his brain.

Then she flattened her hand to his chest and brought a close to his ability to think. Time to feel. To touch. He traced her collarbone with his tongue, working kisses and nips lower to her tempting curves until his mouth closed over the peak of one breast, drawing it tighter, then shifting his attention to the other equally sweet swell, in need of more, more of her, sooner than he'd expected after their mind-blowing encounter in the hall. She arched against him and then they were both tumbling onto the bed.

She slid her hands down his back and cupped his taut buttocks, digging in her fingers, urging him closer. "Now, Matthew."

He clasped her wrists and gently eased them to the side. "Slower this time, remember?"

"Forget about slower. We have all flipping night for slower." She wriggled temptingly under him.

He trailed kisses between her breasts, shifting his hold on her wrists to link fingers with her. He nipped along her rib cage, working his way south.

He blew air against her stomach, lower, lower still until she gasped.

"Matthew?"

"FTW," he mumbled against her.

"What?"

He glanced up the length of her creamy white body and grinned. "FTW. For the win, lady. I'm going for the win."

Ashley swept her hand through the frothy hot tub waters, reclining back into the warmth of Matthew's naked strength serving as the perfect "arm chair." His Jacuzzi was built into the bathroom with a skylight overhead, which offered the aura of being outside without the loss of privacy.

After making love again in his bedroom, he'd shown her the oversize bathroom that had been an add-on to the carriage house. Just as she'd sunk into the full tub, he'd returned with champagne and strawberries—and joined her. The added bulk of his body eased the water just over the tips of her breasts, the gentle swoosh a warm temptation.

As much as she wanted to relax into the moment, sipping her drink, enjoying the burst of fruit on her taste buds as Matthew fed her, her stomach kept tightening with nerves. Things with Matthew were getting more complicated by the second.

Damn it, she should be happy. She'd fantasized over what it would be like with this man. He wasn't hotfooting toward the door like after their first night together. So why did his ring suddenly feel so utterly heavy on her finger?

Matthew's hands landed on her shoulders and he began a soothing massage. "I'm sorry you're so tense.

I hate to think this campaign put those kinks in your muscles."

"I'm managing." She sipped from the fluted crystal, the fine vintage tickling her nose as surely as the bristly hair on Matthew's chest teased her back.

"You're more than managing." He rested his chin on her head while continuing to knead her kinked muscles. "But you don't care for the spotlight?"

Just what she needed, reminders of Brent Davis's concerns that she could actually hurt Matthew's chances of beating that Martin Stewart. She stayed silent, finishing her drink and splaying her fingers through the rose-scented bubbles.

Steam saturated her senses. The mirror may have fogged a while ago, but she still carried in her memory the reflected image of the two of them together in the gray-and-white marble tub.

His firm caress continued its seductive magic. "Not much longer and hopefully things will settle out."

She couldn't imagine how. Every scenario that played out in her mind—continuing this charade or walking away—spelled frustration.

Perhaps her best solution would be to avoid the whole subject altogether tonight and focus on the sensations of the here and now. "That feels amazing."

His thumbs worked their way up her neck. "This Jacuzzi has eased a lot of tense muscles after working out with my brothers."

"I was talking about your hands, but yeah, the hot tub is awesome, too."

He circled the pressure points along her jaw. "I'm glad to hear you like my touch."

"Very much." Too much. This had been easier when he'd been the unattainable fantasy of a woman convinced he would never look twice at her.

She tapped her left shoulder, the one still slightly raised and blurted, "I had scoliosis as a girl."

His massaging fingers tensed for a second, an understated indication he had heard her.

"I'm lucky Aunt Libby aggressively addressed the problem with my spine early." She knew that now, although she'd hated the brace as a child. "For the most part it doesn't affect the way I live anymore. Although I shy away from higher heels, and standing for too long without moving can give me a headache."

"Well, as I understand it, megahigh heels aren't good for anybody's back, and standing still for an hour is highly overrated."

His easy acceptance of the subject released more tension inside her than the massaging tub jets ever could. "No way did I just hear what I thought I heard."

"What did I say?"

"A man actually dissed high heels for women?" She glanced over her shoulder and crinkled her nose at him. "No freaking way. I thought the whole male species stopped for a woman's legs extended by spike heels."

He cocked one eyebrow at her. "How un-PC of you. You make us sound very shallow."

"You said it. Not me."

"Ouch. Low blow, but well played. Perhaps you should stand in for me during the debates." He slipped his arms around her, just below her breasts. "Certainly everybody has physical traits that they're attracted to."

"Like legs?"

His hands slid up to cup her, his thumbs brushing against her nipples. "Or breasts." His head dipped to her ear. "Or the soft feel of your skin." He nuzzled her neck. "And there's your amazing hair."

"You're quite a smooth talker."

"I'm only being honest." His hands stilled again, clasped over her stomach. "Why do you have such trouble accepting compliments?"

He'd been so understanding about the subject thus far, she allowed herself the risk of sharing more about the other hurts, the emotional kind, that the birth defect had brought her over the years. "Leftover issues from the scoliosis, I imagine."

"You're blessedly healthy." His eyes blazed with an unmistakable intensity and reminder of how much worse things could have been.

"Yes, and I'm grateful for the amazing doctors who helped me over the years." She hesitated. "But you didn't see me before. Achieving this posture wasn't easy. Some people—my biological parents—didn't want the financial and time-consuming strain I brought."

Matthew's muscles turned to Sheetrock against her back. She looked over her shoulder to find his eyes were equally as hard.

"They didn't deserve you." His words were gentle, but his body was still rigid.

With indignation. Fury, even. She read it all there in his eyes so gemstone sharp they could cut. He was angry *for her.* People had been sympathetic, helpful, but she couldn't recall anyone being flat-out mad for that ill-treated little girl she'd been.

Matthew touched her soul and wiped away years of pain. "Thank you."

"No need to thank me, I'm just stating a fact." He held her gaze. "And while I'm on the subject, you're undoubtedly a tough lady."

That felt good to hear as well, especially after Brent's scathing assessment of her character.

"I had to be. Children can be cruel to a kid who doesn't look like the rest of them." Even adults—her biological parents—could be horribly unaccepting of their daughter's twisted gait.

Matthew was right. They hadn't deserved her. How mind-blowing that she'd never before considered that they simply weren't cut out for parenthood.

Muscles she hadn't even realized were still tensed eased at the new level of understanding. She'd talked about this with Aunt Libby and her sisters often over the years. Interesting—and a bit scary—that it had taken just one conversation with this man to help her see things with a different perspective.

Matthew skimmed a knuckle down her spine. "You wore a brace all the time?"

"Until college, then I only had to wear it at night." She cast another quick glance over her shoulder. "That's why I'm so addicted to silky fabrics now. They feel all the more fabulous on my skin."

"You're obviously a sensualist." His hands glided back around her with a touch as light as any fabric.

"I'm an accountant."

"So? People who like numbers can't like sensations and even adventurous sex?"

"When you put it that way…" And touched her that way…

"You're perfect the way you are." His thumbs grazed the undersides of her breasts while he dipped his head to tease along her collarbone. "All of that in the past made you into the sexy, smart woman you are today."

His arousal throbbed an agreement against the base of her spine. She slid her hands under the churning water to caress his powerful legs, wriggling in his lap, her pulse already pounding in her ears as loudly as the blasts of water through the Jacuzzi jets.

He cupped her waist and lifted her slightly, urging her to turn around until she knelt, her damp legs on either side of his. She leaned forward until the core of her pressed to the hard and ready length of him. Her breasts teased his chest as she leaned forward to capture a kiss.

Tonight wasn't over yet, and she was determined to make the most of it.

She arched up until the heat of him nestled against her, then she slid down, slowly taking him inside her, tantalizingly so, torturously so. "FTW, Matthew. For the win."

Chapter 9

"FTW, brother."

His brother's ill-chosen words echoing in his ears, Matthew choked midway through his golf swing and shanked the ball into a water hazard near the clubhouse. Wading birds swooped upward and out of the way.

Matthew scowled over his shoulder at his middle brother who knew the no-speaking rule. "Thanks, Sebastian."

He'd been looking forward to this afternoon of golf with his brothers, even if the event also happened to be a benefit tournament. However, if he kept playing like this, the foursome on the fairway behind them would have to stop for lunch before they could move ahead.

"No problem, bro. Always happy to cheer you on." Their lawyer sibling did have impeccable timing. "Nice slice, by the way."

The other two Landis brothers stood by the golf cart applauding with grins as smug as the one on the gator's face as the reptile slid through the salt marsh. Nope, not gonna wade in after that ball. He would take the drop for a penalty stroke.

Matthew pointed his titanium driver at the youngest, Jonah, first and then at Kyle, the next to oldest. "Your turns are coming up soon enough, and I feel a coughing fit coming on."

They'd all grown up competing with each other, and nothing had changed now. He couldn't fault them for it, and of course Sebastian had no way of knowing just what a kick in the gut his FTW would apply. He and Ashley had both won in a major way throughout the night.

Matthew reached into the tiny trash can on the side of his cart and scooped out a handful of the grass seed mixed with sand. He leaned down to pack it into the divot he'd chunked out of the course when his swing had gone awry.

Thoughts of Ashley tended to send his brain off-kilter in much the same manner. He leaned on his club, images of her facing him in the hot tub threatening what little concentration he had left. They hadn't gotten much sleep, but he wouldn't change a minute of their night together.

He glanced at his watch, wondering how much longer until she would finish her meeting with her sisters to review insurance paperwork. Claire and Starr had driven down from Charleston to spend the day with her, which left him free to attend this benefit golf tournament *and* hang with his brothers. They were just finishing up the ninth hole, so he would be home before supper.

Sebastian clapped him on the back with a solid thud, the two of them the closest in height and build. "Are we going to play or are you going to laze around for the rest of the afternoon staring at your watch?"

The sun beat down unrelentingly on his head. Matthew shrugged his shoulders under his golf shirt, flexed his hand inside the leather glove, but still tension kinked through him. "Just gauging the course."

Jonah chuckled low, his attention only half with them as he watched some college-age girl in a designer sun visor driving the course's drink cart around. "Yeah, right. We saw you say goodbye to your fiancée earlier," he said, no doubt referring to the kiss still scorching Matthew's veins. "What's up with her, dude? Why didn't you bring her by before? You wouldn't let us get away with that."

He hated lying to his family, but… Now he had this notion of letting things keep going as they were with Ashley. See where it led.

Keep enjoying what they did have.

Sebastian elbowed Jonah and pointed to the cluster of reporters gathering around the ocean-side clubhouse in the distance. "Shut your trap. There's media everywhere."

Jonah pulled his gaze off the bleached blond coed in the drink cart with obvious reluctance and checked out the press gathering. "Yeah, right." He shoved a hand through his unruly curls in need of a haircut. "Gotta keep up the good family name."

Kyle swished through practice swings with lanky grace. The workout fiend was always in motion, keeping in shape for his military career. "Damn, bro, thanks to you we can't do anything together anymore without it turning into a photo op."

Matthew dropped a new ball on the ground. "I figured leaking this outing of ours would take some heat off Ashley for the day."

Kyle shaded his eyes against the harsh summer sun as he peered off in the direction of the press. "Giving them something else to talk about?"

"Pretty much." He swung.... Watched... The ball landed on the green. "It's not like we haven't been dealing with this kind of coverage for most of our lives. I figured you could handle the heat."

Matthew climbed into his golf cart, Sebastian settling in beside him while their other brothers drove along behind. He guided the vehicle past rolling dunes with sea oats blowing in the muggy breeze.

Sebastian reached for his soda can in the holder as their clubs rattled in back. "So this woman's really gotten to you, then."

"I'm engaged to her." That in and of itself was a step he'd never expected to take again.

"Ah, come on. Be real around me, at least."

"Who says I'm not being real?" There had been more than a few moments with Ashley where he'd forgotten they were playing roles.

"You're actually going to marry her?" His brother peered over his Armani sunglasses.

"I didn't say that." Yeah, he was quibbling, but this wasn't a conversation he was comfortable with. Not after a night that had jumbled all his carefully made plans. "I simply said we're engaged. She's a special, honest person who doesn't deserve how things went down."

"Bro, you are so toast." Sebastian shook his head,

humor fading from his face as he replaced his drink in the holder. "Just be careful. Don't rush into anything until you're certain."

Hell. He should have seen where this was going given Sebastian's recent separation from his wife. They'd married too young, grown in different directions, and it was tearing them both apart. Now that Matthew looked closer, he could see that his brother had lost weight in recent months, his angular face almost gaunt. He'd gone so long without a haircut, he would soon be sporting Jonah's length.

And he still wore his platinum wedding band.

Sebastian served as a great big reminder for how badly two well-meaning people could hurt each other in the end. Matthew hated that he couldn't do a damn thing to make this right for his younger brother.

He clapped his hand against Sebastian's shoulder. "I hear you and I'm sorry for the hell you're going through."

"I hear you, too, and I'm not trying to interfere, only adding my two cents from the hard-knocks side of the romance world."

Matthew gripped the steering wheel as they whirred past a pelican perched on a wood pole. Damn it all, he'd been so caught up in his campaigning, he hadn't been there for his brother the way that he should have during what was undoubtedly the most painful time of his life. And how was that for a kick-in-the ass wake-up call about ill-advised marriages born of out-of-control emotions? "How much longer until the divorce is final?"

"This fall," Sebastian answered, his voice flat.

"A lot could happen between now and then." Look how quickly his life had been turned upside down.

"Too much already happened between now and then. We both simply want to move on without sacrificing any more blood in the process."

"I'm sorry, damn sorry. I really hoped you two could beat the odds."

"Me, too, bro. Me, too." Sebastian nudged his sunglasses firmly in place and looked away.

Message received loud and clear. Back off.

Silence stretched between them, broken only by the ever-present rustling of creatures in the underbrush that remained after the golf course had been hewn out of the wild area.

Finally, Sebastian's face spread into a smile, a little forced, but obviously where he wanted the tone to go. "Enough of this heart-and-guts bull. Let's get back to the game and I'll show you who's going to blow the odds to hell and back."

Matthew stopped the cart and retrieved a club from his leather bag in back. "I'm starting to think Mom has it right."

Kyle loped alongside them. "What do you mean?"

"The way she picked a friend to marry the second go-round rather than signing on for all that roller-coaster emotional crap. Maybe we should all learn the lesson from her."

Jonah stopped short, a hank of curls falling over his forehead. "Are you flipping blind? Mom's absolutely crazy about the general."

"Yeah, yeah." Matthew waved aside his youngest brother's comment. "I know they're—God forgive me for saying this—hot for each other. Remember, I was there with you guys when we accidentally walked in on them in bed together."

Matthew shuddered right along with his brothers. What a day that had been catching their sainted mother *in flagrante delicto* with her longtime friend turned lover, a man she had since married.

Even their playboy brother, Jonah, looked rattled by just the mention of that brain stunner of an event. "I really would have preferred to go through life believing we were all four immaculately conceived."

Sebastian made a referee T with his hands. "Okay, let's not go there again, even in our minds. But I think Jonah has a point," he continued in his naturally lawyerly logical tone. "Mom isn't just attracted to him, she really loves the general."

Matthew forced his ever-racing brain to slow and think back to his mom's Christmas wedding to Hank Renshaw. Sure, the event had been romantically impulsive, but could there have been something more in his mother's eyes then? And now, as well? He thought of all the times her face lit up when her cell phone rang with the distinctive ringtone she'd programmed for only the general's calls.

Aside from successful, high-power political careers, his mom and her new husband shared a lot of views in common and didn't hesitate to take an hour from their busy schedules to sit on the porch swing and talk over glasses of wine.

Now that he looked at it from more of an analytical perspective, it seemed obvious. His mother and General Hank Renshaw were totally in love with each other.

How could he have been so self-delusional? Because he'd wanted reality to fit his need for low-key commitment—while still holding on to Ashley. Problem was, now he didn't have a solution to the mess he'd made of his and Ashley's lives. Although he did know one thing for certain.

No way in hell could he live without a repeat of what they'd shared the night before.

Back in the main house, Ashley stared out the guest-bedroom window over the ocean, not too different a view than the one she'd grown up with at Aunt Libby's. Lordy, but she'd never needed the woman's support more than now when she faced the toughest decision of her life.

Even the ocean view and the soothing decor of the guest room's delft-blue flowers accented with airy stripes did little to lower her stress level. Spending the afternoon with her foster sisters crunching the numbers and detailing the massive amount of work required to get Beachcombers up and running as a business again had been tougher than she'd expected. Once she rebuilt the place, it would be time to move on with her life— apart from Matthew. Even the thought of that hurt more than she'd expected.

However, continuing with this charade hurt, too. How long could she keep falling into bed—and tubs— with him without making a decision about their future one way or another?

Fantasizing about the man had been easy. Being with him was far more complicated and exciting. And scary.

Why couldn't he have been a regular, everyday kind of guy, with a regular, everyday sort of life?

She stared down at her engagement ring and practiced pulling it off her finger. Her hand felt so blasted bare. She clenched her fist to resist the urge to put the solitaire back in place and to hell with the consequences to her heart.

Ashley held the diamond up for the sun to glint off the facets. So many angles and nuances could be seen depending on which way she looked at the stone. And wasn't that much like her life? She had an important choice to make and her decision changed depending on which way she viewed the situation.

The air conditioner cranked on, swooshing a teasing gust over her neck almost as tantalizing as a lover's kiss. Then stronger, warmer.

She shivered, reflexively closing her fingers around the ring.

Matthew's lips pressed firmer against her skin. "Hello, beautiful."

She tried to force herself to relax as she turned in his arms. "I didn't hear you come in."

He skimmed his knuckles over her forehead. "You were certainly caught up thinking about something important. Did things go all right with your sisters?"

She blinked quickly as she shifted mental gears. God, she hadn't even been thinking about Beachcombers, which should totally have been her focus. "Everything went fine. There are lots of positives to focus on. The fire investigators tracked the problem to old wiring failing. Nothing we're liable for, so our insurance payment will come through smoothly. We can start contacting contractors right away."

He pressed a firm kiss to her mouth before hugging her. "That's great to hear. I'm glad for all three of you."

With his heartbeat under her ear and his musky scent all around her, the queen-size bed only five feet away seemed too enticing. "Let's go out to the living room. I know we're adults and all, but it doesn't seem right for your mother to find us in here together."

He winced. "Banish that thought here and now." Matthew backed up a step but stroked her arms. "Don't worry, though. She just left, so you can relax."

"I can't do that." The ring seemed to gain weight in her grasp. "Relax, I mean."

He looked behind him and back again. "Are your sisters still here somewhere?"

"They left a half hour ago." She gathered up her words and let them roll free before she could stop herself. She unfurled her fingers, the engagement ring cupped in her palm. "Actually, I can't do this anymore."

Any hint of a smile faded from his face. "Do what, precisely?"

Ashley raised her hand holding the solitaire, her hand already shaking at the thought of giving it back. Aside from her own reservations, she couldn't ignore fears of the opponent gaining momentum from her decision.

She would do her best to persuade Starr to step forward. Perhaps that would even encourage others who might have received the same treatment to open up.

Regardless, she couldn't be party to perpetuating a lie, even as much as breaking things off with Matthew tore her apart inside. "Pretend to be engaged. Lying to the press has been difficult enough. Lying to my *sisters* this afternoon was hell. They probably already suspect anyway."

"Well, as a matter of fact—" he clasped both of her hands in his "—I was thinking about that myself while golfing with my brothers."

Her stomach twisted. So this was it. They would break things off and she would be back in Charleston with real memories to replace the fantasies. Except reality had been so much more amazing than any make-believe. "And your thoughts led you to what conclusion?"

His grip tightened on her arms. "What do you say we give it a try for real? No more pretending."

She couldn't have heard what she thought. Her stomach clenched tighter than his hold on her. "I think you're going to need to repeat that because I'm certain I couldn't have heard you correctly."

He lifted her left hand and thumbed the bare spot. "Let's keep the ring in place and get to know each other better, hang out—"

"Have sex?"

"I sure as hell hope so."

Matthew's resurrected grin left her in no doubt of how much he wanted her. Except she needed more than that now. She deserved more. "While you were golfing with your brothers, you decided we need to hang out more and have sex?"

"I'm not expressing myself well, which is damned odd considering I'm used to crafting the right sound bite—which should tell you something about how you screw with my head." His smile went from charming to wicked in a flash of perfect teeth. "How about I try this again. Let's get to know each other better, build a, uh…" He gestured for the word, his gaze scanning the boat-speckled horizon as if answers bobbed on the gleaming waters.

"Relationship. The word is *relationship,* Matthew." It was tough for her to consider, too, but at least she could say the word without becoming tongue-tied.

"Yeah, right. That." He skimmed a finger along his collar, which would have been understandable if he hadn't been wearing a freaking polo shirt with the top two buttons undone.

"Sounds to me like you're describing sex buddies. and sex buddies don't exchange rings." How odd that a few weeks ago, sex buddies would have actually sounded like a fun fantasy come true. Except now this ring screwed up everything because it taunted her with the deeper sentiments that she wanted—deserved— from life someday.

"What do you expect from me?" Matthew stared down at her, frustration sparking in his gem-green eyes. "Do you want me to say I love you? I've been in love before and it takes a while. I haven't known you long enough to be sure about something like that. But I can say that I think I could love you someday. So why break things off when there's that possibility out there?"

Could love her *someday?* Talk about a rousing endorsement.

Then her mind hitched on one phrase to the exclusion of everything else he'd said. "You've been in love before?"

He went stone-still.

"Matthew? Who was it?" She couldn't resist asking, too darn curious about the woman who had managed to steal his heart. "The press has linked you to plenty of women over the years and certainly speculated about more than a few of them recently, but nothing serious ever seemed to come of those liaisons. I think that's part of the reason they've gone so snap happy over our fake engagement."

"You're probably correct," he conceded, although still neatly dodging her question.

Her curiosity only heightened. She wasn't sure why it should matter so much when she was determined to break things off. She should be running for the door before her will faltered.

Still, she had to ask. "Then who is the woman? I think even my pretend-fiancée status gives me the right to ask."

He started to reach for his collar again before dropping his arm to his side as he stepped around her to peer out the window. "Someone I knew in college—Dana." He stuffed his fists into his pockets, his jaw hard. "Dana and I became engaged unexpectedly fast and before I could introduce her to the family, she died."

Her heart squeezed inside her chest with sympathy, and an impending sense of how he'd never been hers from the beginning.

"I'm so sorry." She tentatively touched his shoulder, unable to resist offering comfort for those long-ago hurts. She knew well from her parents' abandonment how long those emotional aches could persist. "It must have been horrible to lose her."

"It was," he said simply, but the two words carried

more pain than any lengthy monologue could have. His muscles tensed under her touch.

"What happened?" she asked gently.

"She—Dana—had a heart defect, something rare that had gone undetected." He scrubbed his hand over his face, his jaw flexing. Pain pulsed from him as palpably as if he'd shouted the words.

"You really loved Dana." Part of her ached to comfort him. Another part, a new, stronger piece of herself, asserted she deserved that same intense love. She couldn't accept being a second-best sex buddy.

Ashley stepped away from Matthew. She carefully placed her fairy-tale diamond and all the precious multi-faceted dreams it had held onto the bedside table. "I'm sorry, Matthew, this is just how it has to end—"

The phone jangled by her engagement ring, jolting her back a step.

Matthew hesitated, his eyes holding hers while the ringing continued. She waved him toward the call. She should call her sisters for a ride. They shouldn't be too far away since they'd dropped her off less than an hour ago.

His eyes still narrowed and locked on her, he crossed to pick up the receiver. "Landis residence."

She started to reach for her cell when something fierce in Matthew's expression as he took the call made her hesitate.

No more than four thudding heartbeats later, he scowled and reached for the television remote resting beside the lamp. "Right, got it, Brent. I'm tuning in now."

He thumbed the remote, activating the flat-screen

television mounted on the wall. What could the press have come up with on them this time? Pictures of them would be embarrassing but useless. Still she could see from Matthew's frown this wasn't happy news.

The TV screen blazed to life with a newsflash that was already in progress. A photo-inset box appeared in the upper right-hand corner behind the newscaster's head, complete with a picture of Matthew at the golf course…

With his arm around a blond hottie plastered to his side.

Chapter 10

"So do we shoot him outright or do we torture him first?" Her expression fierce, Starr leaned her elbows on her restaurant table across from Ashley and Claire.

Ashley tried to shake free the numb sensation still dogging her even two hours after the call from Matthew's campaign manager. There had barely been time for Matthew to turn to Ashley and state, "The photos aren't what you think," before his family had begun pouring into the house for a troubleshooting session.

Sure, he'd had an explanation about the water girl at the golf course throwing herself at him, which left him instinctively steadying her at an inopportune time since the press packed the parking lot. His brothers affirmed he didn't know her—although unlucky for Matthew, his brothers had been in search of food at that particular moment.

He'd been so busy trying to convince her, yet the whole water-girl incident felt like nothing to her in comparison to his revelation about Dana. Ashley believed there was nothing to those golf course photos.

Her problem boiled down to trust on a larger scale. The need to trust he could ever have deep feelings for another woman again. The belief that he could someday fall for *her*.

Her sisters had called almost immediately and turned around to come back to Hilton Head. Claire had told her—in a tone that brooked no argument—that they were on their way. Ashley had been more than grateful for the opportunity to escape the mayhem of campaign central working damage control.

Which was how she ended up in a dark back corner of an out-of-the-way seafood restaurant, wearing sunglasses and a ball cap.

Ashley scratched under the hat. She didn't want her life "spun" anymore.

Starr dragged the bread basket over from the middle of the table, the pregnant woman's appetite apparently insatiable. "So? Quick death or torture?"

Claire unfolded and refolded her napkin precisely. "To think, the press missed the real story when they actually bought into that engagement story hook, line and sinker."

Ashley snatched the perfectly creased napkin from her sister's hands. "Who says it isn't real? I never gave you any indication otherwise."

"Oh, come on, we know you." Claire patted Ashley's hand, still bare of the engagement ring. "You're too much like me. You wouldn't get engaged to someone you didn't know well."

"You've never done anything impulsive in the romance department?" She waited to see how her sister would dodge that question, since they all knew Claire had gotten pregnant in a one-night stand with a friend who was now her head-over-heels-in-love husband and father to their beautiful baby girl.

Claire raised a perfectly arched blond eyebrow. "Somebody's not playing nice today." She reached to the empty table next to them and snagged a new napkin. "But you're forgiven because of the stress."

Ashley struggled to shrug off the defensiveness. These were her sisters. She couldn't lie to them anymore. Perhaps it was time she also stopped lying to herself.

She rubbed the bare spot where the engagement ring had rested. "It doesn't matter now anyway. Matthew and I are over."

Or rather, Matthew had been trying to bring up the possibility of staying together and she'd cut him off short.

Claire studied her with a gentle concern reminiscent of Aunt Libby's maternal care. "Is this about the suggestive photos?"

"The ones of me and him, or the ones of her and him?" Ashley crinkled her nose. "The one of him at the golf course actually doesn't worry me beyond what damage it could do to his campaign. I'm certain the picture was a setup."

And oddly enough, she was sure. She trusted him with physical faithfulness. Totally. He'd never been anything but honest with her, even when it hurt. She'd heard clearly enough in his voice how much he'd loved that woman from long ago, a real romance that concerned her far more than any manufactured one on the evening news.

Starr sagged back in her seat, tearing into another piece of bread while the other guests and televisions buzzed loudly enough to afford them privacy to talk. "I guess this means we don't get to enjoy torturing your hunky senatorial candidate."

Ashley allowed herself a half smile. "I would appreciate it if you took a pass on that this go-round."

Claire patted her hand, her nail tapping the spot where the ring used to nestle waiting for a wedding band to complete the set. "Now your schedule is free and clear again."

Ashley tugged the sunglasses off. To hell with anonymity. She wanted to see life clearly now more than ever. "Don't worry, I will uphold my end of the obligations with reopening Beachcombers."

Claire and Starr exchanged a loaded look before Claire tugged a folder from her overlarge purse. "We were actually getting ready to turn around and come back when the news story broke."

"Turn around? Why?" When they still hesitated so long a waitress managed to work her way past with a steaming platter of crab legs, Ashley pressed harder, "Please, don't hold anything back. I've been up front with you and I'm going to be hurt if you aren't equally open with me."

Claire twisted her napkin in a totally un-Claire disregard for order, which relayed just how nervous she must be. "We weren't lying about anything earlier. We simply omitted some thoughts we've been having about the whole rebuilding process."

Starr shoved away the now nearly empty bread basket. "What do you plan to do with your future, after the election—if you and Matthew don't stay together?"

"I imagined we'll be busy renovating Beachcombers." The possibility of taking him up on his offer still felt so alien she hadn't thought that far ahead. She needed to get her head together and in the present. She looked from sister to sister. "What are you both keeping from me? Was there something wrong with the insurance adjustment after all?"

"No, nothing like that," Claire rushed to reassure her.

Ashley relaxed back in her chair. "Okay, then. I appreciate all the times you helped me and protected me and built me up over the years." She injected strength in her words to match the steel in her spine. "But I'm not that shy, insecure little kid anymore. Could you please stop treating me like a child and welcome me into your grown-ups club?"

Starr covered Ashley's hand with hers. "We love you. It's hard not to worry."

"Thank you." She squeezed Starr's hand and reached for Claire's, as well. "I love you both, too. So tell me. What's with all the secret looks? Come on, Claire. Spill it."

"We're just wondering if we should look into options other than reopening Beachcombers."

Claire's words hovered over the table between them, heavy and unexpected.

Ashley finally got her brain off stun long enough to speak. "You mean level Aunt Libby's house?"

"No, not that." Starr waved aside that possibility, thank God. "We could use the insurance money to restore the place to its former glory. Then sell it. Let a family live and grow and flourish there."

Claire angled forward. "We could split the proceeds three ways and it will still give us each the chance to pursue any career dreams we want. I can open my own catering business with more flexible hours for the baby."

Ashley turned to Starr. "And you feel the same way about this?"

"Yes, sweetie. I do. I've always wanted to go back to art school and study abroad. Sure, my husband can afford it, but I appreciate the chance to finance it myself. You have your degree and this would give you a nice financial cushion. But we don't want you to feel like you don't have a home."

Their plan made sense. They both had husbands, homes, children and unique career dreams of their own. And she had...

A wonderfully unconventional family who loved her and a quirky old lady who'd taught her to value herself. None of that would change because of owning or selling a particular house.

Ashley squeezed her sisters' hands. "We have a bond, the three of us, that goes beyond any house. The memories Aunt Libby gave us are a far stronger link than any home could ever be. And I think she would like the notion of a family being brought up in her home."

Across the restaurant, one of the patrons reached to turn up the volume on one of the televisions. Starr's eyes widening gave her the first hint that she'd better check it out.

Ashley pivoted in her chair for a better view of the screen. A local news announcement had interrupted the sporting event. "Senatorial candidate Matthew Landis's campaign has just announced he will be making a statement to the press outside his headquarters."

What could he be planning to say? She'd left the family gathering before a consensus had been reached. No doubt if they didn't act soon, his opponent would beat him to the punch and no telling what he would concoct. Damn shame nobody ever seemed interested in posting compromising photos of Martin Stewart. But then, Matthew was the forerunner right now, so tearing him down made for better news and a tighter race—which generated more public interest.

Where did she fit into all of this?

She looked at her sisters and thought of how even logical Claire had begun following her heart. Ashley stared at the pictures of Matthew on the television screen—one of him with her, then the one from the golf course, followed by an image of him alone.

From the moment she'd seen that image of him with the blonde, she'd known he wasn't seeing anyone else. Aside from the fact he'd been with her nearly every second of every day, she knew him to be an honorable man. He'd even been willing to put his campaign, his life's dream, in jeopardy to make things right for her.

How come she'd been so comfortable trusting him, but unable to trust in herself? She wanted to be part of his life. He'd told her he wanted to be part of hers and then shared something intensely personal and painful about his past. That indicated a willingness to take things to a deeper level than before and she should be brave enough to explore the possibility.

Life wasn't going to get less complicated if she

walked away from him. In fact, already her heart was telling her turning her back on the feelings developing between them would lead to complications that would hurt her for the rest of her life.

He'd supported her through a scandal that was every bit as much her own fault as his. He deserved her support now. She was ready to fight for her place in the forefront of Matthew Landis's life.

Ashley pushed back her chair and stood, gathering her purse. "My dear sisters, I agree. Renovate and sell Beachcombers. It's time—time for a lot of things." She gathered her purse and her resolve. "I'm going to Matthew's press conference to be with him."

Where she now knew she belonged, beside the man she loved.

Matthew stood in the foyer of his campaign headquarters, gathering his thoughts. In less than ninety seconds, he would step outside and address the media about his plummeting poll numbers.

His staff stayed in the main office, their conversations a controlled low buzz as they gave him the space he needed to collect himself before stepping outside. He blocked out the noise from television monitors and kept his eyes off all the posters packing the walls.

He had speech notes tucked in his pocket, words that could end his political career, but unavoidable. He had to stop this press war that was tearing Ashley apart, and if that meant he lost the election then so be it. A man had to make a stand for what mattered most.

He hadn't been able to do anything for Dana, but he damn well could fall on his sword for Ashley. He couldn't live with himself if he ruined her life to save a career.

In losing Ashley, he'd blown the biggest opportunity of his life, way bigger than any senate seat.

He would find another way to change the freaking world. He had the resources and the drive. Ashley had shown him there were other effective approaches to life than just his bullheaded full-speed-ahead manner.

Matthew checked his watch again. Thirty seconds. He reached for the knob to step out and join Brent on the porch.

A hand fell on his shoulder. Matthew jolted. Damn. He'd been so preoccupied he hadn't even heard anyone approach.

He pivoted to find… "Ashley? What are you doing here?"

Her brown eyes gleamed with a wide intensity, totally focused on him in a way that lured him, distracted him, at the worst possible moment.

"I came in through the back. Your mother met me and let me in." She gripped his lapels, energy pulsing from her, her long hair rising in a staticky halo around her. "Matthew, what are you planning to say to those reporters?"

"The truth. That I've let them dictate my decisions in a way that has hurt others. That if I'm going to be an effective senator for my constituents, I have to be willing to take the flack that might come my way from the press." He resisted the urge to gather her against him even as he ached to skim his hands along her sweet curves under her lemon-yellow sundress. "I'm going to say whatever it takes to protect you *and* set you free."

She slipped her hand through the crook of his arm. "I'm going with you."

"Like hell." He scowled.

She scowled right back. "Just try to stop me."

Before he could blink, she'd ducked under his other arm and slipped out the front door, straight toward the press conference. Hell, she was determined. And hot.

And headed for trouble.

He bolted after her, almost slamming into Brent, who was attempting to hide the panicked look on his face that appeared whenever things weren't following his perfectly scripted agenda. The instant spent working his way around his campaign manager cost Matthew the precious time needed to catch Ashley before she took her place in front of the podium.

Complete with a microphone and a captive media audience.

"Good afternoon, ladies and gentlemen of the press. I know you expected to hear from Congressman Landis today, but I have to confess to being a bit pushy in wanting to get my two cents in first for the record."

She flashed the gentle smile of hers combined with her shy way of glancing through her lashes at the crowd. How odd that he'd never before noticed her ramrod-straight steely spine under that gorgeous mass of red hair. Those years in a back brace had honed strength in her nobody was going to cow, not even the most shark-like members of the media.

"I imagine we've gathered to talk about revealing photos."

Her bluntness stunned everyone still. For all of three

heartbeats, and then photographers started snapping away again.

"Oh, but wait, we already discussed those pictures of me."

A giggle started in the back, slowly working its way to the front until everyone relaxed and joined in. Interesting how everyone seemed to be perspiring from the summer heat—except for cool, collected Ashley.

"I appreciate that you're all here. You offer a valuable service in getting the message out. Today, I simply want to make sure the message is factually correct so we're not wasting time with messy legalities later."

Whoa, she had the spine set on megastrong today.

Brent shook his head slowly. "My God, she's got the press eating out of the palm of her hand. I've never seen anything like her."

Matthew turned back to stare at Ashley bathed in the beauty of her glowing self-confidence that radiated stronger than even the South Carolina sun. "Me, either."

Ashley nodded to the crowd from the podium. "Now, I happen to believe that a photo of a popular candidate, in his golf clothes, on the golf course, standing by a golf course employee isn't particularly scandalworthy. But that's easier for me to say because I know Matthew and I trust him. I realize that trust takes time."

He didn't doubt the surety in her words and wondered why he'd ever thought she couldn't handle whatever life threw at her. Ashley was a helluva lot stronger than he'd ever given her credit for.

She was absolutely incredible.

Her tone shifted subtly from congenial to factual.

"That's what a campaign is all about—taking the time to get to know the candidate. Learning to trust him to see to our best interests in the senate. I, for one, would like to hear more about Matthew's strategy for guiding our country rather than about photos that divert your attention from getting to know the smart, dynamic leadership style of Matthew Landis."

Listening to her talk, Matthew felt a kick in his gut he'd never expected to experience again, one far stronger than anything he remembered experiencing before but recognized all the same. *He loved this woman.*

She glanced his way with a steady smile that sent a fresh surge of emotion through him. "If you're ready to speak now, Matthew, I would especially like to hear more about your innovative plans to sponsor legislation targeted at helping to strengthen benefits in our foster-care system."

He wanted to talk to Ashley, tell her he loved her and yeah, he wanted her, too, but it was definitely about more than being sex buddies. However, the things he had to say to her were private, and the sooner he dispensed with the press, the sooner he could get Ashley all to himself.

Matthew collected his thoughts and stepped toward the microphone. He could present that particular talking point of Ashley's proposed speech blindfolded with his hands behind his back. And after he finished the press conference, he had an entirely different discussion in mind. Except the dialogue with Ashley wouldn't be as easy to deliver and the outcome odds were shaky at best.

But he wouldn't let the opportunity of a lifetime pass him by.

* * *

Ashley applauded the end of Matthew's speech with a mix of pride and trepidation. While they'd averted a campaign catastrophe today, would she be able to turn things around for them after she'd all but pitched his ring in his face earlier?

If she trusted the look in his eyes when he smiled at her, then they weren't anywhere near over. Lucky for her, she'd learned to trust him—and more important, she'd learned to trust in herself.

Brent ducked his head close to her ear. "You took a real risk out there, Ashley."

"He's worth it." She soaked in the broad set of Matthew's shoulders, the honest connection in his eyes when he spoke with individual voters.

Brent extended his hand. "I'm sorry for underestimating you. I should be a better judge of character than that by now."

"Apology accepted." She clasped his palm and shook firmly. "You were only looking out for Matthew, which I appreciate."

Matthew waved farewell to the crowd and joined her, leading her and Brent back inside headquarters, where the televisions already blared with reports of the media conference. "Hey, Brent, get your own lady. This one's taken."

Ashley elbowed Matthew in the side. "Did you ever consider you're the one who's taken?"

"Good point." Matthew scooped her into his arms as he'd done a week ago when he'd saved her life.

She may have squeaked in surprise, but she didn't even bother protesting and simply settled in for the ride while his campaign staff cheered them on. How far she and Matthew had come in just a week since he'd carried her from the flaming Beachcombers.

He stepped into his office and kicked the door closed. Keeping her arms around his neck, she slid her feet to the floor, leaning into him, urging his face down to meet hers. How could she have ever thought she would be able to turn her back on this, on him?

Matthew nuzzled her ear. "You were…"

"Amazing?" She angled back to grin up at him.

"Absolutely," he confirmed without hesitation. "I can't believe I was worried about protecting you from the press. I should have turned you loose on them right from the start."

She wouldn't have credited herself with the ability to field them that first day when they'd captured revealing pictures of her. But the past week spent learning about herself, learning about real love, she'd discovered there were things out there far more important than worrying what others thought of her. "I'm just glad to have been of help. I believe in you and your message."

"Thank you. That means more to me than I think you realize. I'm sorry about the way we left things earlier." He clasped both of her hands in his. "I want to talk to you about Dana."

"It's okay." She brushed her fingers over his mouth. "I understand."

"I need to say this." He clasped her wrist and lowered her hand. "I should have said it the right way earlier, but I don't have much practice speaking about the past. In fact, I don't have any experience with it at all."

"You haven't told *anyone* about Dana?"

He certainly hadn't mentioned that earlier, and the admission touched her heart in a new and unexpected way. He'd chosen her over anyone else when it came to sharing such an important part of his past. What a time to realize that Matthew *had* put her first, even before his own relatives.

"Since my family hadn't met her and she didn't have any family to meet me, nobody knew how serious things had gotten. Nobody until you, now."

No way could she miss the importance of him sharing this with her and how that linked them. "Thank you for choosing me to be the one you told."

She only wished she'd been less defensive earlier when he'd tried to discuss it with her.

He cupped her face in his hands, his green eyes glinting with intensity. "I want you to understand that the past doesn't, in any way, detract from what I feel for you." He tapped her lips, paused to stroke a slow, sensual circle. "And just to clarify, in case there's any doubt about how I feel for you, I love you, Ashley Carson. I. Love. You."

The magic words. Even in her fantasies she hadn't dared go there, but then perhaps that was good. Reality definitely beat any dream relationship in a landslide victory. "I know you do, but it's still awesome to hear you say it." She nipped his thumb. "And quite convenient since I happen to love you, too."

His ragged sigh shared just how much her words meant to him, a strong man so determined to take on the world full speed ahead.

Matthew slipped his hand into his pocket and pulled it back out to reveal… Her engagement ring rested in his palm. "I'll understand if you would rather have a different one to mark our new beginning, but either way, I want our engagement to be real this time."

She placed her hand over his, over the diamond and the real promise it now held. "This is exactly the one I want. I wouldn't change a thing about our past because it brought us to this perfect moment. Yes, I'll marry you."

He pressed a hard, quick kiss to her lips before pulling back with a smile. "I'm not going to give you time to change your mind, you know."

Matthew slid the solitaire back in place.

She closed her fist, locking the ring on tight. "Nobody's going to pry it off my hand again."

"You're a mighty force to be reckoned with."

And she'd only just begun finding her footing.

Ashley looped her arms around his neck, arching up on her toes for another kiss she knew would lead her to the perfect end to a perfect day. "I'm more than ready to make this relationship real."

Epilogue

"Latest polling reports are in," the wide-screen plasma television blared in the family great room at the Landis compound.

Ashley held her breath as the second before the announcement seemed to stretch out with a slow-motion quality. Sitting with Matthew on the sofa, she gripped his hand, their family and friends around them. Five months ago, she never could have imagined how her life would change because of one impulsive decision to take a risk with the man of her dreams.

But here she was after months of campaigning, totally loving Matthew and finding she also fully enjoyed the new world he'd opened for her.

She'd once thought herself a background, live-in-the-shadows kind of person. Now she'd discovered the rush of being at the epicenter of reaching out to others. And when she needed to recharge? She had an even larger new family to embrace, a family who'd all come to share in this moment.

Her sisters and their husbands blended right in with the Landis brothers and General Renshaw's adult children. The general and Ginger had been an unexpected blessing in her life, taking her on as one of their own. Nobody could replace Aunt Libby, but lordy, it felt good to experience the warmth and acceptance of parental love again.

Ashley squeezed Matthew's strong hand as the television announcer continued, "With ninety-one percent of the precincts reporting, the numbers indicate a clear victory for…"

She forced herself to breathe, keep her focus on Matthew and the TV rather than the hubbub behind them from the small media crew that had been allowed into the Landis compound to report about this moment.

"…the new senator from South Carolina, Matthew Landis," the announcer concluded.

The already crowded room overflowed with cheers. Matthew gathered Ashley into a tight hug. As much as she wanted to stay right there and revel, she knew there were others in the room who deserved to celebrate with him.

She kissed him quickly, intensely, before pulling back. "Congratulations, Senator Landis."

He nuzzled her ear, the gentle rasp of his whiskers sending a shiver of excitement mingling with the surge of joy. "Thank you, Mrs. Landis."

And what an added rush to hear her new name.

They'd quietly eloped two weeks ago, unable to wait any longer to make it official. While the immediate family already knew, she and Matthew would tell the rest of the world during his acceptance speech. They hadn't wanted their marriage to be tied up with the election outcome. The vows they'd spoken were all about them and not any political agenda.

After a final searing kiss, they eased apart and the rest of their huge wonderful family surrounded them in hugs and congratulations. Ashley leaned into his muscular side since Matthew seemed determined to keep his arm around her waist.

Cameras continued to flash while streamers unfurled in the air. Hats, bunting and posters instantly redecorated the house with Senator Landis paraphernalia. A champagne bottle popped somewhere in the distance, and thankfully Ginger seemed to have the first interview well in hand so Matthew could enjoy more celebratory time with the family.

Kyle clapped him on the shoulder. "Don't be getting the big head now, brother. I can still whoop your butt in golf any day."

"Of course you can." Matthew grinned good-naturedly. "Golfing is like a college degree for you air force guys."

Laughing and nodding along in agreement, Jonah passed Sebastian folded cash.

Matthew slugged his youngest brother in the arm, laughing. "Jonah, bro, you bet against me?"

Jonah slugged right back. "Dude, we were only betting on the spread of your landslide."

Ashley patted her brother-in-law's cheek. "You're forgiven, then."

Matthew toyed with Ashley's ponytail streaming

down her back from the gold clasp. "So tell me then, guys, who bet for the largest win?"

Sebastian—the most reserved of the group—offered up one of his rare smiles as he pocketed the cash. "We'll carry that secret to our grave."

Ashley basked in the moment as the general and Ginger beamed with parental pride. It didn't even bother her that the small handpicked media group in the back recorded each embrace and high five and hug. She had nothing to hide and total confidence in the love she and Matthew had found.

As the media's attention swapped from Ginger to the general for a comment, Ashley turned to Matthew. "When will we be heading to campaign headquarters to give your acceptance speech?"

"Soon enough." He skimmed his lips over her temple, the warm scent of his aftershave teasing her senses. "First, I want to have a minute alone with you before we leave."

She flattened her hand to his chest, the cotton of his button-down shirt offering a tormenting barrier to the muscles beneath. "I think everyone would understand us stealing a moment to freshen up."

Matthew took her hand and led her through the throng with amazing speed. As they made their way toward the hall, her sisters each gave her another quick hug before exchanging secretive looks. Ashley started to quiz them, then Matthew distracted her with another kiss and before she knew it they were inside the bedroom she'd used when first staying in this home.

He kicked the door closed behind them, gathering her to his chest and sealing his mouth to hers for the kind of tongue-tangling, soul-searching kisses they wouldn't have dared exchange in front of any camera.

Matthew eased away only to rest his forehead on hers. "I want to thank you for making all of this possible."

"You would have won with or without me." She cupped his handsome face in her hands.

"Since I've had enough of debates for a while, I'm not going to argue your point." He turned his head to press a lingering kiss in each of her palms. "But I want you to understand how much more this moment means because you're in my life, how much more connected I feel to what I'll be doing because of the insights you've given me."

His compliment touched her as deeply as any intimate caress they'd exchanged. "That's a lovely thing to say. Thank you."

"I want to give you something in return."

"You already have." This whole experience had helped her mine for depths inside herself she'd never known she possessed. "I have you, our family, our future."

"But I want you to have a home."

"Home will be where we're together."

"While I agree with you on that one, I also know how much you're giving up by splitting our lives between D.C. and here." He reached to the end table and picked up a folder she hadn't even noticed when they'd entered.

Probably because whenever he touched her she didn't notice much of anything else.

Matthew passed her an official-looking document. Ashley frowned, studying the crisp paper in her hand, her mind scrambling to make sense of the words she saw but couldn't bring herself to comprehend, to believe. "This is the deed to Beachcombers, to Aunt Libby's mansion."

"Yes it is," he answered with a smug smile.

"But it already sold." An event she had accepted even though a piece of her heart still ached over that farewell. Except now that she stared at the name on the deed... No wonder her foster sisters had exchanged that knowing look a few moments ago.

"It sold to you. Sebastian took care of the purchasing process so as to mask my name from any of the transactions, and then I transferred the title to you." He thumbed a tear from her cheek she hadn't even known she'd shed. "We'll obviously spend a large portion of time in D.C., but we have to keep an official residence in South Carolina. So I thought we could make Aunt Libby's house in Charleston our official South Carolina residence."

She clasped the deed to her heart. "Are you sure? What about your family home here?"

"Absolutely sure." His green eyes glinted with unmistakable certainty. "Charleston is plenty close enough to Hilton Head for family visits. And you'll be near your sisters. The carriage house here will be too small once we start having kids."

Children. Hers and Matthew's. "I like the sound of that very much. Thank you. Those two simple words don't seem like enough, but there aren't words for how much this means to me."

Already she could envision all the ways she would want to shape the place into a home for them. Basic repairs had been completed and she wanted to stay true to the original decor of the traditional Southern mansion. But also with central AC, a state-of-the-art kitchen and adjoining rooms for her sisters to visit with their families.

Noise floated from the floor below, reminding her their alone time would be short tonight. A doorbell rang, no doubt more staff stopping by to congratulate the new senator. Fireworks popped in the distance; dogs barked in response. A light strobed right through the shades on the window as another news van pulled up outside.

Yet Matthew never once looked away from her face, his whole attention totally focused on her. "I'm glad you're happy about this. I want us to have our own place. The family-compound idea worked well for a bachelor blowing in and out of town, but you and I deserve some privacy to explore the vast benefits of married life." His eyes took on an altogether different gleam, decidedly wicked.

"You're totally not a bachelor anymore." She relaxed into the arms of the man who'd stolen her heart and given her his own in return.

He raised her ring finger to his mouth and kissed the spot where her engagement ring and wedding band rested side by side. "Lucky for me, I went for the win."

* * * * *

We hope you enjoyed reading

IN BED WITH HER BOSS

by *New York Times* bestselling author

BRENDA JACKSON

and

RICH MAN'S FAKE FIANCÉE

by *USA TODAY* bestselling author

CATHERINE MANN

Both were originally Harlequin® series stories!

Harlequin Desire stories feature sexy, romantic heroes
who have it all: wealth, status, incredible good looks…
everything but the right woman. Add some secrets,
maybe a scandal, and start turning pages!

H HARLEQUIN®

Desire

Powerful heroes…scandalous secrets…burning desires.

Look for six new romances every month
from Harlequin® Desire!

Available wherever books are sold.

www.Harlequin.com

NYTHD0414

SPECIAL EXCERPT FROM

HARLEQUIN

Desire

Turn the page for a sneak peek at
Kristi Gold's
FROM SINGLE MOM TO SECRET HEIRESS,
the second novel in Harlequin® Desire's
DYNASTIES: THE LASSITERS series.

The Lassiter family lawyer has some surprise news for one stunning woman...

She looked prettier than a painted picture come to life. Yep. Trouble with a capital *T* if he didn't get his mind back on business.

"After you learn the details of your share of the Lassiter fortune, you'll be able to buy me dinner next time." *Next time?* Man, he was getting way ahead of himself, and that was totally out of character for his normally cautious self.

Hannah looked about as surprised as he felt over the comment. "That all depends on if I actually agree to accept my share, and that's doubtful."

He couldn't fathom anyone in their right mind turning down that much money. But before he had a chance to toss out an opinion, their waiter showed up with their entrées.

Logan ate his food with the gusto of a field hand, while Hannah basically picked at hers, the same way she had with the salad. By the time they were finished, and the plates were cleared, he had half a mind to invite her into the nearby bar to discuss business. But dark and cozy wouldn't help rein in his libido.

Hannah tossed her napkin aside and folded her hands before her. "Okay, we've put this off long enough. Tell me the details."

Logan took a drink of water in an attempt to rid the dryness in his throat. "The funds are currently in an annuity. You have the option to leave it as is and take payments. Or you can claim the lump sum. Your choice."

"How much?" she said after a few moments.

He noticed she looked a little flushed and decided retiring to the bar might not be a bad idea after all. "Maybe we should go into the lounge so you can have a drink before I continue."

Frustration showed in her expression. "I don't need a drink."

He'd begun to think he might. "Just a glass of wine to take the edge off."

She leaned forward and nailed him with a glare. *"How much?"*

"Five million dollars."

"I believe I will have that drink now."

Don't miss
FROM SINGLE MOM TO SECRET HEIRESS
Available May 2014
Wherever Harlequin® Desire books are sold.

Copyright © 2014 by Kristi Goldberg

HARLEQUIN®

Desire

Powerful heroes…scandalous secrets…burning desires.

Save $1.00 on the purchase of

FROM SINGLE MOM TO SECRET HEIRESS

by Kristi Gold

available May 6, 2014,
or on any other Harlequin® Desire book.

Available wherever books are sold, including most bookstores,
supermarkets, drugstores and discount stores.

- ✂

Save $1.00

on the purchase of
FROM SINGLE MOM TO SECRET HEIRESS
by Kristi Gold
available May 6, 2014
or on any other Harlequin® Desire book.

Coupon valid until July 1, 2014. Redeemable at participating retail outlets
in the U.S. and Canada only. Limit one coupon per customer.

52611403

Canadian Retailers: Harlequin Enterprises Limited will pay the face value of this coupon plus 10.25¢ if submitted by customer for this product only. Any other use constitutes fraud. Coupon is nonassignable. Void if taxed, prohibited or restricted by law. Consumer must pay any government taxes. Void if copied. Millennium1 Promotional Services ("M1P") customers submit coupons and proof of sales to Harlequin Enterprises Limited, P.O. Box 3000, Saint John, NB E2L 4L3, Canada. Non-M1P retailer—for reimbursement submit coupons and proof of sales directly to Harlequin Enterprises Limited, Retail Marketing Department, 225 Duncan Mill Rd., Don Mills, Ontario M3B 3K9, Canada.

U.S. Retailers: Harlequin Enterprises Limited will pay the face value of this coupon plus 8¢ if submitted by customer for this product only. Any other use constitutes fraud. Coupon is nonassignable. Void if taxed, prohibited or restricted by law. Consumer must pay any government taxes. Void if copied. For reimbursement submit coupons and proof of sales directly to Harlequin Enterprises Limited, P.O. Box 880478, El Paso, TX 88588-0478, U.S.A. Cash value 1/100 cents.

5 65373 00076 2   (8100)0 11911

® and TM are trademarks owned and used by the trademark owner and/or its licensee.
© 2014 Harlequin Enterprises Limited

HARLEQUIN®

Desire

ALWAYS POWERFUL, PASSIONATE AND PROVOCATIVE.

THE SARANTOS BABY BARGAIN
Billionaires and Babies
by Olivia Gates

Now guardian to his orphaned niece, Andreas Sarantos
wants only the best for her, which means marrying the
baby's adoptive mother—his ex-wife. But their arrangement
becomes less than convenient when his passion for
Naomi reignites….

Look for THE SARANTOS BABY BARGAIN
in May 2014, from Harlequin Desire!
Wherever books and ebooks are sold.

Don't miss other scandalous titles from the
Billionaires and Babies miniseries,
available now wherever books and ebooks are sold.

HIS LOVER'S LITTLE SECRET
by Andrea Laurence

DOUBLE THE TROUBLE
by Maureen Child

YULETIDE BABY SURPRISE
by Catherine Mann

CLAIMING HIS OWN
by Elizabeth Gates

A BILLIONAIRE FOR CHRISTMAS
by Janice Maynard

THE NANNY'S SECRET
by Elizabeth Lane

SNOWBOUND WITH A BILLIONAIRE
by Jules Bennett

—— www.Harlequin.com ——

HD73314

Love the Harlequin book you just read?

Your opinion matters.

Review this book on your favorite book site, review site, blog or your own social media properties and share your opinion with other readers!

Be sure to connect with us at:
Harlequin.com/Newsletters
Facebook.com/HarlequinBooks
Twitter.com/HarlequinBooks

HARLEQUIN®

A *Romance* FOR EVERY MOOD™.

**Stay up-to-date on all your
romance-reading news with the
Harlequin Shopping Guide,
featuring bestselling authors, exciting new
miniseries, books to watch and more!**

The newest issue will be delivered right to you
with our compliments! There are 4 each year.

Signing up is easy.

EMAIL

ShoppingGuide@Harlequin.ca

WRITE TO US

HARLEQUIN BOOKS
Attention: Customer Service Department
P.O. Box 9057, Buffalo, NY 14269-9057

OR PHONE

1-800-873-8635 in the United States
1-888-343-9777 in Canada

Please allow 4-6 weeks for delivery of the first issue by mail.